GALAXY∞BOUND 02

Galaxy Bound
Sovereign Earth Book 2 of 6

Vidar Hokstad

No part of this publication may be reproduced, distributed or transmitted in any form, or by any means, including photocopying, recording, or other electronic or mechanical, methods without the prior written permission of the author, except in the case of brief quotations embodied in reviews and certain other non-commercial uses permitted by copyright law.

© 2021 Vidar Hokstad. All rights reserved.

Galaxy Bound

Chapter 1 1
Chapter 2 5
Chapter 3 10
Chapter 4 14
Chapter 5 17
Chapter 6 22
Chapter 7 26
Chapter 8 28
Chapter 9 30
Chapter 10 34
Chapter 11 38
Chapter 12 41
Chapter 13 45
Chapter 14 49
Chapter 15 52
Chapter 16 55
Chapter 17 59
Chapter 18 62
Chapter 19 65
Chapter 20 69
Chapter 21 73
Chapter 22 77
Chapter 23 82
Chapter 24 86

Chapter 25 91
Chapter 26 95
Chapter 27 98
Chapter 28 102
Chapter 29 105
Chapter 30 109
Chapter 31 113
Chapter 32 116
Chapter 33 120
Chapter 34 123
Chapter 35 127
Chapter 36 131
Chapter 37 134
Chapter 38 137
Chapter 39 141
Chapter 40 145
Chapter 41 149
Chapter 42 152
Chapter 43 155
Chapter 44 159
Chapter 45 163
Chapter 46 165
Chapter 47 169
Chapter 48 172
Chapter 49 176
Chapter 50 178
Chapter 51 181

Chapter 52	185
Chapter 53	189
Chapter 54	194
Chapter 55	198
Chapter 56	202
Chapter 57	206
Chapter 58	210
Chapter 59	214
If you enjoyed this book . .	218

Chapter 1

Soka'li Em-Sckirrrnie Three—Soka to friends and family—entered the administrators' palace on the first moon of the planet Thestias orbiting a star about fifty light years from Sol.

He had been summoned to this remote outpost for a mission of some importance, but had not been given any further detail, other than a vague suggestion to read up on the recent connection to the Sol system and the Earthers that inhabited it. Hence how he knew the distance to Sol, and was aware the Earthers did not even have a proper name for this unremarkable system that he'd only learned the grid reference to a few days ago.

Soka had grown up some 250 light years from Thestias, and considered himself a refined man used to the pleasures of life close to the traditional Home World of the Kriii'nai Empire. He was certainly not used to slumming it in these kinds of remote locations.

But sometimes one has to accept that duty comes first, he thought to himself, as he brought out a pocket mirror and ensured he looked appropriately attired. He was only visiting a local administrator, but it was still important to look good. Soka adjusted his makeup slightly, and sighed.

He had not enjoyed the trip, and missed being home with his family.

His wife had been gracious, and pointed out she would manage with her other two husbands. They only had four children so far, but two of them were still toddlers, and Soka already missed them.

He entered the palace, and reported to the security guard on duty, who pointed him to a waiting secretary. The secretary welcomed him warmly, if in a voice that to Soka seemed rehearsed and somewhat fake.

"We are so pleased to have you here. The Lady Xine-Zor Li'mor Four will be with you shortly."

Soka waited in the ante-chamber the secretary showed him to. Even Soka had to admit the chamber was quite tastefully arranged for such a remote location.

The Lady Xine must have a strong masculine influence in her life, he thought, *to ensure these kinds of tasteful flower arrangements.*

He was soon shown in and introduced to the administrator, a woman with an air to her that signaled to Soka that she was a confident, assertive woman. She looked at him with a stern expression that instantly made him feel like he was about to be scolded. Her overpowering presence impressed him before she'd even said a word.

He could not help but wonder what a woman like her was doing in a backwater like this.

"Soka… May I call you Soka?"

He nodded eagerly, instinctually seeking her approval.

"We have an important mission for you."

She motioned for him to sit on a sofa along the side of the office, and sat down opposite him.

"Have you heard of the expansion towards the planet called 'Earth'?"

Soka confirmed that when he had been summoned, he had been told to read up on it, but that his knowledge was very much superficial. The Lady Xine filled him in, in short precise statements about the essentials—as she saw them. In her words they sounded even more like a truly backwards civilization to Soka than what the public information suggested, and he shuddered at the implications.

"Only a few gates in the system are active as of yet. The Lynians got there first to secure a secondary connection to our network. The Earthers connected only recently as a result of the transponder set up when our gate reached the system. A couple others. But it's shaping up to become an important hub once more of the gate cores underway arrives."

Soka nodded; he'd studied the charts and seen the projections of incoming gates both from existing trading partners that wanted additional connections, and the notes on radio contacts with civilizations further out. The Earthers had gotten lucky—they were only about four lightyears away.

"We're having some trouble. There have been accusations of attacks on their trade ships, and they're pressuring us to allow military vessels to protect their interests. Of course, such a thing would be entirely unacceptable as a matter of principle. We cannot allow savages to build up forces along our trade routes, no matter how primitive their weapons."

The Lady Xine almost spat out the words, and her forehead wrinkled in a most unattractive, aggressive way.

"We have consented to allow a small civilian ship to investigate. It will be armed, but no more than normal freighters, and it will bear no visible military markings or transponder codes. It will have a representative of the Earth military, and one of our own…"

Soka was intrigued. An Earther investigation with one of theirs. Suddenly it was getting interesting.

"We want you, Soka. We want you to find out what this nonsense is. Clearly we have not been attacking anyone, so we need to know who has, and why."

Soka was so taken aback he gasped. Even when Lady Xine had mentioned she wanted one of them on the Earther ship he had failed to make the connection from that to his summons.

In retrospect that was sloppy, he thought. *It was rather obvious. How could I have missed that?*

"But I have young children to get back to, and you want me to travel even further out from the core of the Empire?"

"Pull yourself together, Soka. I've read your file. You can do this."

"I will consider it, Lady Xine. But I must confer with my wife."

The Lady sneered.

"I understand, but do it quickly. We do not have time to waste on this kind of masculine hysterics."

She waved for him to leave her, and he bowed. He was somewhat embarrassed, and backed out of the office then turned and hurried back to his quarters.

It did sound a bit exciting. "Earth." Such a weird name. It would be an opportunity to learn about a truly backwards civilization.

It was too early at home to call his wife, so he took a leisurely route along the banks of the river. It was evening local time. He must admit that for a backwater, the terraformers had done a lovely job making this moon into something resembling a liveable location. Temperate, with tolerable gravity. On the low end of the comfortable range, but enough to hold things in place. Soka hated being on ships and having to deal with shifting gravity or none at all.

As he wandered deep in thought, he was coming around to the idea of this mission. If his wife was amenable, it might be a chance to prove his worth and solve what had sounded like an awful situation. It made him feel positively young again.

Soka had been an engineer on a cruiser for the better part of forty years in his youth, and knew his way around a spaceship very well. Slumming it on one of those little "Earth" ships might give him opportunities to learn about their engineering as well, quaint as it probably was, as well as learn about their culture.

*It **is** a long time since I've gone somewhere truly **new**,* he thought. And Sol was new not just to him, but to the Kriii'nai Empire. *They're young even to themselves*, he thought. Kriii'nai was old enough that its pre-interstellar history was shrouded in the mists of time, hidden by the fog of interplanetary wars believed to have happened hundreds of years after they achieved space travel.

For a moment he looked up at the darkening sky, with a few stars becoming visible. *I wonder if there are empires out there vaguely aware of us as young upstarts the way we are of Earth,* he pondered. He was coming around to this task.

He made it to the villa he had been assigned, and grabbed a drink while waiting for a suitable time to call home.

When he did, he had already decided: If his wife would permit it, he would go.

"Dearest… How are you this morning?"

"Soka, you sound like you're in a good mood. Just yesterday you hated being sent to that provincial outpost."

Soka could already tell she was suspicious at his cheerful demeanor.

"Oh, I am in a good mood. But first, how are the children?"

"They're well. They miss you of course."

"And how are Alai and Noki?"

Alai and Noki were their other two husbands. Soka had grown up with four parents too, and wanted the same for his children. He had two mothers and two fathers, but three fathers were also good.

"They are well too. Now tell me what is up, Soka."

"I've been asked to assist on a matter near 'Earth.'"

He had to explain to his wife where and what Earth was, and like Soka, she was initially uncertain and displeased at the thought.

But after pleading with her a bit, she conceded that she could manage with Alai and Noki for a while.

"Thank you, dearest. My love to everyone."

Soka ended the call, and fired off a quick message to the Lady Xine confirming his acceptance. Then he cleaned off his makeup and went to bed, dreaming about the savages of "Earth."

Chapter 2

After decades, the wait had finally been over. The gate was ready. The synchronization signal from the other end confirmed the other end was ready to go as well. The countdown had started.

To some it meant the start of a new era of adventure. To others, boundless opportunities for trade, for science, for knowledge. To some—expansion...

And then again there were those cowering in bunkers, or hidden in ships, waiting for the armada of Centauri invaders they believed to be the inevitable outcome.

The official opening of the Earth side of the Earth-Centauri gate took place aboard Vanguard II, the most monstrously large space station constructed in the system, at a radius of 5 km and a length of 30 km, five times both the radius and length of the smaller Vanguard.

The station was a concession to those who feared the Centauri: filled and surrounded by ships custom built to match the maximum volume the gates could handle, and complements of smaller support ships.

If anyone had paid close attention, they'd certainly believe Sol was planning an invasion of Centauri. But, of course, if anyone did pay attention, until the gate was switched on there would have been no faster way than a roughly four-year radio transmission to pass the information along.

Ambassador Erika Tran waited impatiently in the lavishly appointed reception hall aboard Vanguard II. Set in a parkland on the "ground" level that provided a simulated outdoor space, the reception hall seemed to be inspired by some sort of nondescript temple, with pillars, and open views "out" as there was relatively little weather to protect against.

Clouds did form around the center spire sometimes, but giant air-conditioning systems worked day and night to ensure the humidity never rose to levels where there'd be actual rain, and they got mild winds at most.

The reception itself was relatively small. A selection of leaders from Earth and the colonies, including a number of military leaders, but a conscious choice had been made to avoid the top leadership from Earth and the military—nobody cared who the colonies sent—in case the Centauri did turn out to be hostile.

A number of camera-drones provided press coverage.

Tran was young for her post. She'd been born two years after the Centauri signal, and so she had grown up with the anticipation, never knowing a world where humanity wondered if it was truly alone.

She'd grown up wondering what that was like to her parents and grandparents. Looking up at the stars and wondering if anyone were there, instead of counting down the years until we got to see them, and what that would mean.

Her era was one where the biggest polarizing issue that cut through all of society was the question of whether the Centauri would be good or bad. Whether they'd invade or change everything. If it'd end all conflict and poverty, or relentlessly exploit them like imperialist colonizers.

"Ambassador? If I may, the gate should initialize within minutes—may I show you to your seat?"

An assistant led her to a seat at the head of a table of dignitaries, most of whose names she did not remember, and she sat down.

Tran was one of the hopeful ones. She could hardly contain her excitement when she was appointed Sol's first ambassador to the Centauri, and given the job of receiving their first envoy. Though the cynic in her realized she got the job in part because a number of the more senior candidates in the diplomatic corps were either considered indispensable, and so were far from Vanguard II and the gate, or were too scared.

She was qualified, but she was not the most qualified. She was the most suitable when considering the intersection of qualifications, guts, and the acceptable range of seniority which made her a possible candidate yet not yet indispensable.

She could live with that if it meant she got to be the first human to shake hands with an alien. No matter what happened next, she was guaranteed a name in the history books.

It made it easy for her to smile to the assembled crowd.

A large screen at one end of the reception hall gave a composite view of the area around the gate, Vanguard II C&C, and news reports.

The military had a massive job keeping a suitable volume around the gate clear of a large number of civilian ships ranging from curious explorers, hopeful colonists wanting to seek out new worlds to settle, religious nutjobs who saw the gate as a gateway to heaven, religious nutjobs who saw the gate as the work of the devil, and groups similar to Sovereign Earth and others who believed the Centauri would send an armada through the moment the gate opened and who wanted to be the first line of defense.

The latter were the most dangerous. Tran was aware of several attempts at destroying the gate over the last year, and the investigation into Sovereign Earth had ground to a stand-still—trench warfare by court motions someone had described it as.

There were fears the first Centauri ship through might be immediately attacked, and so a significant exclusion zone had been created, and any ships found to be attempting weapons locks would be destroyed immediately.

Still... Tran was worried something would go wrong.

***

"Ambassador, we have word C&C says the gate data feed is indicating it is going online in seconds."

No sooner had the aide informed her, than a brief flash of light occurred on the cameras facing the gate.

The operators soon zoomed in on a tiny ship, what looked like a small one-person shuttle.

Tran stopped breathing then and there, and just stared. It didn't matter that she'd expected something much bigger and more stately for an occasion like this. She was looking at the first alien ship to visit the solar system.

"This is Vanguard II on behalf of Earth to unknown ship. Please identify."

The voice boomed through the reception hall, from the video feed.

"This is local vice administrator Krrrt'li Al-Sqirel Two of the Kriii'nai Empire. I am happy to report the gate is operational, and if I may, I would like to meet with you."

The 'Kriii'nai Empire' was the real name of the Centauri. Even after hearing it pronounced, Tran was not at all sure how to produce the sounds with an Earth vocal cord, and so she made a mental note to find out how to broach referring to them in official communication.

The name "Centauri," it struck her, was about as insensitive as when Europeans had "discovered" America and called the native population Indians without bothering to reflect the names they used for themselves, or even if they'd found the right continent.

She listened as Vanguard II C&C tried to pronounce Krrrt'li Al-Sqirel Two's name, winced when they asked if he minded being called Kurt, started breathing again when he answered that was indeed acceptable in an entirely neutral tone, before they coordinated his docking procedure.

An aide was hovering by her side to bring her to the assigned docking bay so she could be the first person to welcome "Kurt" in person. While they walked, she played back his name on her pad repeatedly and tried to get her pronunciation flawless, and kept failing, and she soon decided maybe it'd be "Kurt" after all.

At the docking bay, the only people present were a military honor guard, herself, the aide that brought her there, and the station commander. The small ship had landed and interfaced flawlessly with the docking system.

The doors opened, and Kurt walked out. He was a tall, very slim man, skin like bronze, dark and somewhat shimmering. Tran was not sure if that was normal, or if it was glitter or makeup of some sort. He was dressed in a long figure-hugging gown, and gracefully swayed down towards Tran in a manner which struck her at the same time as very feminine and utterly alien and suiting the character before her perfectly.

"Hello, everyone," he said, in perfect English, and she was taken aback even after she'd heard his radio communication just minutes before. She knew they'd talk English—they'd been asked, in the early days of communication, to provide recordings for purposes of having the Centauri emissaries learn the language, but she'd expected to hear at least a trace of an accent, and if she heard any accent it was the very faint trace of an archaic British accent, nothing alien. She found that faint trace mildly amusing, and made a note to look up the sample recordings that had been provided.

"I'm Krrrt'li Al-Sqirel Two, or as your station staff seemed to find easier: Kurt. Rest assured I'm happy to be called whatever is easier for you to pronounce. I extend my deepest appreciation of being welcomed here, and in turn welcome you to our trade network."

Tran decided to forgo any attempt at saying his real name.

"I'm ambassador Erica Tran," she replied, "and I welcome you on behalf of the whole of Sol system."

She was transfixed by Kurt's long lashes, and high cheekbones.

"Please accompany me to the reception hall."

Kurt extended his hand.

"Please lead the way, ambassador."

She felt a bit childish, but took his hand, and marveled at how soft it was, before she got giddy at the thought that she was now indeed the first human to have taken an alien hand as she led Kurt towards the reception.

Chapter 3

"Zo!"

Clarice spotted her first, and ran towards her to give her a long hug.

"Are you okay?"

Zo fought herself loose from Clarice's firm grip, and smiled.

"Never better."

"Have they told you why we've been let out?"

"Only that there is some mission."

Captain Zara Ortega, Zo, looked at Clarice, and then the rest of her crew—her family—waiting right behind her. She shook their hands in turn, exchanged greetings, grabbed a chair and sat down and motioned for the others to sit as well. They were in a conference room at the space port of Kampala, Uganda, the nearest major space port to the detention center they'd been held in.

Zo had been there before. The Kampala Space Port was a sprawling and impressive complex. She knew it was located there because it was near the equator—as space had become increasingly important, cities near the equator had grown massively in importance for some time until further engine improvements reduced their advantage. And as the African Union had coalesced into a single federated state, before the world-wide unification, it had become one of the wealthiest cities on the planet.

She had not seen any of her crew since their conviction after their raid on Vanguard. Thankfully it had not been nearly as long as she'd worried it might. In total they'd been detained for a bit over a year. Most of the crew had been given two years—a very lenient sentence given what they'd done. She'd been given five as the captain.

They'd all been quietly informed they'd likely be let out early, because they'd helped bring to light Sebastien Terrell's conspiracy, but "politics required" at least those sentences, apparently.

"It's got to do with the gate… Some Earth ship has been attacked, and they said their attackers were Centauri before they were cut off."

"Knew it," her second in command, Mons, muttered in the corner.

"The Centauri denies it, of course. Earth command don't know what to believe and they're all arguing. Apparently, the Centauri refuses to allow a military presence on the other side."

"Where do we fit in?" Jonas asked.

"We're to go after them. The Centauri has agreed, as a compromise, to a single armed civilian ship, with one Centauri diplomat and one Earth military representative."

"We're to take on a Centauri?" Mons spluttered. Zo had many conversations with Mons about the Centauri before their Vanguard mission, and knew he'd been sympathetic to Sovereign Earth before it—as had she, she admitted to herself—but she'd not realized until their trial just how worried he had been about them. *I guess some of that worry is still there,* she thought to herself.

"We're to take on *military*?" Vincent sounded as annoyed as Mons, for different reasons. Zo knew that Vincent had left the military because he didn't want to fight for others any more, and now they were going to take on a job for the military.

"I know. Strictly as an observer and crew member, Vincent. They'll not be in charge."

"The officer we're getting is also apparently a trained medic in addition to having worked in intelligence. She's supposedly an excellent all-rounder."

"We're taking on *another medic*," gasped Rob, their ship medic, in a dramatic mocking tone that to Zo, at least, seemed mostly intent on making fun of Mons and Vincent. She smiled at him.

"One more thing. Colonel Williams is worried that Terrell might try something if he finds out about this attack. Maybe sabotage the mission to prevent us from tracking down who did this. It's in his interest to play up any conflict with the Centauri, after all. Nobody can know unless we find evidence, to prevent information getting to Sovereign Earth sympathizers. He's worried there are Sovereign Earth people inside his unit too. Their influence is spreading even after the shit last year."

They all knew Colonel Williams after their cases. He'd been the one to ensure their sentences were brief, by presenting the outcome of the military investigation that supported the case that they had helped uncover a major conspiracy. He'd also met with each of them in person to thank them.

"When do we leave?" Clarice seemed the most eager to get back out in space.

"As soon as we've inspected the ship." Zo rose.

"Yeah, what about our ship?"

"Come and see for yourself, Jonas. Everyone."

Zo led them out of the conference room.

"Why did you think they brought us *here* in the first place?" She smiled.

"I just thought it was a convenient place to dump us to let us get transport out," Jonas offered up.

Zo took them to the docking area, and produced identification to the guard.

There it was.

Zo had already been inside and had a first look, but the others had not seen it for a year. The *Black Rain* stood on the launch pad, and the gantry they were on was connected so they could walk straight in.

She heard several gasps, as her crew realized it'd definitively been repaired and refurbished, and best of all: cleaned.

"I can't even smell your dirty clothes, Vincent."

"Fuck you, Jonas."

She led her crew inside, and led them to the bridge, which was locked with the floor towards the engines.

"Fuck me, look at the weapons stations," Vincent yelled and stared at the display showing the upgraded pulse cannons and what looked like several missile launchers. His priorities were clear.

"The engines have been upgraded too," Zo told him. "And the bulkheads have been reinforced."

"You all know your jobs. Williams arranged for a first-rate contractor to fix and upgrade the ship, and it should be fully stocked, but I don't want to leave anything to chance, so before the mission we need to check everything."

"I know it's a bitch to get around the ship in this orientation, so we check the basics here. Once we're launch ready, we head for Vanguard II, as that's where we'll pick up our military liaison. Anything we can fix or stock up on at Vanguard II can be checked once we're out of this damn gravity."

The bridge orientation could be changed—it rotated on a gimbal. It was not used very often during normal flight, but during fights the ability to adjust the floor to match acceleration even when they accelerated at odd angles made it a lot easier to avoid nausea.

Zo had long thought that in practice it was a lot less useful than the designer of this old model had probably expected—the reality was that the nav thrusters were so much weaker than the main thrusters that usually you'd use them mostly to spin the ship so the main thrusters could accelerate you in the best direction, and that meant too short burns with the nav thrusters to be worth the hassle of relying on the gimbal to adjust the bridge orientation. *One of those nice ideas that turns out pointlessly impractical.*

Most of the rest of the ship was built with the assumption that in gravity, the floor would be towards the main engines, so they could walk around and could climb up and down, but hauling things around was still a massive pain, as in this orientation they had many small floors. In zero-g they also had far more work surface, and the ship was small enough that this made a huge difference to comfort.

They all checked their bridge-stations first, and confirmed all systems appeared normal, and checked out the upgrades. Then they filed out one by one to check their assigned systems and cargo.

Soon Zo was alone on the bridge, in her captain's chair, content to know that in a few hours she'd be back in space. She didn't mind Earth. But she minded being there for more than a few days here and there. It didn't help that she'd been locked up, of course, but she was *used* to being confined to small spaces for long periods of time during flight. What she disliked the most was the damn gravity.

More than just getting back out into space, she was eager to get through the gate. See the Centauri system up close.

Chapter 4

The trip to Vanguard II was smooth. After launch from Earth and the exhilaration of being back in space, and the even greater exhilaration of not having gravity for a while after a short acceleration burn set them on a course to coast at low speed towards the Earth-Moon gate while they checked out every detail of the rest of the ship, they finally had a chance to talk. Some of them were more talkative than others.

"How about the Centauri?"

Clarice had consumed every little bit of information she had been allowed to get her hands on while locked up, and they'd been quite lenient with her news access. She'd watched every interview with "Kurt," read every news report and opinion piece. Read all the gossip from the first trade missions. She found them immensely fascinating. So different from what she'd expected.

"At least they didn't attack." Jonas shrugged.

Clarice knew Jonas was joking, but there was a serious tinge to it as well. They'd all gotten caught up in the original mission, and it hurt to have been misled like that, but more than anything, it had been scary waiting to see if they'd gotten it wrong in the end when they turned on Terrell.

"Do any of you think the Centauri were really behind the attack we're going to be investigating?" Rob asked.

"Doesn't make any sense for it to be their government at least." Vincent's face looked as serious as Clarice had ever seen it.

"They're traders. They've proven that. Attacking ships that provide revenue in the form of tolls makes no sense for them. On the contrary, it damages them." Vincent's military training made him see everything in terms of tactics and force-projections and payoffs.

"These people are renegades," he went on. "Some renegade Centauri faction that they might not even want to admit exists."

The conversation raged back and forth. Some of them, like Mons, were still highly skeptical of the Centauri. But overall, they agreed it couldn't be the government.

***

They passed through the Earth-Moon gate, and when they materialized in Lunar space, Vanguard II was there in plain sight.

None of them had been aboard it. It was still mostly military, but after the lack of a Centauri military action some concessions had been granted for civilian use.

But of course they'd been locked up when that happened.

Vanguard II was the first station other than some small experimental projects to have a hull constructed in part using a concrete-like material, as churning up asteroids brought in through the gate system meant there was a huge supply of suitable material available on the cheap without boosting it up a gravity well.

It made Vanguard I look like a toy.

In light of their previous encounter with a station like this, Clarice did a quick calculation to realize that though the station's rotation took about three times as long as for Vanguard, the speed the outer rim moved at was well over twice as fast.

Good thing we're not trying to fake a crash into that, she thought, still quite pleased with how believable she'd made the "crash" into Vanguard to prepare their breaking. She'd been questioned repeatedly about that point during their trial—the prosecutor found it hard to believe they'd successfully faked a crash into the station to deposit Zo and Jonas and kept trying to get them to admit to having brought them aboard by some other means. She wasn't sure why. It was not as if it would have made a difference to the case.

Vanguard II C&C made contact, and after identifying themselves, they were directed to one of the military docking bays, and set down and locked in place without incident.

Inside they were met by a couple of guards that informed them they were to be escorted to the security office to be introduced to their liaison.

"Familiar feeling. This is just like when they took me to complain about crashing into Vanguard," Clarice said to Zo. Zo hadn't been there for that—she'd been working her way up from the lower decks with Jonas.

The guards announced them, and motioned for them to enter.

"Welcome. I'm Lieutenant Monique Salinger."

Before them stood a serious-looking woman in the uniform of the Earth Space Corps. Monique was average height, appeared to be mixed race, with a kind of oval face that Clarice associated with ancestry somewhere in Eastern Africa. *Maybe Ethiopia, or Somalia.*

Monique was curvy, attractive, and standing in a broad, domineering stance that Clarice thought seemed like stereotypical of young military officers eager to demonstrate they were *very* serious about their jobs. *Bet she's no fun at all*, Clarice thought. *But the guys will try to impress her anyway.*

She greeted them all with a firm handshake, and turned back to Zo once she'd greeted all of them.

"My job," she started, "is to be your liaison to Colonel Williams, and to the Earth Space Corps."

"It is also to ensure you behave. We can't afford this to escalate. There are already people trying to whip up the mood to push for a military incursion into Centauri space."

"You people know what these kinds of groups are capable of better than most. I had friends on the *Ariane*; I know they died saving you, and you better show me you were worth saving. And we better find out what went down before those groups convince more people the Centauri are the enemy."

Clarice wanted to express her sympathy, but the look of anger on Monique's face made her decide to hold off until another time.

"Captain Ortega, while I'm on your ship I'll be under your command, with certain caveats. I will report to Earth whenever I consider it necessary, and I'm authorized to take charge if you deviate from the mission parameters. I'm also to represent Earth in any communication with the Centauri authorities if I deem it necessary. Is that understood?"

Zo nodded. Clarice could tell from her facial expression that she was not particularly happy about it, however.

"That's all understood."

Monique's face changed. Suddenly she had a broad, friendly smile. *I'm not sure it suits her.*

"Are you ready to leave? I'm eager to get through the gate, and pick up our Centari diplomat."

"We're all ready, Lieutenant Salinger."

"Monique, please. Let's go."

Chapter 5

Zo felt like a child as they passed through the Centauri gate. Decades of regular space travel was nothing like passing through more than four light years of space in a moment and materializing in the middle of, not just another starsystem, but a system so fundamental to human dreams of the stars.

Not just the nearest system, but such a fundamentally alien system—a trinary system...

The binary pair, Rigil Kentaurus and Toliman, and the more distant cousin, Proxima Centauri, a red dwarf. Though most people referred to the three as Alpha Centauri A and B and Proxima.

Proxima tantalizingly named because it's the nearest star to Earth, for so long so near and yet totally out of reach.

She'd of course seen A and B from near Earth, plainly visible in the night sky, though easily mistaken for a single star. And she'd seen Proxima as a faint dot on enhanced pictures. *I've heard some people can see it with their bare eyes. Wonder if Clarice's augments can pick it up on Earth*, she thought briefly.

Here, as they rematerialized, A and B were similar in size and brightness to the sun seen from Earth—Rigil Kentaurus brighter, and Toliman roughly half the brightness, and no enhancements necessary to spot Proxima, only about a fifth of a light year away.

"It changes language, doesn't it? It's a star when it's a dot like Proxima is for now. It's a sun when they look like disks like that." Zo spoke to herself as much as to the crew.

All of them just stared at the images for a while, letting it sink in that they were there.

Mons pointed out the sun to them on one of their cameras. There it was as small as Alpha Centauri had been from Earth, just a little dot in the dark sky.

Not only were they further away than they'd ever been, but they were about to meet an alien for the first time, in an alien space station...

It was hot on the bridge, but Zo still shivered briefly.

"This is Alpha Centauri gate control. Please proceed out of the gate area." They were greeted in near flawless English. Of course gate control knew very well that they were an Earth ship. And who they were. And probably exactly who were onboard.

Zo shook herself out of her daze.

"Acknowledged."

"Clarice, take us out of here, and request clearance for Outpost 164A-79."

"Who named that thing," she heard Rob whisper.

The Centauri, Zo had learned, did not consider the Alpha Centauri outpost significant enough to warrant a name. It only had a designation following some system they were not privy to, but the size of the numbers still hinted at an immense reach for the Centauri trade network that she could not yet wrap her mind around.

Clarice sent the request, and relayed the credentials they had been given to prove they were there to pick up the Centauri diplomat assigned to them.

"*Black Rain*, this is Outpost 164A-79. Course and docking arrangement to follow."

They were given a precise course and speed that'd leave them coasting for about an hour, and then a slow deceleration burn. Altogether they'd have about two hours to take in the images and to process the feeling of adventure that was overtaking Zo as the immensity of it all washed in over her.

"Can you believe we're here?"

Clarice couldn't contain her excitement as well as Zo and the others. Normally she was quiet and closed off, but this clearly brought even her out of her shell, and Zo could see she struggled to stay seated.

Zo smiled and enjoyed seeing her get excited like this. She had missed Clarice the most.

"Look, they've sent us the transit map!"

Clarice was practically jumping up and down in her seat at this point. She was intoxicating to Zo when she on a rare occasion got this worked up about something.

"There's a gate to Proxima," Clarice practically yelled.

"And Barnard's Star! Epsilon Indi! Wolf 359..."

The Centauri system had several gates marked as leading out of the system, though a handful of them were marked as under construction. Who knows how many of those systems again had gates leading even further. The Centauri released information to Earth in small drips. The system had a further half a dozen gates internal to the system itself, like the one to Proxima Centauri.

"Does that mean those all have civilizations?" Jonas asked out loud, though none of them knew the answer to that, and the information that had been relayed did not say.

Maybe, maybe not, Zo thought to herself. After all, the Centauri system itself had been barren when the Centauri got there. What was there was what the Centauri had built in a few decades.

It's incredible there are already gates to other systems at all… The solar system is so close, and yet we didn't know there were civilizations in those places, and they **beat us here**… It struck Zo that somewhere in the explanation for that, the answer to the Fermi paradox could be found. *They were there all along, but we didn't see them.*

Zo knew that so far Earth had been limited to direct trade only with the Centauri in any case, and had not been given much information about which other civilizations were within close reach.

So far most of the trade had been in rare minerals. Some trade in artifacts had begun. The limitation was, of all things, bureaucracy. The Centauri insisted on lengthy negotiations of standards and customs rules and duties for each and every good. *And no direct contact* with the other systems, yet.

Repeated requests for information on which goods might be available, and which other civilizations might be there were only occasionally answered, and when they were, only bits and pieces of information were given.

Zo recalled an article on the subject she had read in prison that had stated that the Centauri insisted information would be released, but that Earth had to be patient. Earthers were newcomers, and not everyone trusted newcomers. *Earthers.*

Then there were customs considerations and protectionism. Medical and health considerations—nobody wanted *Earthers* to start spreading nasty alien viruses around. *It's funny to think of* **us** *as the aliens.*

She had only gotten halfway through that article before she was too bored to continue, however, and she did not know all that much about the current state of negotiations.

Of course plenty of people on Earth still did not trust the Centauri, and insisted this was further evidence of plotting and intrigue and that we could not trust them and should force the issue.

Maybe they were all plotting against Earth.

More likely, thought Zo to herself, *they can't be bothered, and have more pressing concerns.*

As willing as she had originally been to believe Sovereign Earth, their lies and deceit and the subsequent lack of an invasion after the gate opened had changed her outlook.

But each gate was a doorway to another star, and another new adventure. *Pick the right doors, and who knows, maybe you'd get all the way to the Galactic Center.*

Sagittarius A*. A supermassive black hole with dozens of stars orbiting it. *Wonder if we ever get to see that?*

She got dizzy just thinking about it, even though she knew full well the distances were so vast it'd be little different from a regular night sky.

She also began wondering about the opportunities. If they did this job well, and impressed the Centauri diplomat, maybe they could leverage it into access. Opportunities to travel and see what lay beyond Centauri. Travel the galaxy, even if only a small corner of it.

The Centauri outpost was, unlike the far away stars Zo was fantasizing about, already visible without magnification. Compared to the size of it, Vanguard II was insignificant.

"From what I can tell, it's got a radius of fifty km, and it's several hundred km long."

Vincent was staring at the screen in disbelief at the scale of it.

Zo magnified the display, and they could make out the structure. It looked pretty much like an Earth station in most respects, because a lot of things, like parabolic antennas, just make sense for purely functional reasons. Physics and geometry may be expressed differently, but the rules don't change.

But there were also all kinds of details they could not make sense of. Architectural flourishes maybe, or functionality they did not understand.

"Make sure to record everything," Monique said, facing Clarice and Mons.

Zo glared at her.

"Next time direct your requests to **me**," Zo told her. "You don't give instructions to my crew without my approval."

Clarice looked at her, and Zo nodded for her to go ahead with the recordings.

"Sorry… *Captain.*"

Monique didn't *sound* sorry to Zo, but she let it go.

It was time for their deceleration burn and they all strapped in before the nav thrusters carried out the final adjustments as specified.

It had been a long time since she had felt a rush like this; her heart hammering in this way. Even during the events last year, she felt she knew what was coming most of the time. Sometimes there was fear, sure, but she knew what to expect.

Nothing she had ever experienced involved anything as totally new and alien as they were about to see up close.

Chapter 6

Soka had waited at Outpost 164A-79 for two days when he was finally alerted that the Earthers had passed through the gate.

He had absolutely detested every second of it.

He was there to learn about the Earthers and solve the problem at hand, not rot away on some tiny little insignificant station like this.

The outpost was claustrophobic like all remote outposts. Though it was large enough to have tolerable gravity and an "outdoor" space that had some nice parks and markets, and a delightful but busy beach, it was still too small to be believable. You could even now look up and see the ground rather than the sky past the clouds.

And the food.

He detested the food.

The variety was tolerable, but little of it was fresh. He was told when he spoke to the station commander that more and more hydroponic capacity was coming online weekly, and the new nearby trade routes meant more fresh variety, but he was far from impressed. Artificial meat and other replacements did not satisfy him at all.

He'd spent some time on the observation deck the first day, taking in the views of Alpha Centauri AB and Proxima, but when you've seen one trinary system you've seen them all. *They're almost all just close binaries with a more distant little hanger-on,* he had thought to himself. *Entirely unremarkable.*

Soka yawned.

These Earthers better be interesting, he thought. *Or taking this mission will not have been worth it.*

He'd spent the tedious trip to this outpost reading up on all the material he could find about Earth in the databases Lady Xine had made available to him. The trip had not been that long—only a couple of gate passages, but the low acceleration travel between the intermediate gates had felt agonizingly slow.

Most of what he found during his reading confirmed his suspicions that the Earthers were indeed backwards savages, but he did also find some things he liked.

Their fashion sense was a bit on the muted side for him, and the reversal of the traditional gender roles confused him. Earth men were so feminine. And most Earth women so masculine. It was decidedly a massive turnoff, but oddly fascinating at the same time. He had briefly looked into the databases selection of material Earthers found… titillating, and had immediately been thoroughly grossed out and vowed not to see an Earther nude again. Then he took another look, and made the same vow again.

Then again, I won't be looking to these savages for a partner.

He had been waiting in the docking bay for half an hour now, after being informed they were on the final approach. He wished he'd had his lunch first.

Finally their ship was descending to the docking platform, and the gantry extended, and the docking adapter got a fit.

A few minutes later he could see the humans walk towards the port, and be allowed in by the station staff.

"There you are. Finally! I have waited a long time for this moment."

Soka rushed towards them, his elegant dress robe almost tripping him up.

"I…"

He paused for effect. Possibly a little too long.

"… am Soka'li Em-Sckirrrnie Three. But you may call me Soka, as I know you people have problems with our names."

He smiled his broadest smile and hoped he hadn't sounded condescending to the savages, and offered his hand up to the woman who looked to be in charge.

"Pleased to meet you, Soka. I am Captain Zara Ortega. You may call me Zo."

Zo took his hand and shook it. Soka was dumbfounded. Nobody had done that to his hand before. He looked at his hand for a moment in confusion, then smiled again.

"What a weird greeting. So delightfully quirky."

While he found the handshake weird, the firmness, and the confident stance of the woman who called herself Zo impressed him. Together with her practical and austere uniform, he was pleased that at least some Earth women knew how to dress and act feminine.

He looked over the rest of them, and found it somewhat disturbing that the men dressed and acted the same way, however. No colorful robes, and they looked like they didn't know what makeup was.

"Delightful," he said to himself to gloss over that he stood there staring at them, while holding on to an increasingly forced smile.

"Why don't we get you a meal while we discuss the mission and get to know one another," he found himself saying, driven more by his own hunger than concern for his guests at this point.

"I've read up on Earth, and do you know there's a whole report on which kinds of food are compatible with Earth digestive systems? I think it will prove most helpful, and I know just the place to take you."

He held out his hand for Zo to take, and was pleased to see he did not have to explain, as she held his hand firmly. At least they had *some* minimum level of social graces.

Soka led the group to the nearest elevator, and up to "ground" level. He was somewhat dismayed when heard the crew gasp at such a pedestrian view—quite literally—as they stepped out into the plaza.

***

Zo had been very taken aback at first at seeing Soka—a tall, shimmering bronze man in a flowing colorful dress and what seemed to be heavy makeup to Zo, who rarely wore any.

But his smile was infectious, and his demeanor was very friendly, and she soon relaxed to the point that she automatically took his hand when he offered it to lead them to somewhere to eat.

She was still in a daze, taking in every little bit of alien-ness.

When she'd gone into space with her father for the first time as a child and visited Mars, it'd been the same. All the new impressions had left her exhausted day after day, but that was just another human-populated world, with people mostly speaking a language she understood.

Here everything was alien.

Even the lift looked different, smelled different, and the lift panel had recognizable buttons but the numbers—one of the few things you could expect to always recognize on Earth—looked nothing like Arabic numerals.

And then the lift doors opened, and she saw what a big space station looked like, just to hear Soka utter beside her, "I know it's cramped."

It was then that she noticed he was still firmly holding on to her hand, and it felt awkward, but it was also very clear from his grip that he had no intention of letting go of it.

Where Vanguard looked like you were at the bottom of a deep valley, here you could look to the sides and see the landscape disappear in the atmospheric moisture in the distance, and there were proper clouds in the "sky," not just the occasional little haze of Vanguard, and birds flying above them. And instead of the strip of lighting from the spire in Vanguard, there were two central "suns" set on spokes offset sufficiently to minimize shadows from the spokes themselves.

On the plaza in front of them, there were masses of people. Centauri, but also far more alien-looking humanoids, and possibly even some non-humanoids in a group in a distance, but Zo did not get a chance to look at them properly before Soka was pulling her along.

Soon they were in a side street, and Soka motioned them into a small restaurant where he was clearly already on good terms with the owner.

"I always study the eating places before I come to a new outpost," he explained. "I ate here last night, and for a tiny backwater outpost like this, it is quite alright and most of their food is edible to Earthers."

He sat down next to Zo and eagerly started explaining the bewildering menu to them.

Chapter 7

"So what do you think of Soka?"

Vincent was lying back in a chair in the shared living space on the *Black Rain*.

They were all back on the ship apart from Soka, who needed to get some paperwork sorted out with his superiors first, and get his luggage. It was late afternoon, local station time, when they'd gone back to the ship, and they agreed they might as well leave their departure until the morning, and they agreed they'd see him then.

"Is that shimmer his actual skin, or glitter? I saw most of them seem to have it, but not as strong." Rob looked around the room.

Zo shrugged. "Not sure. The first envoy was reported as shimmering like that too. If it's glitter, they seem to all like to use a lot of it."

"Did you notice how all their men dress feminine, and all their women very masculine?" Jonas sat up.

"I think they see it as opposite," Zo answered. "He told me he thought it was very weird how feminine you dressed, Jonas. And the rest of you guys too."

Clarice and Monique burst out laughing.

"Hey, I don't have a problem with it. I mean it's not like it's unusual at home, it just struck me how almost all of their men were in robes or dresses," replied Jonas. To Vincent he sounded defensive.

"He seemed genuine and curious, though," Zo said while looking off into space.

"Did you notice what he said when we got to the plaza?" Rob said.

"He told me 'I know it's cramped.' Imagine what kind of stations they must have if this is cramped, and a 'tiny backwater outpost' as he said in the restaurant…"

"He complained about the food too," added Monique.

They all agreed the food had been incredible. They did not know what any of it was. Soka had translated and attempted to explain, but they were left with tastes they had never before experienced and names like "Xarian Eight-armed Starfish" and "Congealed egg of Ge'thian Lavasnake" that sounded gross, but told them very little, and their lack of anything visual to connect the names to made it easier to eat things that might otherwise have put them off.

"I asked where he was from," Jonas said, "and he got all cagey. I don't think they trust us with that yet."

"He did say, though, that it took him about a dozen gate transfers to get here, and that he was more around 250 lightyears away. Of course he might have been exaggerating." Jonas looked around, and Vincent thought it looked as if he was expecting applause for having revealed something major.

He liked Jonas, but he also thought Jonas seemed to depend too much on others for validation.

Vincent glanced over at Monique, and he noticed how little she drank, and how she seemed to hang onto every little word about Soka. He knew her sort well enough to know she'd go back to her cabin and write down every little thing that had been said for her report. He'd have done the same in her place—he didn't blame her. But he wasn't sure he trusted her yet.

He found her very attractive, though. He was too drunk tonight to try chatting her up, but he was definitively going to try to get to know her better.

"How about his English? Do you think he's using a translator?" Mons asked.

"I don't know," said Zo. "I didn't see any, and if he does, they're doing something very clever—I can't see or hear any signs of him originating speech in any other language. Maybe something subvocal that vocalizes before him. Or direct neural interface."

"Oh, I'd *love* that." Clarice lit up at the thought. "Imagine learning a language this fast."

They kept talking about Soka well into the evening, and one after the other drifted off to their cabins to sleep.

Chapter 8

Soka turned up first thing in the morning, and Clarice was the only one already up and ready to meet him. He was dressed in a figure-hugging short blue dress that Clarice thought looked surprisingly good on him, though it seemed highly inappropriate for an official representative to a space ship.

"Good morning, Soka. Pleasure."

She took his hand as he seemed to want, and led him inside, and showed him around the ship.

Clarice noticed he scrunched his nose a number of times, and wondered if that indicated displeasure the same way it did on Earth, but she decided against asking.

"How do you manage with all of you on this small a ship?" Soka asked as she showed him the common area.

"It's not that small by Earth standards. Are Centauri ships all much bigger?"

"Oh, I wouldn't really know what our freight or courier ships are like. I hope I didn't offend… The diplomatic corps ships I normally travel on are quite large. At least the guest quarters are. I did serve on a military ship in my youth, but it was a big cruiser so not really comparable."

He smiled apologetically to Clarice, while Clarice tried to guess his age.

In his youth, he said, she thought to herself. He looked young to her. She'd have guessed he'd be maybe in his thirties.

When they got to the bridge, Zo and Mons were already there, and Soka greeted them both with an excitement and intensity that Clarice could see tested their morning mood to its limits, especially given the late night they had. She knew Zo would have found that intensity grating under any circumstances.

Clarice quickly derailed him before he tried to turn it into a more extensive conversation.

"So, here is all the data we've been given about the incident. Why don't you review it, and let us know if anything stands out to you?"

Soka agreed with the same enthusiasm he had shown in his greetings, and sat down by the terminal and started scrolling through the information, stopping a couple of times to ask for Clarice's help with the wildly unfamiliar computer interface, but overall ingesting the information at a surprising speed given it was all in English.

I bet he's augmented. Maybe ocular implants like mine, she mused to herself as she observed him more closely than she observed what he was watching.

The information they had on the incident was extremely limited. They had sensor readings and logs that had been transmitted alongside the last message. The message itself involved a desperate plea for help, and an identification of the ships as Centauri—something that seemed consistent with the sensor data.

The logs showed a trading run to a small outpost near the Proxima gate where trade in certain minerals had been authorized, apparently to feed needs at a Centauri colony on Proxima Centauri b.

Clarice hoped perhaps Soka would recognize anything in the data of the scans of the Centauri ships. Be able to tell anything about their type or class, or any way to identify them, but he seemed to be drawing a blank.

Why did they send us a diplomat? she thought. *Surely someone with a military background would be better. Military intelligence even.*

"We're ready to leave when you're ready, Soka," Zo said. She sounded like she'd recovered from Soka's excited greetings.

Soka turned around. "Excellent! I'm ready. Let's go!"

Clarice looked to Zo, and caught her trying not to roll her eyes at Soka's excitement. Zo nodded her confirmation, and Clarice turned back toward her console and asked C&C for clearance.

"Everyone to stations."

The rest of the crew were in place within minutes, and soon they were given clearance to leave as well. Zo took control herself, and they slowly boosted out of the docking bay.

Once out, Clarice laid in the course, and waited for Zo's order, and then they were away—their first job in another star system.

Chapter 9

"Those are definitively parts of an Earth ship."

Monique was maneuvering carefully among the wreckage alongside Vincent and Jonas. It was hazardous work, and complicated. To avoid any risk of flying off accidentally, they were all three tethered to a "sled"—effectively a crate with compartments they could put whatever worth securing into, and strap equipment to, and which had extra oxygen and small thrusters. They were not powerful enough to get much speed, but significantly more powerful than the tiny emergency thrusters in their suits.

The sled was tethered to the *Black Rain*.

But that meant four tethers total to avoid getting all tangled up as they moved around the debris field looking for evidence.

It had taken them hours of painstaking high-energy scans to find the debris field, but when they did, it was obvious it was there—they got hits for higher than natural concentrations of a number of materials to be expected on an Earth spaceship.

They'd carefully approached the debris field and Monique had insisted she needed to be part of the salvage party. Zo had looked annoyed when she did, and had offered Soka an opportunity to go out too. Monique didn't know if it was a show of diplomacy or if Zo just thought it'd annoy her to have him tag along. But the Centauri had very dramatically expressed his pleasure—no, deep gratitude—at being asked and then politely declined, and insisted he trusted the Earth crew would act with integrity. He would, of course, look at what they brought back.

Monique had frowned. She didn't know what to make of Soka. She found him physically attractive, but his femininity confused her. She had no issue with feminine men, but she usually didn't find them attractive. She preferred her men to look strong and rugged, and Soka's mannerisms put her off. At the same time she had already come to like how sensitive he was, and how openly he expressed his feelings about… everything. Even when his dramatic flair for how to do it made her frown.

"I think I have components of an engine here," said Vincent, as he brought a twisted bit of metal back to the sled.

Monique continued combing through the endless sea of pieces around her. It was hard to decide what mattered. What should be collected. They certainly did not have the time to try to collect everything. She found pieces from people's cabins… It probably mattered to someone, but it wasn't priority. Evidence had priority. She found broken pieces of circuit boards, and brought them back.

A charred and then desiccated piece of someone's head, reduced to a skull with blackened, freeze-dried pieces attached.

Whoever attacked this ship had done a very thorough job. They did not find many body parts. But then they did not find many parts bigger than a fist of the ship itself either.

"What the hell have they done to this ship?"

Vincent expressed what Monique felt too. She did not know what weaponry the Centauri had, or if the attackers were Centauri, but this didn't look like Earth weapons.

"A normal plasma cannon would have punched holes in the ship, and maybe make it break apart or explode, but there should be bigger pieces… I don't know what could do this, unless they've spent ages afterwards shooting every piece they saw into smaller pieces, or unless they used excessive amounts of explosives or a broad plasma beam."

Pulverizing a ship this way… It was wasteful as well as seemed cruel. *They must have gotten no chance to surrender,* she thought. *Unless they pulverized it after they'd already killed them.*

Monique lowered her voice, which made no sense, and replied. "Much broader than anything we have. The energy required would be ridiculous."

"We can rule out nukes," Vincent added. "There's nowhere near enough radiation."

They'd scanned for radiation before they went out, and he was right. There were some minor sources of radiation, likely from weapons and parts of the engine, but they were if anything surprisingly low—the sources of radiation on the ship clearly had been pulverized and dispersed like the rest.

"Fuck, I hate this," Monique muttered mostly to herself.

Monique had investigated destroyed ships before, but this felt ominous to a degree nothing else had. There used to be closure. You found something to bury. You understood what had happened, and you could say who did it, and promise retribution.

And it was rare it looked like purposeful, intentional outright slaughter.

But here they'd found what might or might not be pieces of four people so far, out of a manifest of nineteen, and only fragments, and they were further from understanding what had happened than they were before they'd set out. It looked very much like a hostile Centauri ship was the only possible perpetrator.

Unless it's another species entirely. Who knows who might be out here.

Soka had been very adamant there was no way it could be the Centauri government, and seemed very earnest and offended it was even suggested. *Maybe he's a good liar, but he doesn't seem the type.*

Vincent had also very strongly expressed the belief it'd make no sense tactically or strategically for the Centauri government to be behind this, and Monique tended to agree with that.

If it was Centauri, and not sanctioned by the government, then that seemed worse—from everything Monique had read about the Centauri, all Earth intelligence on them suggested a social system that strongly frowned on and restricted private control of weapons of any kind. In fact, it appeared most Centauri vessels were unarmed, and relied on the ability to rapidly dispatch military for protection, coupled with a reputation for swift and ruthless vengeance when wronged.

A privately armed Centauri ship destroying an Earth trader might be as big a challenge to the Centauri as to Earth.

Monique didn't want to contemplate the political implications.

"I may have the black box. It looks damaged, but maybe we'll be lucky."

Jonas sounded triumphant. They had most of the data from the ship—the emergency message had been accompanied by an emergency data dump of prioritized information, but it had been incomplete, and would also not include anything picked up by critical systems after it was sent.

"I don't know what else we can find here. Let's head back and analyze what we have so far, and continue tomorrow if we have to."

Monique was not technically in charge, but both Vincent and Jonas appeared to have let her lead.

If Zo heard me taking charge, she'd have been pissed off, Monique thought, and briefly smiled.

She knew Vincent was skeptical of her. She'd seen his record, and knew he'd left the military because he'd decided he didn't want to fight Earth's wars any more, and she respected him for that—more than she was willing to say out loud as serving officer, but also understood why he would not trust her as a result. She got the sense Vincent let her lead anyway because he wanted to observe her, and get a handle on her. *I'd have done the same.*

And she was pretty sure Jonas let her be in charge just because Vincent did. He clearly looked up to Vincent more than either of them was prepared to acknowledge.

They fastened their equipment to the sled, rolled up their tethers, and let the winch on the sled pull them back to the ship.

Chapter 10

"Hey, Clarice. How are you doing?"

Clarice turned and greeted Monique as she entered the common area.

"I'm good. *I* haven't just spent seven hours scouring a debris field and getting the dust of charred people all over my suit."

Clarice was disgusted, based largely on the comms she'd listened in to while bored on the bridge.

"Yeah, well, I've scrubbed unreasonably much. I felt dirty even though I know logically nothing could possibly have gotten on my skin through the suit. You know? Trying to feel clean in zero-g without a proper shower doesn't make it any better."

Clarice knew perfectly well what she meant.

"Sounds like there's not going to be much to work with," Clarice replied.

"Yeah, we found a few components, and a few charred body parts, but I have no idea how we're going to be able to figure out what went down here from that."

"While you guys were out, we ran long range scans and high intensity as well, and found nothing else of interest. Despite many 'helpful' suggestions from Soka."

Clarice rolled her eyes. Soka had inundated her with suggestions about frequencies, criticized the sensitivity of their "primitive" equipment, and generally annoyed Clarice until she wished she could take one of their larger antennas and insert it into some orifice or other on Soka.

As an "experiment."

I don't even know how many orifices he has, she thought, and smirked.

She'd not spent much time on Centauri anatomy. She'd read everything she could about their tech, on the other hand. What little they had access to.

She'd glared at Soka to the point where Zo had to point out to her that her eyes were pulsing in a fiery red that Soka seemed to find quite alarming.

To make him relax, she had to explain her augments to him, but had lied about why they'd pulsed red. *Maybe I should fine-tune the automatic response.*

Afterwards she'd spent the last hour or so trying to relax in the common area, and had been quite happy to have it to herself, though she'd had enough time to calm down, and was pleased to be able to talk to Monique now that she was back in.

The common area was quite cramped in flight, but now that they were not accelerating, it felt spacious since they could use all six sides. In zero-g they had no need for chairs or sofas, as they'd just push themselves off them anyway if they tried to sit down on something. Instead they had numerous clips and other things they could attach themselves or various objects to in order to avoid floating around if they moved too much.

Clarice had been reading on what in forward acceleration would have been the ceiling, attached to it with a small clip that would certainly not hold her if they suddenly accelerated, but which held her enough that she could push her feet gently against the "ceiling" to hold her in a weird sort of sitting position with nothing as a seat. This was how she preferred to "sit" while she was otherwise occupied.

She was reading as if a virtual screen was projected on her eyes. Really, nothing was being projected on them at all because of her augments—the display was sent straight to her optic nerve. It was an efficient way to read—though "speed reading" had been largely found to work poorly and reduce retention. Her optical interface nevertheless allowed her to get the illusion of having the text "projected" into her view for the optimal amount of time, and optimal size and font to maximize both her reading speed and retention.

Rob had described her as bat-like once after coming across her late one evening in the common area hanging from the "ceiling" in her reading position in near darkness, with her eyes mostly blacked out apart from a faint red glow. There was no functional reason for that glow. She just liked how it looked. *And how uncomfortable it makes people.*

He'd told her it was the scariest thing he'd seen, and she knew he'd been a wartime medic in several bloody conflicts, so she was sure he'd seen all kinds of nasty things.

She'd feigned indignance, but had secretly been quite pleased she was able to put some fear into him. She'd toyed with getting her incisors sharpened just to really scare him one evening, just for fun, but had decided cosmetic dentistry just for the sake of scaring a crewmate was a bit far even for her.

She suddenly realized what time it was.

"Shit, I need to get back to the bridge. I promised to relieve the captain. Talk to you more later, Monique."

Monique smiled at her, and Clarice unclipped and kicked off the wall and into the hallway.

***

"Sorry, Zo. I was talking to Monique and didn't pay attention to the time."

"It's okay. How do you find her, anyway?"

"She seems okay. Vincent seems sure she's going to spy on us, but she seems pretty laid back. Not asking anything she shouldn't. So far anyway…"

Zo frowned.

"And she seemed freaked out by what she saw out there today," Clarice added.

"I don't blame her, it doesn't make any sense. Keep scanning, okay. Jonas will relieve you later. I need some sleep."

Zo brushed her hand against Clarice's arm, and slipped out.

The hairs on Clarice's arm stood up. She did not quite know how to be around Zo after last year. She'd thought about that evening while in prison more than she cared to admit to herself, even if nothing had happened. Maybe she wished it had. Zo hadn't said anything. Yet. But they'd hardly had a moment alone.

Clarice clipped into her seat, and checked her screens. Same boring scans, with nothing showing up. She thought about Soka's suggestions. It occurred to her they were oddly detailed for someone ignorant. *Maybe he knows more about the technology than he lets on. Maybe he's just ignorant about the limitations of Earth technology.*

She resolved to push him on the subject in the morning.

In the meantime she was stuck doing the same scans, and trying to think of ways to improve the resolution.

Suddenly there was a blip. She wrote it off as just noise, but when she scanned the same area again, it was still there. It was too weak to resolve to more than a higher than usual concentration of certain metals, but it was at the very least not normal, and it was above the noise threshold.

She was not yet sure whether to raise the alarm.

It moved. Of course everything moved. But it moved-moved. As in, its direction changed. Slowly, but it changed. And it very gently accelerated.

It must be a ship, she thought to herself. But if she fired thrusters, it'd know they'd been spotted, and the size had to mean it was a tiny scout ship or cloaked in some way.

Soka, she thought. She paged his quarters, and got a very drowsy response.

"I need help. Oh, this is Clarice, on the bridge. Could I have your help?"

"Now? Can it wait until the morning?"

"No… I think there's a ship. I need you to help me with the scanner."

She said the last part with a very pointed tone. She did not know if he understood Earth intonation at all, but at least he stopped objecting and promised he'd be there shortly.

If you're a ship, she thought, *what are you doing here?*

Chapter 11

"Where is that ship you needed help with?"

Soka looked puffy and sleepy and not at all happy at having been woken up when he got onto the bridge.

Clarice showed him the scans.

"Those suggestions you had about the scanners. You know the tech better than you wanted to let on, don't you!"

Soka groaned.

"I may have dabbled on some scanner tech when I was an engineer. It was a long time ago. And I'm not even sure your tech can handle it, and I don't know how to program your system."

"That's okay… Just tell me, and I'll let you know if we can adjust our software or if it'll take hardware upgrades."

She flashed her eyes in a light blue for emphasis. He sighed, and started explaining to her the equations needed to infer additional resolution based on resonance between the responses in various bands. As far as Clarice understood the theory, what he described was beyond any Earth tech, and she got the distinct feeling he was still holding back.

Even if he wasn't holding back, as far as she understood, Soka's own understanding of this was the understanding of someone with several decades outdated engineering background in the tech, not someone who at any point knew what the state of the art *was*, much less the current state.

It was a humbling realization.

She updated the ship's systems as rapidly as she could, but it took several false starts and listening to an exasperated Soka moan about the primitive computer systems they had to deal with, and how slow everything was, and how poor her grasp of "basic mathematics" was before they had something even worth trying.

The first attempt was far from perfect, but they'd increased the resolution of their scans at the requisite distance several times over. After some further tweaks, Soka gave a contented grunt.

"You're a fast learner, Clarice. I had my doubt any of you could understand this at all, but you're starting to."

He smiled at her. Clarice was not sure exactly what the smile meant. It felt to her as if perhaps it indicated the kind of pride a parent might feel when a young child achieves something that is in the big picture not the slightest bit impressive, but a first for *their* child. There was a hint of condescension even in his limited praise.

When they reran the scan, the resolution was over a magnitude higher than when they started.

"That'll do," Soka said, mostly to himself, it seemed.

Clarice looked closely at the image of what had before been a blob of matter. It was now very clearly a ship. It did not look like an Earth ship.

She called Zo's cabin.

"Sorry to wake you, Cap, but we've got a ship. A small one. I wasn't sure, so I talked Soka into helping with the scanners."

"Coming."

Zo was there a few minutes later, and Clarice walked her through the scans and explained roughly what they'd done to improve them.

"If they know the limitations of Earth scanners, odds are they think we haven't spotted them. They're holding very much at the edge of the scanner range of normal Earth scanners," Clarice said.

"It seems you're more than just a diplomat, Soka…" Zo stared him down, and he just smiled an awkward smile.

"What do we do, Cap? Do we move towards him? He'll realize we've spotted him."

"For now, let's just wait. Since we know it's a ship, and given the scanner modifications, how far behind can we remain and reliably track them?"

She looked at Clarice, and then Soka, and back.

Clarice made some quick calculations and conferred with Soka and gave the captain her numbers. They could safely stay about twice the current distance away and have a decent margin to track them even on the move.

"Okay, so let's keep a close eye. If they start moving, follow them. Let them increase the distance before you follow."

Zo clipped into her seat.

"I'm going to nap here… Don't you dare wake me unless they move."

"I need my beauty sleep too, dear Clarice. Can you manage without me?" Soka quipped in a voice Clarice didn't know whether it implied the kind of sarcasm it sounded like.

She almost growled at Soka, but settled for a red flash of her eyes instead, and was pleased when he yelped and backed out of the room.

Zo laughed. "Don't scare the man… The poor guy is intimidated by you."

"I know, but he's so infuriatingly condescending sometimes. At least I think he is."

"Good night, Clarice…"

Zo smiled at her, then closed her eyes, and Clarice looked at her softening face. She liked seeing Zo's face soften for a change. On duty she was always so tense.

Clarice set her eyes to alert her if anything changed, in case she were to fall asleep, and tried to get more information while waiting. It took two hours before she was alerted, just as it felt like she'd been dozing off with open eyes.

The ship had started slowly accelerating away from them. She waited a few more minutes to be sure, and woke Zo.

"Okay, let's get everyone up."

Zo alerted the rest of the crew, while Clarice started very gently accelerating to follow them. She pulsed the nav thrusters in short bursts at first, adjusting their position in what might be mistaken at distance for a search pattern. As the scout ship accelerated faster, she moved the ship out of the debris field in time to fire the main engines just as the ship had doubled its distance to them.

No sign of being detected.

They increased the rate of acceleration as much as they dared, and carefully tried to maintain the distance to the scout ship while zig-zagging behind them, hoping that if they were spotted there was a chance their prey would think *Black Rain* had not seen them.

The ship was heading towards an area that should have no stations, off the typical shipping paths, beyond the Proxima gate. There'd be no reason to fly there unless they were meeting someone. Especially not in a ship this small.

Suddenly several larger blobs appeared at the very edge of the range of their improved scanners… Seconds later they resolved to large ships. The structure indicated Centauri.

"What would our ships be doing out here?" gasped Soka.

Chapter 12

"Full stop!" Zo yelled, and Clarice flipped the ship around and braked hard.

Soka almost vomited. It was a long time since he'd had to deal with those kinds of sudden maneuvers and he'd had no time to prepare.

"Anything you can tell us about these ships, Soka?"

Zo turned to him and her voice was hard and icy.

"The scans don't tell me much yet. The data is consistent with Centauri destroyers of the Atrycc class. If that's what they are, this ship would be torn to shreds in seconds if they engage."

Soka was sweating.

"But… but… They shouldn't have any weapons that should be able to do what was done to that Earth vessel without spending time methodically destroying every piece afterwards… If those ship are Centauri military, they have weapons I've not been informed about."

He paused.

"Weapons like that makes no military sense. And if they're not military… Then something is very wrong. I need to talk to them."

Zo stared at him for a moment before she spoke.

"Not on my life; until and unless they spot us. We wait and see if they react first. If we can avoid a confrontation and sneak away, maybe we'll live."

Soka clasped his hands together as he did not know what to do with them. He'd found the idea that Centauri ships would be behind the attack preposterous, but he could not explain the signatures. He tried to keep calm, but the data was more than consistent with Atrycc class. It looked like a perfect match. *Of course this ship's scanners still aren't great,* he thought. *Even so.*

He had been assured there were no Centauri military in this sector at all, so any ships that were here were, as far as he was concerned, unauthorized.

It was the worst possible outcome, unless it was a mistake. Maybe they'd been sent here to investigate too, without his knowledge.

Clarice turned to Zo. "They've definitely spotted us."

Soka was just barely coming to grips with the ship's tactical displays, but one of the ships was using a high-energy active scan on them, and he again implored the captain to let him talk to them.

"Okay, Soka, you have your chance."

Zo motioned to Clarice to arrange it. Moments later Clarice indicated to Soka he was good to start his message.

"Centauri Ship, this is Ambassador Soka'li Em-Sckirrrnie Three aboard the Earth vessel *Black Rain*. You are ordered to stand down and identify yourselves," he said, in English in deference to his host. It took a short while before they got a reply.

"*Black Rain*... Ambassador whoever. We do not answer to you. You stand down."

"What... Insolence... I am authorized by the Lady Xine-Zor Li'mor Four to investigate an attack on an Earth ship in this sector. You may check my credentials."

"Our authority exceeds yours. You have no business here. Stand down, shut off your engines, and wait to be boarded, or you will be destroyed."

"I demand your rank and name. The Lady Xine will hear of this."

"You demand nothing. You have thirty seconds to comply or be destroyed."

"Cut the connection," Soka could hear Zo whisper to Clarice.

"It seems they don't want to talk, Soka. And there's no way in hell we're surrendering. Everyone, I want options. Fast."

Soka looked down. "You need to at least start slowing down, so they think we're complying," he almost mumbled in Zo's direction.

Zo nodded, and Clarice cut the main engines and used nav thrusters to adjust their speed.

"The Atrycc class is built for long range fighting. Nobody in a serious conflict sends big ships close... It's all about long range acceleration of mass. The destruction of the Earth ship still confuses me, but I don't think these ships did it."

Soka was speaking rapidly. He was more confident now.

"If they get too close to us without launching fighters or anything else, they'll be vulnerable. No experienced Centauri commander would bring these ships close. They'd send something else."

"Yes!" he exclaimed, half turned away, as if he was having a discussion with himself. "This is someone who doesn't understand these ships." *But why,* he thought. *It still makes no sense.*

Clarice had brought up the latest scans, and Soka bounced over to her.

"Look here," Soka pointed, "and here. The weapons ports are recessed too far into the ship to be able to adjust direction much. They're meant to launch huge self-propelled projectiles, but those projectiles are too big to detonate this close to their own ship, and have too long a turning radius anyway. They're meant for major targets."

"The plasma cannons," Soka said and pointed again, "don't provide comprehensive cover at short range. By the time someone gets close they're meant to have a fighter wing launched, and support ships."

Vincent nodded. "You're right. Whoever is flying this doesn't know the capabilities, or they're hoping we don't. And either way I'd say they probably don't have the support they should. Maybe they're stolen, or there's been a mutiny or something."

Soka was pleased that Vincent understood, but he scoffed loudly at the idea that someone had stolen ships from the Centauri military. *What other explanation can there be, though.* He could not think of any.

"We're close enough now." Soka pointed to the scans. "At the moment they can't hit us with their plasma cannons."

Zo turned to Vincent and Jonas. "Boys… I want you ready to hurt them. I want them to hurt bad enough to try something stupid."

"I know just the thing, Cap."

Vincent grinned.

"Soka, what happens if we launch a missile into their missile port?"

"I truly don't know. I don't think that's ever happened. It'll be closed… But if you hit it enough times, you might just penetrate. Even with your old-fashioned missiles."

Soka held up his hands. He'd studied the specs for the *Black Rain*, and he knew how primitive the Earth missiles it had aboard were.

"Full barrage, then, with a plasma appetizer…"

Vincent and Jonas set to preparing it.

"Soka, help Clarice plan an escape path that minimizes their chance at firing at us before we have decent speed," Zo told him.

"Cap, they've launched a shuttle," Mons yelled.

"Good, clearly they think we're ready to surrender," Zo replied. "Or at least they don't expect us to put up a fight if they try to board."

Soka was impressed. Perhaps there was something to these people after all. If it was up to him, he'd almost certainly have surrendered faced with a ship like this, but they didn't even consider the option, and in the excitement, neither had he. He felt exhilarated, and almost clapped before thinking better of it and clasping his hands together to suppress his display of exhilaration. Zo in particular impressed him. So determined.

He showed Clarice the path he thought would maximize their chances. They worked rapidly together, turning his explanation into a program to allow them to change thrust more rapidly than Clarice would be able to do manually.

If the ship had—and launched—a fighter wing, they'd have a problem, but Soka felt confident that if they did, they'd have launched it already. Maybe they had other ships, but it'd likely be minutes before they could react. It did seem very odd for a ship like this to be out here without proper support.

Clarice concurred with the path he'd argued for, and Soka was pleased.

"All ready, Cap," Vincent said.

It looked like Vincent and Jonas had the firing pattern programmed in.

Clarice pointed her thumb up to Zo.

Soka could guess from context that it meant she was ready. He tentatively tried to copy the gesture to himself, and found it curious.

He was thrown back in his seat when Zo gave the order and Clarice maxed out the main engine.

Oh dear! he thought. He'd not felt acceleration like this since his military days.

Chapter 13

On Zo's order, Clarice had immediately triggered the flight path Soka had helped plan out.

It was rare for the roar of their main engines to be that loud. Zo kept an eye on the execution of the flight plan on her contact lens views, while the main shared viewscreen on the bridge showed a tactical display.

They were subjected to much higher perceived g than normal. Nothing they could not handle, but enough that it'd be uncomfortable. The bridge had been unlocked, and would rotate to match acceleration for some of the burns to try to at least keep the g-forces somewhat consistent.

They would accelerate straight past the destroyer's torpedo hatch.

"Fire!" she yelled to Vincent and Jonas. The two launched the plasma cannon barrage straight at the torpedo hatch first. They would not know if it had penetrated before they launched a full missile barrage. Unlike the giant torpedo hatch on the destroyer, the *Black Rain* had been refitted with a small bank of deadly but far smaller and more maneuverable missiles, and they were now all programmed to hit the torpedo hatch, or as far inside it as they'd get, in quick succession.

The ship had not yet shown signs of a reaction. The shuttle that was headed for them started veering off.

Zo watched the tactical display as it indicated two of the missiles had slammed into whatever was left of the torpedo hatch… The third one was about to hit… And continued in.

The explosion was much bigger than the first two. Clearly, it'd set off explosives. It was hard to tell how much damage it'd do. They did not know what kind of warheads this ship might carry.

She hoped they weren't suicidal enough to try to fire a torpedo at them from this distance. It didn't look like it.

Zo watched out for any signs of launches from the destroyer, but so far their scanners showed nothing.

Suddenly the main thrusters cut out for a few seconds, as the nav thrusters rotated the ship 120 degrees, before the main thrusters hit again, forcing a brutal turn before they leveled out at 90 degrees from their original heading, now hugging the "top" of the destroyer as closely as they could to stay out of view of the plasma cannons turning radius.

They'd now be on a maximum burn as long as possible, hoping that they'd accelerate enough while alongside the first destroyer that they'd have enough speed to be a hard target for the others once they were no longer protected by the bulk of the first destroyer.

Zo looked back to the tactical display, which showed major energy buildup inside the ship. The fifth and sixth missile had also exploded far inside the torpedo hatch, and it looked to her as if perhaps they'd set off one or more of the ship's missiles.

Seconds later she got confirmation, as the explosions started breaking through the outer hull and the destroyer started breaking apart.

"The other two destroyers are breaking formation to avoid the wreckage." Even Mons was excited for a change.

It looked like they had their chance. It'd take the others too long to correct their course and avoid the ship to be able to get up to match their speed. They'd be most of the way to the Proxima gate before then.

Zo felt optimistic, but just then Mons announced two smaller ships had been launched from one of the destroyers.

"Shit. Assessment?"

"They're larger than fighters. We should be able to fight them, but if they harass us or keep tagging us until the destroyers can get up to speed, they'll be a problem."

Mons asked Soka to have a look and help with the threat assessment.

Zo turned to Clarice. "Clarice, make sure we record all of this data and broadcast it."

"On it."

"Massive radio interference. Not sure if anything will get through."

"Keep trying, Clarice."

"Looks like the smaller ships are armed with light plasma cannons. Few or no missiles. But they're likely to be faster than us according to Soka."

Zo nodded to Mons to acknowledge his report, then turned to Monique.

"Monique, help Vincent and Jonas man the weapons stations."

One of the upgrades they'd gotten that Zo was particularly pleased about was additional plasma cannons on the sides of the ship that could rotate fully to fire backwards. They were in a far better position to keep firing at attackers without having to flip the ship and lose acceleration while firing.

She was hopeful they'd take out the two smaller ships without having to lose the speed advantage their initial maneuver had given them.

The plasma cannons were powerful enough that the extra thrust of firing them shook the ship rhythmically as they started firing. Their followers were surprisingly agile, and it proved hard to pin them down.

Clarice yelled out, "Cap, the second destroyer has completed turning, and we're far enough out they might try firing."

"The moment they do, you thrust in whatever damn direction necessary. Everyone, pay attention, this will get rough."

"Try to keep the smaller ships in between us and them. We're minutes from the Proxima gate."

"I think they're going to fire regardless... Shit, shit, shit."

Without warning, the ship flipped and thrust hard in a new direction.

"Status!"

"They fired a massive missile, Cap, the ships in between are trying to avoid it too. Not sure if they'll make it." Clarice sounded panicky, but Zo knew she'd react with precision.

She watched the path of the missile on the tactical display, and saw their ship changed course fast enough that she was pretty confident the missile would not manage to turn in time to hit them.

In fact, she need not worry, because the ships following them did not react nearly as fast as Clarice had, and clearly the destroyer had failed to appropriately lock the missile targeting. The missile hit the slower of the two smaller ships, and exploded in a massive blast.

It tore the smaller ship into pieces, and flung them as massive projectiles straight into the second of the following ships.

They looked on, dumbfounded. If they'd been unsure if these people knew how to operate these ships before, they knew now they lacked experience with large-scale battles entirely.

If they're really this shit, maybe we'll be okay, Zo thought.

She ordered Clarice to adjust course again. They were less than a minute from the gate when the destroyer fired again. They had time.

They counted down the seconds, as the missile accelerated faster than they could hope to.

And then they rematerialized near Proxima. Zo was not sure she'd ever get used to just suddenly being somewhere else.

"Head for Proxima Centauri b. Full speed."

They needed to find somewhere to hide before the destroyers reached the gate too.

Chapter 14

Proxima Centauri is a small red dwarf circling Alpha Centauri A and B roughly every 550,000 years. Soka had eagerly read up on what the Earthers knew about it, and was bemused at how recently in their history they'd spotted it given how near them it was.

He understood it was not visible to the naked eye from Earth, but it would not take a powerful telescope to spot it, and it had led him down a chain of searches that just emphasized how underdeveloped and savage these Earthers were.

The *Black Rain's* star charts showed it had four planets, and gave embarrassingly little detail.

Soka had pointed out to Zo that Proxima Centauri b had a Centauri scientific colony on it, which was why they were heading there. The planet was near, and they could potentially get help there, though he dreaded going there. That planet was cold and miserable.

"Soka! We're out of the range of their jammers. At least until they get through the gate. Contact your government. Try to find out what the hell is going on."

Soka was pulled out of his thoughts and nodded to Zo, and quickly brought up communications. He was getting the hang of the ship's controls, but had not yet gotten comfortable with the contact lens screens, so he used the terminal screen.

Zo moved over to his left side so she could see what went on.

Soka punched in confirmation codes to bypass the call screening, and got through to a colonel in the Centauri Space Force.

"Colonel Yuta'ri Li-Skiln Two, here. Who is this?"

Soka introduced himself.

"I'm on a diplomatic mission, and we're being attacked by several Atrycc class destroyers."

"Impossible."

"It's very much possible, Colonel. I am forwarding you sensor data and footage."

Zo had Clarice attach the data Soka mentioned.

"We have no destroyers in that sector. This data must be fake."

"I assure you, Colonel…"

"I don't know what you're up to 'ambassador,' but you're on an Earther ship, attacking the integrity of our forces, blaming us for unprovoked attacks, sending fake video clips."

"I demand to speak to your superior officer." Soka was not used to raising his voice and try to assert this kind of authority, and he was not sure he was any good at it.

"Your credentials must be fake. There is no other reasonable explanation. Maybe Earther trickery. I will not bother my superiors with this."

"Your head will roll for this," Soka yelled in attempt at dramatics, before he turned to Zo to whisper "not literally" in case she'd get the idea they were backwards barbarians, as he seemed to recall humans had still *actually* beheaded people in their quite recent history.

The colonel laughed.

"You're not even one of us, are you. You must be an Earther simulacrum. If our forces are after you, I'm sure it is for good reason. Good bye 'ambassador.'"

The call was cut.

Soka faced Zo with his eyes cast down.

"I had never expected they wouldn't believe me. This is unprecedented."

Zo put a hand on his shoulder.

"It's the problem when records are so easy to fake, Soka... Believe me, we've been there before."

"But what do we do now?"

"Are there anyone else you can call?"

"I can try my wife. She can try to get the message out."

Soka tried establishing connection again, but was unable to get through.

"We're getting a carrier from the Centauri relay stations, Captain, but then we're cut near instantly," Clarice said.

Soka scrunched up his mouth in an unbecoming pout. "The colonel must have blacklisted us. We won't be able to contact anyone far enough away to require a relay."

Zo looked worried. "Do you believe that the colonel told the truth, or at least what he thinks is the truth, when he said they have no ships here?" she asked.

"I really don't know, Captain. Before this mission I'd have considered it unthinkable for one of our officers to lie, but I'd also consider it unthinkable for any of our ships to be part of anything like this."

"I don't know how to read your kind's body language, Soka. Did you see or hear anything that made it seem like he might be lying?"

Soka thought about it. The colonel had seemed arrogant and confident, but seemed shocked when Soka made his claim, and the shock changed to disgust. There was nothing in his demeanor that suggested deception to Soka. He'd spent many years learning to read people, and he was pretty certain the colonel genuinely believed what he'd said. He told Zo that.

Then again, maybe he's just not privy to that information…

They were most of their way to Proxima Centauri b, and hopefully most of their way to being able to hide, at least for a bit, as the destroyers following them would not know where they'd gone.

Soka looked on their tactical display and confirmed they expected the first of the destroyers to be through the gate in minutes. Their hope rested on a course that'd get them sufficiently inside the planet's gravity well before any of the destroyers entered the system, so that they could flip and brake into orbit with their plume obscured sufficiently by the body of their ship that there was a chance they'd go unnoticed until the planet was between them and the gate.

It was pretty much guaranteed at least one ship would still be dispatched towards the planet, as there were not many other options, but they were hopeful the destroyers would at least split up, and they'd have some chance of trying to shake them by flying closer to the planet than the big, bulky destroyers would want to risk.

This was far too much excitement for Soka. He'd left the Centauri military to get away from this kind of stuff, and he did not particularly miss it.

"Everyone strap in, it's about to get shaky."

Soka sighed. Clarice was about to adjust thrust and flip the ship and get them into orbit.

No sooner had she confirmed it was all done before their long range scanners showed a bulk of mass that had to be the first destroyer.

They immediately went as dark as possible, but they still had to burn their main thrusters for at least thirty seconds before they'd have slowed down enough to let the much smaller nav thrusters do the rest of the job. As much as their orientation should hide most of it, there was every chance they might pick up a sign of it on their scanners.

Chapter 15

"What the hell is going on, Soka?"

Monique had followed Soka to the common area when he left the bridge, and she was seething.

Soka folded his hands and looked calmly at her.

"I don't know any more than you do, Lieutenant Salinger."

"I don't believe you." Monique got right up in Soka's face and yelled.

She stared into a pair of oddly non-human eyes. She hadn't noticed them before. He had nice eyes, but the patterns of his irises were curved in a way she'd never seen on a human.

She found herself drawn in by his eyes, but she intended to be intimidating, and pulled herself together.

"All the intelligence we have on you people indicates large armed ships in private ownership just does not happen. So how do you explain those destroyers?"

"I don't. I have no idea…"

Soka was leaning back to get away from her, and slumping down where he sat.

Damn it, he seems genuine, Monique thought to herself and felt it get harder to maintain her anger, but she pressed ahead.

"Here's what I think, Soka. I think nobody is going to admit to anything while you're talking from the bridge of an Earth ship, and I think you knew that before you tried."

She pointed right in front of his face, and he outright whimpered like a scared animal.

"Maybe… I mean, maybe they won't admit to it, but I don't know anything about that."

He looked so apologetic, and scared of her.

"I'm sorry, Lieutenant Salinger… Monique. I was trying my best, I really am. It's unheard of to have military ships like these on deployment this far out without a well-publicized diplomatic spat or open war. Our forces are always kept back. It's bad for trade when people see destroyers everywhere, you see. It makes them jumpy, and asking questions about why the show of force is necessary."

"I really don't know what they might be doing here. I expected to find Earther ships. I really did. And frankly, according to the communications from your superior before the mission, I suspect so might they. I have a whole dossier on what *this* ship was involved in last year—it seems you Earthers are much more factional than we are. To find our own ships. It's distressing. Truly distressing."

It looked to Monique as if Soka was on the verge of crying, and she felt sure that this was not a man employed to keep secrets. She softened. She found it impossible to continue to yell at him when he looked this upset and intimidated.

She sat down next to him and put an arm around him. She felt odd about having to comfort someone. Doubly so knowing he wasn't human.

"Relax, Soka. I believe you. We'll figure it out, I promise."

Monique could not believe she was comforting an alien diplomat because she'd almost made him cry.

She had to stifle a laugh. He was so human in so many ways. Very feminine compared to most of the military men she was used to surround herself with. But in a way it made her feel comfortable with him that he was different. Vincent, Jonas, even Mons and Rob had all tried the tough guy act around her, though Mons and Rob mostly failed miserably.

Though she found Vincent physically attractive, she found the way they all acted tedious. Exhausting at times.

Soka, on the other hand, as strange as he was, seemed to never play games. Something she found bizarre in a diplomat, and she was not quite ready to trust that it was genuine. Maybe he was just really good at deceiving her. But she found his earnest reactions attractive. And he looked good too… If only he hadn't been quite so emotional.

Damn it, I'm wondering if I'm attracted to an alien—to a simpering alien. What is wrong with me, she thought, and quickly pulled her arm back.

"Something is wrong…" Soka looked up at her, and she was glad to be pulled out of her head.

"What do you mean?" she replied.

"Their strategy is off. They don't know how to handle those ships. And they should have more supports."

Monique nodded. They'd all agreed whoever was in command was inexperienced, and the lack of fighter wings was really strange. This wasn't new.

"We know that. Is there anything specific, Soka? Think. Both anything we can use against them, and any clue to what is going on."

"I'm not sure." He straightened up. "If this is some sort of secret op, perhaps they had limited choice in who they picked. People without proper flight experience or tactics." He paused briefly.

"But there's no way anyone would authorize ships this powerful for that, and these aren't ships you sneak about in. They must be stolen."

That sort of made sense to Monique as well. Maybe the reason they were so dismissive to Soka was that it was being covered up. *But we've been over this.*

"Who could steal several destroyers and get away with it? And pretend to be military when challenged?"

"I don't know, Monique. As far as I know nothing like this has ever happened before. If they've been stolen it'd be a total outrage. The government would likely be forced to go. Maybe that is why they were so dismissive. Maybe it's a cover-up."

They sat in silence for a moment, and Monique observed Soka's expressive face in a way she hadn't before, and her pulse increased a bit.

"My wife might know someone who could help. But those damn relay blocks… Maybe I'll be able to reach her from a station."

"First we need to survive until we get to a station," Monique pointed out.

Chapter 16

Zo watched the tactical display with trepidation. So far there was no sign that the ships that had come through the gate had spotted them, but it was hard to tell. They were avoiding active scans, and though it did not leave them totally blind, especially given the size and drive plumes of the destroyers, it did significantly reduce their ability to keep close track of them. However, it also made them significantly harder to spot.

One of the destroyers had set course in their direction, but not precisely. Zo had Clarice try to ascertain whether this was a ploy or not, but they could not really say for certain. Their course would not give them any particular apparent advantages or disadvantages. The fact the other two remaining destroyers were heading for the other two bigger planets in the system suggested the incoming force genuinely did not know where to look for them. *But that too could be an attempt at deception,* Zo thought to herself.

The *Black Rain* was about to "disappear" behind Proxima Centauri b, and Zo worried it was possible their followers would change course once they were out of view and wouldn't be able to spot course changes. Worst case they'd face all three destroyers converging on them from different angles.

As a result, once the following destroyer was out of view, she did not breathe any sigh of relief.

Instead, she ordered Clarice and Mons to start scans of the planet surface to have a clear idea of what they were facing if they had to land, and where best to approach the Centauri colony from.

The planet was dark and cold. That was the first impression from the data she got. It was slightly larger than Earth, in an orbit taking it around Proxima Centauri roughly every eleven Earth days. It orbited Proxima only one 20th of the distance Earth orbits the sun, but given that Proxima is a dim red dwarf, and most of the radiation from Proxima is in the infrared, as far as they could tell the planet never got brighter than twilight on Earth in normal conditions.

But Proxima flares heavily. On days with heavy flare activity the sunlight might get up to eight times as bright, though still only a third as bright as a Mars day.

Zo got miserable just thinking about landing there.

The biggest problem, though, would be radiation. Background radiation at ground level was high enough that unprotected they'd get a year of Earth-level background radiation in a day. If they were unlucky and got a day of heavy flare activity…

She had Jonas and Rob look at to what extent they could get away without wearing full EVA gear without getting fried. Rob had also prepared a suitable cocktail of potassium iodine and whatever other radiation treatments he could concoct with what limited medical supplies they had. They were not exactly prepared for this kind of situation, though they did of course carry some stuff intended for first aid in the case of minor leaks. Nobody cared about major leaks—on a ship, if a major leak happened it'd be too late to do anything anyway.

It'd be peak irony if we got burns, given how cold that damn place is.

The colony itself should have a heavily radiation-shielded dome according to Soka, but they were not sure if they'd have a choice in where to land, or for that matter if they'd be welcome, given the response of the Centauri so far.

The initial scans of the planet's surface were not much comfort. Rocky ridges with ice, a substantial proportion of which appeared to be water-ice in the valleys across the poles, with an equatorial belt that was mostly ice free, but still inhospitably cold radiation-soaked mountain ranges with no sign of plant life, and hardly any atmosphere.

Why the Centauri had decided to put a colony there, Zo had no idea, and Soka was not sure either. Or wouldn't say. Maybe they hoped to terraform it, but the low light and high radiation made it less than ideal. Maybe there were minerals there of value. Though Soka had insisted there'd be no point in putting a colony there just to hollow it out.

"We'd just have built a space station in that case," he'd said, as if throwing together a huge space station was not the slightest challenge. But she remembered he'd described the Centauri outpost they'd visited as "cramped."

"Anything else," she probed Clarice and Mons, who were still pouring over scans. The detail levels of the scans were not great—they avoided amping up the power to reduce the risk of being noticed.

"The colony is there," Mons said, pointing at a mountain South of equator. "It seems to be mostly dug out, with a tiny dome and a number of buildings outside."

"There are a couple of small landing pads here. They're full… We've identified two possible landing spots nearby that should be flat enough for us. The nearest is half an hour's trek at least through difficult terrain."

Half an hour doesn't sound too bad, in proper suits, she thought. With the giant caveat that if the destroyer got here and spotted their ship, they might well find themselves with no means of escape if they couldn't get help at the colony.

"Okay, tell everyone to prepare. It won't be long until that destroyer is here. If we're going to hope to get help, we need to try now. And get Soka here so he can try talking to them first."

An alarm blared.

"It's not the destroyer, but a smaller ship is headed for us, high speed. They've definitively spotted us." Mons brought the ship up on the main display.

"From the surface? Or from the destroyers?"

"From the destroyer, or at least from the other side of the planet, Cap."

"All hands, brace. We're about to go into battle. Monique, Vincent, take weapons."

Jonas was not on the bridge, so they were short. No time to wait for him to return.

"I'll help out with weapons. Clarice, prepare evasive flight pattern, but try to keep our main guns on them. Mons, you're our eyes."

"They have weapons lock, Cap," Mons yelled out.

"Fire at will!" Zo yelled the order.

Clarice did her best to get them out of the firing angle of the other ship's plasma cannons as Monique, Vincent, and Zo started blasting away at the other ship.

"Missiles incoming." Mons was keeping track of the weapons platforms on the other ship as best he could.

"On it," both Monique and Zo yelled at the same time. The first two missiles exploded within seconds.

"Two down," Mons confirmed. "Three more left."

Vincent took out the ship's missile launcher while Monique and Zo tried to destroy the last three missiles.

Monique almost jumped in her seat. "Got one!"

Before anyone had a chance to respond, the last two slammed into the ship, and shook it hard.

"Status?"

"We're venting air, Cap. Fast. And main engine is damaged and we're hurtling towards the planet. We should be able to land. Sort of."

Mons' report was exactly what Zo didn't want to hear. Their adversary would know where they'd land. *The destroyer will not just know where, but by extrapolating from the trail, they will know long before we get there…*

"Got a hit… Looks like they're going down too." Vincent laughed like a madman.

"Set us down. Closest spot to the colony you can get to."

"We're going down too fast to be able to get to the closest one… We'll be in for a long walk." Clarice turned and looked at Zo with a concerned expression.

"I don't care, Clarice. Do your best."

"All hands, prepare for emergency landing."

Chapter 17

Mons felt sure they were going to die. He was bracing himself, but then thought *What's the point?* glumly as they hurtled towards the ground. He was sure Clarice would do her very best to land them properly, and he had a lot of confidence in her abilities, but in that moment, he felt more confident in the power of gravity.

Landing them like this was immensely hard. Only one of the main engines was firing properly, and so he knew Clarice had to compensate by firing the nav thrusters properly to balance the ship correctly and prevent it from spinning out of control. Of course the computer would do most of the work, but no amount of simulation and contingencies would perfectly capture a random set of damage to a random set of aspects of the ship, and so Clarice would have to be prepared to handle any situation where the computer sensors—many of which were undoubtedly blown to pieces—and the nav system failed to compensate correctly.

So far, he could see on his contact lens displays while he was tightly closing his eyes that she was doing a remarkable job, but he still felt certain they were about to end up landing on the edge of some ravine and fall down it to a fiery death somewhere cold and dark where nobody would find them.

He'd been so excited when they were let out. Even more so to know they'd been given a job for the military. It pleased him they had a job that was honorable for a change. He'd not gotten over the immense embarrassment of the whole affair with Sovereign Earth, and how he'd been taken in by the original mission. His only consolation was that he had been the one to take out Grant and that in doing so he'd demonstrated his loyalty, even if Zo had never known that he had wavered—only Grant seemed to have picked up on that.

But then they ended up running from a heavily armed opponent again. Already. At least this time it was obvious who the enemies were.

Not that it matters now that we're about to die.

"We're about to set down. It'll be rocky!"

Clarice's voice lifted his spirits a tiny bit. He was still not convinced they were not going to die, but at least it sounded like she thought they might survive. *Maybe there's a chance,* he thought just as they slammed into the ground.

Zo spoke first. "Everyone okay?"

There were words of confirmation, and Mons dared open his eyes.

"Ship is intact... Apart from the damage from those missiles earlier. We're still venting atmosphere, of course."

Zo yelled at everyone to get to Jonas and Rob, all suit up, and grab weapons.

"How long a walk?" she asked.

Clarice pointed to the map and asked Mons for his assessment.

"It's at least a day."

They'd missed several of the nearest possible locations due to the lack of control, and there was at least one major ravine between them and the colony.

"We'll need to make sure we have climbing gear," Vincent said.

Zo smiled weakly, and Mons could guess why: If there was one thing they had plenty of, it was climbing gear. They'd stocked up on more than they ended up taking with them for their break-in at Vanguard Station.

"Any idea where the other ship set down?" Zo asked.

Mons looked at the last data collected.

"Not sure, but they can't have landed very far away. They seemed to descend with better control than us, so they almost certainly did what they could to land near us. I'd be surprised if we have more than a couple of hours head start."

Zo did not look pleased. "Try to get radio contact with the colonists, see if we can get help."

Mons tried to raise them, but got nothing but static.

"Okay, guess we're walking." Zo shrugged.

Zo and Clarice locked down all systems on the bridge, before they all made their way down to the lower airlocks.

The suits were all over the room. Jonas and Rob had been preparing them and only barely had the chance to get themselves strapped in when the attack happened. Rob had a bump on his head, and a small cut.

"Got hit by a damn helmet," he said to nobody in particular.

Vincent laughed. "That'll be a great first battle scar for you."

Rob glared at him, but even Mons could not help smiling.

They all got into their suits as fast as they could, and divided up the equipment. They brought food and water but only enough for a couple of days. If they didn't get to the colony they'd die soon enough anyway.

"Everyone got everything?" Zo asked.

Everyone confirmed.

"Check each other's suits. I don't want any casualties because of stupid mistakes."

It was a long time since Mons had been on any longer trek in heavy gear, and he dreaded it. As far as he knew most of the others hadn't either. Especially in near-Earth gravity. He had no idea about Monique or Soka of course, but from Soka's complaining when Jonas had tried helping him with his suit, he had a feeling Soka had not been in a full EVA suit for many years, if ever.

Mons was in a terrible mood. A day's walk with heavy equipment, with people following them was bad enough, but the ravines on their scans worried him. Climbing on Vanguard was one thing—the most complex climbing they'd done was in very low-perceived gravity.

Here they might have to cross a broad ravine with heavier gear at roughly one-g.

They opened the door, and stepped out.

He was momentarily distracted by the realization that they were, as far as he knew, the first human crew ever to set foot on a planetary body outside of the solar system.

He pointed it out to the captain over the radio.

"Awesome, we'll go into the history books," Clarice chirped cheerfully.

"Yeah, yeah," Zo replied with much less enthusiasm.

"Is that really what you want the history books to say your first words were?" Rob asked her. "'Yeah, yeah'?" he mockingly copied her.

"We'll invent something later," she replied. "When we aren't followed by people wanting to kill us. Mons, point the way."

Mons reviewed the map data and pointed out the direction.

When they turned, the view took his breath away, and he could not help pausing for a moment.

He'd seen Earthrise from the moon, and sunrise on Mars, but compared to this…

He could see the dim reddish disk of Proxima, high in the sky but still not lighting the barren rocky landscape up much. It looked like twilight. In the dark red-brown sky were two bright stars so close together you could mistake them for a single light. It could only be Rigil Kentaurus and Toliman—Alpha Centauri A and B.

"Three suns in the sky… Look at that."

Chapter 18

Rob was not built for this.

His breathing was rapid and his pulse rising. He did not need his suit flashing up notices about this on his contact lens display, because he could feel it.

He had not been marching at this kind of tempo anywhere for a very long time, much less with a heavy backpack, in an environmental suit, at full Earth gravity.

Rob looked at Monique in front of him, and wanted to swear. She didn't seem to be straining at all. In fact, he knew she wasn't as all of their suit bio data was fed to him as the ship medic, and he could see her damn pulse in real-time.

Of course she is active military, he reminded himself. Measuring himself against that was stupid.

Soka, on the other hand, was fascinating. They'd had to disable the alerting from his system because their suits did not know what to do about someone with a pulse that did not fit a human pattern at all. His heart was beating in a weird tempo that Soka confirmed to him was because Centauri heart muscles did in fact contract several times rapidly and then pause. It was disconcerting to Rob to watch. It looked like a severe heart defect to someone used to monitoring human heartbeats.

He didn't know precisely what Soka's normal range was, but given he was keeping up and wasn't complaining—and complaining was something he'd already come to expect from Soka—Rob felt confident it was in normal range. *Not like I'd know what to do if it wasn't.*

The terrain was brutal on his legs. Rocky enough that it took extra effort to walk even when the ground was relatively flat, which it rarely was. They'd walked for only two hours and Rob felt beat already, and he knew they had many more hours to walk before they could afford to risk a break.

The perspiration was dripping down his forehead, despite the suit cooling.

He was second to last, with Jonas keeping up the rear. It made him more insistent not to slow down, as he knew Jonas was in great shape—he could see it on his display, and he did not want to let Jonas notice how much he was struggling.

Rob was happy when they got to a slight downward slope, but changed his mind when he realized that descending a rocky slope like this was almost as tiring as ascending one—it took a lot of effort to avoid tumbling down.

Just then he saw one of the crew do just that. In the shadows he could not see who but he rushed down as fast as he could to find Clarice lying on the ground.

"Check her face plate!" Zo yelled over the radio, and Vincent carefully rolled her over.

"Can't spot any cracks. I'll check for leaks too… Rob, check your data for any pressure drops."

Checking for leaks was their first priority, because if the suit had ruptured, they might have little time to find and fix it before there'd be too little air left for it to be possible to reach the colony.

"Clarice, how are you feeling?" Zo's voice was shaking.

"I feel okay, I think. My leg. My left leg is hurting."

Rob moved over next to her. He'd have to assess the damage without opening her suit.

He'd checked his data for pressure drops, and there were none. He went through the rest. Pulse was returning to normal as she was lying down.

"Someone help her up, we need to see if she can put weight on her leg at all."

Vincent put her arm around his neck and lifted her up as if she weighed nothing.

"Carefully, Clarice, try to step on it."

"Oww… It's a searing pain… I can't step on it at all… And I feel nauseous."

"Nausea is common if you've broken a bone. I obviously can't tell for sure if you've broken it or just sprained it," Rob told her.

He turned to Zo and switched to a private channel.

"We need to look at it closer as soon as we can. I need a pressure tent as soon as we can afford the time. I can pump some painkillers into her air supply, but she can't put weight on it, and depending on how bad the break is she could be bleeding."

"Okay. We can't risk it yet. Do what you can, and we'll set up the pressure tent once it gets darker."

Zo turned to Clarice.

"Rob will give you some pain killers, okay, and we'll sort something out."

"Vincent, can you help her?"

"Don't worry about it, Captain."

Rob brought out a small gas canister and attached it to Clarice's breathing apparatus.

"You should feel the pain subside shortly, Clarice, and hopefully the nausea will get better too. Tell me if anything changes, okay?" *She better not puke in her suit.*

Clarice nodded.

"Jonas, help me with that."

Rob pointed at one of the tent poles for one of the pressure tents they'd brought. He needed part of one detached to use as an improvised brace for Clarice's leg.

Jonas quickly unscrewed it and handed it over, and Rob used one of the climbing ropes to tie it securely above and below where he believed her leg was broken.

"Clarice, that does not mean you should put weight on it, okay? I know you won't feel much, which makes it extra important you don't think it's alright to try to walk on it, because it won't work. Worst case you make things a lot worse. This is just to prevent you from moving it."

She nodded, and Rob confirmed to Zo that they could keep walking. It did slow them down, despite Vincent doing an amazing job at keeping Clarice up and moving.

Rob felt bad for thinking the pace suited him better now, and afraid of whether that meant their followers might catch up to them. He was not built for long walks, but even less built for battle.

He couldn't wait for darkness, but that was still at least a couple of hours away.

Chapter 19

Proxima was finally setting, and the landscape was almost entirely dark. Though Alpha Centauri A and B were brighter by far than the other stars that had come out, they were still far enough away to provide sufficient light to help much.

They would not be able to safely make any headway.

"How long is the night?" Zo asked Mons.

"It should be fully dark probably about five hours."

Jonas could tell it worried Zo.

Who knows how our followers are equipped, he thought. *Perhaps they'll risk walking through the night.*

Clarice's leg had definitively slowed them down.

They set up the pressure tents. The tents were basic. No airlock. Likely to leak. They'd all need to suit up if anyone wanted to leave. They would not risk sleeping without helmets in these—they were to let them eat, and otherwise prepare in a bit more comfort, nothing else.

Rob finally got a chance to look at Clarice's leg properly in one of them.

"It looks like a simple fracture," he told them as he bandaged it up and applied a hardening foam to create a cast.

"Nothing sticking out is always a good sign," Vincent quipped.

"Let the doc handle this, Vincent," Zo said. It looked like she about to say something else, but her voice trailed off.

Jonas didn't know much about medicine, but he knew there was a risk Clarice would need surgery to correct things if Rob hadn't gotten everything properly back in position. But it could wait until they were somewhere with decent medical facilities, and it shouldn't be a lasting problem.

After they'd all eaten, Zo assigned the watch. Jonas and Zo would go first.

Everyone suited up again, and they left the tent, armed with a plasma rifle each.

They switched to a private channel to keep in touch and keep each other awake without disturbing the others.

"How do you feel about being the first on an extra-solar planet?"

"You know, Jonas, I'd feel a damn lot better about it if we weren't on the damn run again."

"It's awesome, though, isn't it?" Jonas was grinning inside his suit, and didn't know if Zo could tell or not.

"Yeah," Zo conceded, "it is a bit awesome. Being on this planet, not being on the run again."

Jonas laughed. "How can something be a bit awesome? It's awesome or it isn't."

"It'd be nicer if it was a more hospitable, planet, you know. With my luck they'll name it Ortega or something, and generations of settlers will use my name as a swearword because they've ended up stuck on this shithole of a planet."

"Hey, who knows, maybe it's a real paradise in the summer."

"Right. Just slightly lethal radiation, so you'll get to freeze to death before you get radiation burns. Come see the wonderful planet Ortega."

Jonas smiled again. It was rare to hear Zo joke.

"I did like the suns, though," Zo added.

Jonas agreed. Even Earthrise on the moon was nothing in comparison—even if you grew up on Earth and never left, you'd at least have seen pictures of Earth from space. But nowhere in the solar system could you get a view like the one they'd had. The three suns of the Alpha Centauri system all in the sky at the same time.

"Wonder what other things we'll see out here," Jonas said quietly, looking at where Alpha Centauri A and B had hung.

"Shh… Lights."

Zo pointed, and he could barely see her arm, but he did see the lights too. They were moving towards them.

They both changed to the main channel.

"Sorry to wake you, but we have visitors. Suit up. Quietly. Make sure you have no lights on when you exit the tent…" Zo's voice was calm and firm.

Vincent and Mons were the first out, pulse rifles ready, and Zo motioned for Vincent to go with her, and for Mons to go with Jonas. They took up defensive positions about ten meters apart.

"Rob, stay with Clarice in the tent," Monique said.

"Guard the opening," Zo interjected before Monique had finished speaking, and Jonas knew her well enough to recognize anger in her voice at Monique's interference.

"But I can still shoot," Clarice objected.

"Yeah, but if they go for you, you can't run like that," Zo replied. "Take a gun in case, but let Rob guard the opening."

Jonas looked around, and saw Monique and Soka had found a third rock to take up positions behind.

"I really don't know how these… guns work," Soka almost whimpered.

"Monique will show you, Soka," Zo replied to him over the radio, with a sharpness to it that made it very clear she still wanted to reinforce to Monique who was in charge.

Jonas saw Monique help Soka position his rifle. He grinned to himself and wondered if Soka had ever shot at anything at all. But he was sure Monique would do well. He looked at her for a moment, and was impressed by how gracefully she moved even in the bulky suit. *She's a real fighter.*

"At the ready. Here they come. Nobody shoot until my word," Zo yelled.

There were five of them. *There must be more of them behind.*

"Now!"

The first of their followers fell nearly instantly, shot by either Vincent or Monique. The rest jumped to the side, and shots flew in both directions. It was not clear if they'd gotten anyone else.

Jonas started creeping along the ground and motioned for Mons to follow him. "We'll try to flank them."

Suddenly they were almost face to face with one of their followers who clearly had the same idea. He fired, and Jonas just barely managed to roll out of the way.

Jonas was about to fire, but Mons beat him to it, and took out their opponent with a shot straight through the face plate. It was instantly covered with a fine mist so they could not see anything else.

"Got one!" Vincent yelled over the radio.

"Mons took one," Jonas added. That made three with the first one to fall. Two left, unless there were more on the way.

Suddenly there were several flashes of plasma rifles in quick succession.

He looked around, and saw the two last ones lying right in front of Soka. Monique was standing over one of them, having shot him the back.

The other one had his head on top of Soka's rifle… Or rather, Soka's rifle poked out of the back of where his head should have been, after a blast straight to his face had apparently obliterated the soldier's head and opened a big hole in the back of his helmet.

Jonas could not help but stare.

"That's all of them," Zo told them without hint of emotion.

"I see more lights. We need to get the hell out of here." Vincent pointed in the distance.

They gathered their equipment up, and Vincent supported Clarice again when they started walking.

Zo went first. "Careful, I can hardly see anything in front of me," she said quietly over the radio.

They started making their way as quickly as they could, but the lights seemed to advance on them.

"What if we use our lights too?" Jonas asked.

"If we do, they know where we are, and can fire at us to force us to turn and take a stand," Vincent retorted.

Jonas turned for a moment to look back at the lights, when he made a wrong step and started sliding down a slope.

"Help!"

Before he knew it, he slipped over the edge and fell.

Chapter 20

"Jonas!"

Mons rushed to where Jonas had gone over the edge and tried to see, but it was pitch black.

"I'm here," they heard over the radio. "I'm hurt, I can't move, I think something is seriously wrong with my back."

Zo got up to the edge next to Mons, and looked down as well. She turned on the helmet light, and they could see him down on a ledge.

"Shit. Getting him up from there if his back is hurt is going to be a problem. Rob... I'm going to need you to winch down. Use lights if you need to, but try to keep them pointed down into the ravine, maybe we can avoid getting spotted."

"Vincent, Monique, prepare to take a stand up here with me. Clarice, you stay behind that rock outcrop, you understand? Take a rifle, but avoid drawing fire unless absolutely necessary."

"What about Soka and me, Cap?" Mons asked.

"I want you two to run as fast as you can to the colony and ask for help. Go carefully and use your lights first when you have some distance, okay? Drop all your gear here."

"Are you sure, Zo? It doesn't feel right to leave you here."

"It's that, or leaving Jonas and Clarice, you understand? We'll depend on you to get there and get us help. And you need Soka with you so it's not some strange Earther just showing up for no good reason."

Mons did not feel good about this at all, but Zo made a good case.

"You heard the captain, Soka."

They lightened their load as much as possible, taking only some oxygen canisters, a few mag grips and rope in case they needed to climb, and set off. A brisk walk at first, which was painful and difficult even without their big backpacks. Once they were past a low ridge, Mons decided it was okay to turn on their headlights. They'd be potential targets if any of their followers got past their crewmates. But at the same time, with some luck, if their followers spotted them, they might be careless and walk past Zo and the rest without realizing.

They sped up, trying to run when possible, but it was more like a slow awkward half-jog half-walk—they were constantly slowed down by rocks or holes or just uneven ground, and had several near misses where one or the other got close to tripping or falling over an edge.

Mons checked the maps. They could not be all that far from the colony. Maybe a few hours if they'd been walking with a backpack. If they could do it in half the time at the speed they were "running," they'd be making good time. It'd take their followers at most half an hour to get to where Zo was. They'd need to be able to beat them or hold them off for at least a couple of hours.

Mons was feeling glum again. It felt to him as if there was a very substantial chance they'd come back there with help only to find corpses. Or worse, get ambushed and killed as well.

Though if the crew is killed while we're off looking for help, being taken out in an ambush might be a blessing, he thought to himself. He was not sure he could live with something like that on his conscience.

Soka tried to talk to him, but Mons was not paying attention. He could not stand Soka's emotional reactions and what Mons considered a too cheerful disposition.

"Mons! Mons!"

Finally he responded and turned to look at Soka.

"Lights. Over there."

Soka pointed, and Mons looked in the direction he indicated. They were lights, and not moving lights from the headlight of a suit, but fixed lights on buildings.

"It must be the colony."

It was closer than he thought. Maybe half an hour's "run" away. They rushed towards it as fast as they could.

Twenty minutes later they reached a small, surprisingly thick dome. *Radiation shielding, I guess.* They looked in either direction for an airlock. There was one to their right, only a few hundred meters further down. It did not require any authorization. *Clearly the colonists don't expect unwanted visitors.*

Inside they checked the atmosphere and pressure, and the suit displays indicated it was safe to breathe the air, but radiation levels were still higher than ideal. Mons opted to open the face plate but keep the rest on. The air was cold and dry, but not unpleasant.

They went looking for living quarters where they could rouse someone. The first buildings appeared to be workshops, and Mons was getting a feeling of urgency.

"Anyone home?" he yelled into the night.

"Sounds." Soka pointed towards a building a bit further in towards the center of the dome.

A couple of minutes later a few surprised Centauri came out to meet them.

"Soka, I think it's best if you speak for us."

Mons stood there and tried to smile, while Soka seemed to introduce them in his language—at least he heard their names—before switching to English. "I told them I'll use English for introductions for your benefit," Soka told him. "Most of the colonists here have done work at the outpost and integrated the basics, but I may have to switch back and forth—they don't all have a full vocabulary yet." Mons did not know what that meant, exactly.

Soka explained their circumstances, leaving out a lot of detail, such as that their followers appeared to come from a Centauri military destroyer.

The colonists were sympathetic, and unlike the military officers Soka had tried to speak to, they respected his title and office and pointed to two big all-terrain vehicles.

"They'll come with us and help," Soka confirmed to Mons.

Eight of them armed themselves and they split into two groups, with Mons and Soka in the first vehicle. The return trip went much faster, and within twenty minutes they could see the blasts of plasma rifles in the distance.

"Can we get there any faster?" Mons asked the colonists while directing it through Soka.

"Not in this terrain, but I can turn on the floodlights. See how they like that," one of the Centauri replied. His English was good but his pronunciation sounded a bit odd to Mons.

The lights from the vehicle did not reach far enough to light up the battle quite yet, but the furthest combatants seemed to pull back as they approached, and soon the plasma fire came only from the nearer fighters. Their crew, he hoped.

Soon Mons could see Zo and Monique, and scanned around for the rest.

They all seemed to be okay. Or as okay as they were when he left them.

Zo waved, and he got out to introduce the colonists and realized they'd been in too much of a panic to exchange names.

Chapter 21

With the help of a winch and an improvised stretcher, they were able to get Jonas up and onto one of the all-terrain vehicles very quickly. Several of them remained ready with their plasma rifles in case their followers would return.

Zo looked carefully across the horizon, but saw no trace of them.

They were able to get everyone and their equipment onboard without too many problems. The vehicles had a lot of space at the back, but few seats, so several of them were shifting back and forth and hanging onto straps on the side.

They were mostly silent on the ride back to the colony. Their adrenaline from the fight wearing off and giving way to fatigue. As soon as they were inside the dome, Zo got Soka to ask the colonists for medical attention for Jonas and Clarice, while the rest gathered together to discuss the situation.

"It looks like there are only civilians here," was Vincent's first observation.

"Soka confirmed as much to me. He spoke a bit with one of the colonists on their way back to us," Zo added.

"Mostly scientists, a few engineers. Some with military experience but no actual combat experience. The people we were up against might be shit at navigating a space ship, but they know their plasma rifles. If we hadn't been in a superior tactical position, we'd have been in trouble."

"We have to assume they'll come. Worst case those damn destroyers will unload a shitload of people and murder us all, unless, for some reason, they want us alive, and we've seen no sign of that."

When even Vincent got this pessimistic, it made Zo worried.

"So we try to get them to get word out… Then what? Maybe they have a ship we can 'borrow.' They can say we stole it. Maybe we actually steal it…" Zo looked around to see if any of the Centauri were within earshot.

"Let's first actually explain the full situation and ask them." Monique stated something that ought to have been obvious to Zo, and Zo felt a pang of resentment that Monique was the one to suggest it, not least because she was the last person Zo would have expected it to come from.

Zo had seen how skeptical Monique had been of Soka at the start, and now she wanted to lay all their cards on the table with a bunch of Centauri.

She nodded, and swallowed her pride.

"You're right. Let's put it to them."

She walked over to a group of the Centauri who had come with them, and asked who could speak for them. She introduced herself with full name and title.

"I'm First Triaton'ai Lem Four," the Centauri spokesperson replied.

Zo was still bewildered about Centauri names, especially the numbers. She'd meant to grill Soka about it. So far she understood it had something to with their relative position within their family, though Soka had seemed annoyed when she'd asked if that implied an order of importance or a hierarchy. She pushed it aside.

"I don't know how much Soka, the Centauri we came with, has explained to you about the situation. First Triaton—my apologies, may I call you that?"

"You may. Soka explained parts of it to us. We've inferred some from the fact you were attacked, but we don't know why."

Zo described the events that had transpired, and she took care to leave out nothing, hoping that brutal honesty would serve them in a group like this of scientists and engineers likely to value fact over politics.

First Triaton nodded along, and looked at her with an expression Zo could not parse.

Finally it seemed he was ready to speak.

"It sounds like you are the victim of an injustice, Captain Ortega." He stopped briefly and looked her straight in the eye until Zo badly wanted to look away, but somehow felt she couldn't. Zo just nodded in agreement.

"I can see no valid reason for a Centauri ship to treat you this way, if you have told the truth, and it sounds like the truth. And though I have not spoken to many Earthers, you act the way I would expect of someone who is being honest."

First Triaton spoke calmly and cautiously. Finally he broke eye contact, and Zo blinked and sighed as she relaxed.

"We will arrange to try to get a connection so you can describe your situation to someone who will listen, and hopefully we can help you clear this matter up."

The Centauri standing around them nodded in agreement.

Zo smiled. "Thank you ,First Triaton, but my most immediate concern is to ensure that you understand the risk you take as long as we're here. I don't want to put you at risk inadvertently. If you want us to leave, we'll leave, though I would ask for your help to get away."

"To us, Captain Ortega, if you ignore injustice you share equal guilt with those who perpetrate it. We cannot let you face this treatment alone. It would not be honorable. Your concern for our wellbeing further reassures me that you are in fact victims of injustice."

His gaze returned, for a moment.

"As long as you are here, you are under our protection. It would be utterly unthinkable for a 'Centauri' force to put us at risk—we're all citizens, and we are here at the direct request of the regional administrator to work on an important project. To harass us would be a direct attack on the authority of the administrator, and by extension the government. I cannot imagine they would do such a thing."

"I greatly appreciate it, First. But to reduce the risk, may I ask that we arrange to have both Soka and my Earth representative try to get messages through as soon as we possibly can? I'd feel a lot better if more people know we are here."

Triaton pointed towards a building, and asked one of his men to bring Soka there. Zo yelled for Monique, and together they followed Triaton into a two-story building with a large array of antennas on the roof.

"This is our communications array. It's not particularly strong, but it has no problems reaching the relay station at the Proxima-Alpha Centauri gate. Heck, we could reach Alpha Centauri directly, but that'd take a long time."

He smiled at his little joke about the distance—a radio signal would take about ten weeks without the gate relay—and Zo humored him with a chuckle. Then he started the connection sequence.

"That's odd. I'm getting a lot of interference. We're not getting a carrier."

"That's not good. Any way of boosting the signal? Earlier the destroyers jammed our radio as well."

"We can try." He walked over to a panel at the back of the room, and rewired some of the power circuits.

"I've made the array draw on both the primary and backup power circuit. Let's try now."

They were still unable to get a connection, though they could faintly detect the carrier wave this time.

"If they're jamming us, it must mean they're not giving up. And if they're not giving up, it must mean they're going to be preparing a larger scale attack," Zo told him. "If you have any concern about harboring us, now is the time. If we stay, you are all in danger."

"I've already told you, Captain. We want no part of the guilt of letting these dishonorable people get to you. That they are jamming us is yet another piece of evidence that you spoke the truth. If you can help arrange the defense, we will help you stand up to them."

First Triaton stood up seemingly a lot straighter than before, with a look of determination on his face that Zo hoped meant the same on a Centauri as it did on a human. Zo decided she liked this man very much, though she found it hard not to giggle at the man trying to look serious while wearing a light flowery dress more suitable for a nice summer day than the dark Proxima colony.

I'm better than this, it's not like they were prepared for us to bring a battle here, she thought to herself as she suppressed her grin, and went to find Vincent.

Chapter 22

Her leg had not hurt since Rob pumped painkillers into her suit air supply, but Clarice had felt it throb the whole time, and the nausea persisted for hours.

When Jonas was hurt and she had to lie there behind the rock with a plasma rifle, she had been adamant she would help fight, and tried to hold herself up to aim, but the others had done pretty much all the work. She thought she'd gotten off a shot or two, but no more.

In the all-terrain vehicle on the way back to the colony, one of the colonists had asked what was wrong in the stuttering, mechanical English of an electronic translator, which made her even more curious as to how Soka spoke so perfectly.

Monique was in the same vehicle as her, and explained while Clarice tried to focus on everything but the sickening throbbing.

As soon as they were inside the dome, two of the colonists helped her to a stretcher, and she could see Jonas on a stretcher next to her, and Soka was there too. She smiled at him, and despite the throbbing she finally relaxed enough to fall asleep.

She woke to find her suit had been taken off, and a Centauri doctor was looking at her leg, and a display showing an x-ray, seemingly more out of fascination than a desire to heal her. She was about to ask why the hell they were not doing anything when she realized the throbbing was gone and her nausea was done.

The doctor was a squat man, not at all how she'd come to expect a Centauri to look, though she realized she'd had few examples to judge by. He wore a white robe not unlike what doctors on Earth wore. The same bronze, shimmering skin as all the Centauri she'd seen, and tight curly nearly black hair with what looked like blonde highlights.

"Ahh, awake, yes."

He smiled at her.

"Your friend Soka told me to take good care of you. Here, see."

The doctor showed her the x-ray.

"Leg was broke here."

He leaned over her to point.

"You're all fixed now. Almost. Don't put too much weight on it for a day."

"What do you mean 'all fixed'?"

"Injected you with a growth hormone and special catalyst to regrow bone. Took us a while, because it's not been used in Earthers before, so we had to take blood samples and run tests first."

"Took you a while? How long have I been out?"

"Oh, I think you've been sleeping for about four hours."

"Four hours?"

"Yeah, sorry it took so long."

Clarice suddenly felt light-headed again for a moment. They were apologizing for taking four hours to mend a broken leg. She pulled herself together and slowly sat up, and tentatively tried putting her foot down. It didn't hurt.

"Careful. Not much weight, remember."

The doctor was observing her carefully, and Clarice put her other foot down and stood up with most of the weight on that leg. She could feel a little twinge when she tried walking, and asked the doctor about it.

"Yeah, that's why you should not put much weight. Limp, okay?"

She was able to walk without pain with just a very light limp, and the doctor reiterated to her it'd take a day for it to heal completely. Once again, he was all apologetic about it.

"What about my other friend? Jonas? The one with the hurt back?"

"Ahh, yes, Jonas with the back. He will take longer." The doctor looked down on the floor and Clarice felt worried.

"How long is 'longer'?"

"A couple of days at least. Maybe a week. Sorry. His back was broken." The doctor made a gesture that looked to Clarice as if he suggested it had been fully torn, and she felt sick to her stomach. *But he said a couple of days?!?* she thought to herself.

Clarice wanted to yell at the doctor for scaring her with the thought that Jonas was in for a long recovery when it was only a few days, and then casually adding his back had been broken. *It must be his English, it can't have been that bad.*

"Come, I'll show you. Spine was completely severed. We've just finished reattaching it."

"His spine was severed? Will he be able to walk again?"

The doctor turned his head askance and his brow furrowed.

"Walk? Of course. Why wouldn't he?"

Clarice's mouth hung open for a couple of seconds before she was able to answer.

"We're not always able to regain full motion when the spine is severed. So many nerves to regrow or reattach. And even when we do it takes much longer."

"Oh? Really? Here. It's a data cube with all the treatment data for your friend, including detailed data on how the reattachment was done. Your doctors might learn from it. If not, they should ask."

He fished a small data cube out of his pocket and handed it to her.

Clarice had seen the reports, and knew there had been requests for medical information, but it had been frustrated by endless bureaucracy and requests for more specific enquiries. She clutched the data cube and suppressed a grin. If it helped to ask specific enough requests just to get surgical information about nerve reattachment and fast healing of bone, that alone would make this mission worth it. *Wonder if he's allowed to share this*, she thought, and thought better than to ask him.

"You can see your friend now."

The doctor led her into another room where Jonas was lying on a bed, eyes open, but strapped down.

"Ahh, you're awake. Good. Your friend is here."

Jonas turned his head towards them, and was clearly surprised to see Clarice walking almost normally. Clarice noticed his surprise.

"They fixed it!"

She grinned, and added, "And the doc tells me your back will be okay in a week at most."

"Really? So it wasn't that serious then?"

"No... Yes... Your spine was severed but they reattached it."

Jonas' mouth hung open, and the doctor gave him an explanation that looked like it went right over his head.

"Sounds crazy, right? They gave me the data on it," Clarice told him, and spun the data cube between two fingers. "Worth its weight in... Any material you could imagine."

The doctor looked at them and shrugged, clearly not grasping how surreal the experience was to them, and how much the data would matter.

"You need rest now. You need to go so he can recover. Please." The doctor opened the door for Clarice.

"Sorry, I don't mean to sound rude. English not fully integrated yet."

"Oh, can I ask you some questions about that?" Clarice was suddenly interested—maybe she could learn how they'd picked up the language so fast.

"Not something I know much about. Find one of our bioengineers."

He shooed her out and closed the door. Clarice looked around what looked like some sort of common area, and found the exit, and she decided to have a look around and find her friends.

It was day, as much as it ever was day on this planet, and the sunlight was augmented by floodlights in a few strategic locations that illuminated the buildings and the small, thick dome.

The dome was a geodesic structure, built of triangles of some translucent material, rather than the thin semi-inflatable non-rigid structures that had become common in the solar system colonies.

Probably the radiation, she thought to herself.

The buildings in the dome were mostly two and three stories nondescript structures of some dark-grey material that looked like a concrete. Most had a few windows, but few of them were large.

It had a feel to it that was very much like one of the older Mars or Moon habitats, built to be fast to erect from local materials and be solid, not fancy and comfortable. The interior in the medical building she had just left had been light and comfortable, though, so clearly they were not content to live in squalor.

She saw a few Centauri walking around. None of them appeared to pay her much attention, though they undoubtedly must realize she was not one of them. She wondered if they all had bronze skin. She'd still not seen any exceptions, but then again there were still pockets on Earth where you might get the idea most humans looked the same, though they were getting rare.

Monique could possibly manage to pass for Centauri with some makeup. But she'd need a ton of glitter.

The ground was mostly the same reddish brown rock they had walked over for hours outside, but with shingle roads, and a couple of concrete stretches emphasizing that the colony was still under construction.

She kept glancing over at the suns as she walked around. They were almost more fascinating than being in an actual freaking alien colony. It was finally starting to hit her that not only was she more than four lightyears from home, but she'd had to make a second gate transfer to get close to the third star she'd been near since they left the solar system.

No other crew from Earth had yet been granted passage through the other gates. All trade had happened in the Alpha Centauri system. They were the first humans this close to Proxima.

For some reason she found it funny to think of being close to Proxima. After all, its human name was given to it because it's the star closest to Sol. Until a year ago, no human had been closer to another star outside the solar system than to Proxima. And now, no humans had been closer to Proxima than they had.

She stopped a woman and asked where she might find her friends, and the woman, in much more halting English than the doctor, directed her to the administrative building next to a small park at the center of the dome.

It was only a couple minutes' walk to get there, and the door was open.

"You're walking! What about your leg?"

Zo rushed over to her, and gave her a hug. Clarice blushed. It wasn't like Zo to show this much emotion in public. Or, usually even in private. *Other than... that time last year,* she thought. Zo pulled back, and seemed to have realized the same.

"They fixed it. I need to be a bit careful for a day. And get this, Zo, the doctor apologized for making it take so long. And Jonas will be fully walking in at most a week."

"They did say he'd fully recover, but when we talked to them this morning, they weren't ready to tell us how long. A week?! That's crazy. I worried he might be in for months of physio."

Clarice held up the data cube again, and triumphantly told them about the data.

She looked around. Everyone was there. Everyone except Jonas, of course.

"So, what are we doing? How are we getting off this place? What about our followers? Tried the radio?" She couldn't help feeling optimistic.

Vincent rolled his eyes at her.

"Calm down. One thing at a time."

Chapter 23

"Hold up. Where are you going?"

Vincent turned around to see Clarice limping at a surprisingly rapid pace towards him.

"The Centauri have asked for my help repurposing their mining lasers as a defensive weapon," he replied.

"Sounds fun. Can I help?"

"Sure, come along."

Vincent wasn't in a talkative mood, and was thankful that Clarice didn't try to push him into a conversation. They'd gone over the available resources with the colonists, and created a defensive plan they hoped would hold. Their problem remained that if they could not broadcast to the relays, they needed to make it out. The colonists had a decent ship available, and a shuttle, but they were unwilling to flee. They had however offered up the shuttle. The shuttle would never survive an attack by the Centauri destroyers, but it might get them to *Black Rain* with spare parts.

Unless the bastards bomb our ship first, he thought.

He was vaguely hopeful their attackers would ignore their ship and focus on the colony. But of course they'd be entirely dependent on pinning them down enough that they wouldn't notice—or be unable to do anything about—a shuttle heading for the ship. They'd need at least a couple of hours to repair the second of the main engines before they could even hope to get it in the air.

And then there were those destroyers.

If they'd left *Black Rain* intact so far, they surely wouldn't if they realized their prey was back there.

"Why haven't they just bombed us from orbit?" Vincent asked out loud, not really expecting an answer.

Clarice replied anyway.

"Either they care about the Centauri, or they want us for some reason."

"What could they want us for?"

"Maybe they want to know what we know. And whether anyone else knows." Clarice shrugged.

Vincent slowed down, and turned to her. "They're taking a big risk, though. So far we've tried to connect to the relays. I'm sure they're aware.

And we've told a whole colony of Centauri. They must realize the colonists know."

"They're alien. Who knows how they think?"

They were at the entrance to the mine near the edge of the dome, and were met by two Centauri who introduced themselves.

"Fascinating how they've all picked up English, but different levels. The doc said something about 'integration,' and told me one of their bioengineers might be able to explain more…"

Vincent looked at Clarice. "Sounds interesting. But not now."

Clarice wanted to help moving the laser assemblies, but Vincent shut her down hard.

"You're still limping, *kid*."

He knew she'd be annoyed at being called "kid." He only ever did so when he wanted to really emphasize that he was twice her age and had spent most of that time in the field. He respected Clarice. She was incredibly smart, but she lacked proper field experience, and sometimes her survival instincts were not quite where Vincent would like them to be.

Clarice looked annoyed at him. *She'll deal*, he thought, and distracted her with another thought.

"Hey, Clarice, why do you think they are mining here anyway? Soka insisted if that was the purpose of the colony, they'd just place a station here and only bring down mining equipment. They wouldn't say."

"Maybe they need to place equipment deep underground for some reason… Or maybe it's easier to mine raw material than bring it?"

Vincent didn't reply.

They were preparing an inner perimeter by blocking the paths between a number of buildings around the administration building, and they'd place the lasers on improvised mounts on the roof of the administration building and a couple of others. The dome could withstand short pulses and still let through enough energy to cause serious burns from within about a 50 m radius, they'd calculated. He hoped their calculations were right.

Once their attackers were inside the dome, they'd have far more freedom, and would be able to take out quite heavy weaponry and vehicles.

Unless they bomb us.

Vincent kept coming back to that. The pessimist in him, or perhaps the realist, always looked for the worst their opponent could do to them, and worried why they hadn't taken that option.

He helped haul the laser assemblies onto carts, and they got them back to the center of the dome. There he helped mount a winch on the administration building first. They almost lost the first laser when it was nearly at the top, but steadied it and got it onto the roof.

The mount would let them rotate it most the way around, and angle it reasonably well. There were some obstacles blocking shots in a couple of directions, but little they could do about that without taking out the comms tower, which Vincent had suggested, given they were being jammed anyway. But First Triaton had refused, still holding out hope he'd be able to boost the signal enough to get through to the relays.

The two other lasers were easier to mount. The roofs of those buildings were flat, and slightly lower and provided plenty of space to get everything mounted.

We can't have much time, Vincent thought to himself. It was late afternoon. Their followers would have had plenty of time to regroup.

Maybe there are too few of them, and they are waiting for reinforcements from one of the destroyers. Or maybe they are waiting for darkness.

He looked out over the endless rocky terrain, and wondered where they were hiding.

"Hey! A ship! Over there!"

Clarice had spotted something with those damn augmented eyes of hers.

"It's landing. From what I can tell it must be landing about halfway between where we landed and the colony."

"Shit. It must be reinforcements. If they bring vehicles they can be here within an hour or two. They'll probably take some time to prep. My guess is they'll attack under cover of darkness. Check what infrared gear these people have. We should have a few spares in our kit, but not enough for everyone."

Vincent paused for a moment, then yelled to Clarice. "Also, let Zo and First Triaton know about the ship."

Clarice ran off. Or bounced off, given her limp.

The Centauri would not be much help if none of them could see. But he was hopeful they'd have infrared equipment. They couldn't rely on the floodlights. Too easy to take out.

Damn it.

They were not nearly ready. There were still gaps in the defensive perimeter around the outer buildings, and if that was breached, the administrative building would be crammed and nearly impossible to defend.

I hope these scientists and engineers know how to fight.

He finished up with the last laser, and he asked the two Centauri who had helped him about that.

"Yes, we've done many hours in simulators," was their answer. It didn't fill Vincent with confidence.

Chapter 24

The colony fascinated Monique. She had her tasks to help prepare, but she also paid very close attention to everything she saw. She was extremely aware that this was, if anything, the first opportunity anyone had to get direct intelligence on the Centauri. Their meeting at the Alpha Centauri outpost had certainly been interesting, but they'd seen recreational areas, a docking port, and a restaurant.

Here she saw *tech*, and could talk to people who were not as well trained as she was certain Soka was, and who did not know precisely which technology their government would sanction for outsiders and not.

Take the data cube Clarice had been given. Monique had made sure she got a copy of the data. It was innocent enough. The doctor was probably used to freely giving out this information. Scientists tend to be open enough about sharing information once it's already published, without thinking about available access to the publications they've been published in.

As far as she could tell, while it was mostly data specifically about Jonas' treatment, it contained detailed specifications of the treatment, including drugs used, their chemical composition, and analysis of their effects on humans based on what appeared to be a remarkably detailed simulation, as well as a precise 3D recording that was a mix of video and 3D models of how their operating equipment had reattached his spine and the nerves.

Clarice had been right to be excited. Earth researchers would be pouring over this for many years unless they could outright get the engineering specifications from the Centauri. And just *having* this data might well help them ask the right questions of the Centauri to get that given how the Centauri bureaucracy appeared to work.

Monique was looking everywhere to see what else she could get hold of. She'd studied the mining lasers, but they'd not been anything particularly special. She'd disassembled a plasma rifle, but they were similar to the Earth designs. There are only so many energy-efficient ways of superheating plasma in a portable way, it seemed.

She visited Jonas in the infirmary, and asked the doctor a lot of questions, and did get some additional data out of it.

But First Triaton had turned her down blank when she asked if she could get access to any of their other data banks. He was willing to sit down with her and answer a number of questions, and he did, and she probed about everything she could think of, and got answers on a number of subjects. But, he pointed out, their databanks contained too much sensitive data on their terraforming engineering and engines, and the research they were doing here, that he was not allowed to release that without permission.

And on that, he had also refused to say what they were researching.

She did find out more about their language learning, and learning in general. Apparently most—not all—Centauri working outside their home systems, in systems where they might come into contact with other species, had augments that interfaced directly with the language center in their brains, that could be fed with data to trigger training that allowed language acquisition in a matter of hours to days, depending largely on individuals' existing understanding of languages and what level of proficiency they needed. She was allowed some very superficial data about this process that would nevertheless certainly be valuable.

They had other augments that could interface with the brain, she was told, but Triaton refused to share further details.

In the end, Monique got enough that the mission would be certain to get her a commendation, or more.

If we survive, she glumly thought to herself.

She was about to leave First's office more frustrated than she entered it, having gotten tantalizing glimpses of technology that could dramatically change the entire solar system, but not getting the data.

Without thinking, she grabbed a data cube that sat unprotected on a sideboard on her way out. Triaton didn't seem to notice. Her heart was racing, and she rushed to the room they'd been given to use to copy it. Her plan was to return it and drop it on the floor near his office door and let him think he'd just dropped it.

But before she could copy it, Triaton and three of the other colonists entered and grabbed her.

"Why did you betray our trust?"

First did not sound or look angry to her, though she was not sure how to judge their facial expressions, still. His face was quite blank and subdued, as if he was disappointed in her. His voice was as calm as it had been earlier.

"I don't know. It was a spur of the moment thing."

She knew there was no point in denying it. All she could think was that she was terrified they'd change their mind and hand them to their followers over this. Or lock them up. Or just throw them out.

There were no good options.

"I take full responsibility, okay? None of the others had anything to do with it."

Zo appeared in the door opening.

"What's going on?"

"I fucked up, Zo. I snatched a data cube. I'm sorry."

Zo didn't say a word to her, but Monique could tell from how Zo's face hardened that she was suppressing anger as she turned to Triaton. "How can we make this up to you?"

"It had weapons data, Captain. This is serious."

"I understand. What do you need to do? What do you need from us? Anything."

"She needs to be punished. Publicly."

Monique was tearing up, but trying hard to not let anyone see. She was not afraid, but she felt concern she had jeopardized the mission and the crew. "Do whatever you need to, just help the crew," she told Zo.

"Oh, we will." Zo's voice was hard and Monique didn't pick up much of a hint of sympathy.

"What do you need to do, First Triaton?" Zo repeated, her voice harder and sharper.

"The harshest punishment we give for a non-violent offence, Captain. I'm sorry, but this is serious." Triaton was still just as calm, and his calmness made Monique feel even more desperate.

"You don't understand, First. We don't know your system. What exactly does that entail?" Zo asked.

First Triaton looked down, seemingly unable to keep eye contact with Zo as he started to answer her.

"Public humiliation, of course. She will need to prostrate herself in the public square and apologize to us all."

Monique couldn't believe what she was hearing, and her anxiety shot up rather than dissipated. *What does he mean?* She couldn't make sense of it, and it made her worry she had misunderstood.

"An *apology*? I stole from you, and all you're asking for is an apology?" She practically yelled, and she realized she might have sounded angry.

"All? It's about honor, Monique Salinger. You have forfeited yours. I'm terribly sorry we have to do this, but it will a long time until it is restored."

He looked deeply upset, and Monique realized he truly did see this as a harsh punishment.

Of all the things she had learned about the Centauri, this was the strangest. Monique had never believed the Sovereign Earth lies about the Centauri standing ready to invade, but now, being forced to make the colony good by apologizing, she almost wanted to laugh at how ridiculous those lies had been.

She held back, fearing expressing the relief would offend.

Even though she'd never believed the lies about them, it was starting to dawn on her that she too had preconceptions about how they'd act based on the reports she'd read, and that her preconceptions were entirely misguided—the reports were human interpretations of outcomes of discussions they had not been party to, following rules they were not privy to, based on a moral code they had no idea about.

Monique felt her skin tingle as her adrenaline levels crashed, now that she knew there was no immediate danger.

She resolved to keep quiet about this punishment in her report, and asked that the crew did the same. Not out of shame, though she felt shame over her preconceptions, but out of fear it'd be exploited. Out of fear that humans, if told the punishment for theft was an apology, would rob the Centauri blind while saying sorry.

***

"What the *hell* were you thinking, Monique?"

Monique had delivered the apology First Triaton had required, in the middle of the central square of the colony. She hated every second of it, but they had not required much ceremony. Triaton had given a brief statement of her transgression, and Monique had given a statement that was short and clear, acknowledging her guilt, and promising not to do it again, with her head hanging down in what she hoped would come across as a sufficient display of shame.

The Centauri were easy to please.

Zo did not appear to be as easy to satisfy. She had grabbed Monique by the arm as soon as it was over, and half shoved, half pulled her into a room in the administration building.

"You got off way too easy," Zo yelled at her.

"I know," Monique answered, with a subdued voice she wasn't sure if Zo would hear.

"What the hell were you thinking?"

"I wasn't. I'm sorry. I guess I just thought we'd not get a chance like this anytime soon."

"You realize these people are risking their lives for us, yes?"

Zo was right up in Monique's face. Monique had not realized Zo even could get this angry and seem this intimidating.

"I… I don't know what to say. I know. I fucked up, okay?" Monique started raising her voice too.

"This is your *one* chance, you understand?" Zo told her. "Anything like this happens again, and I'll fucking leave you behind!"

Monique didn't believe she'd go that far. Zo didn't seem the type to be that brutal, but she did think Zo might well decide to lock her in the brig. *Then again, maybe she might go that far…*

Zo stormed off and left Monique to her thoughts. She thought the Centauri let her off easy at first, but she was suddenly not so sure. Maybe it'd have been easier to face a harsher punishment from the Centauri, than the enduring anger of Captain Ortega.

Chapter 25

After speaking to the colonists, Soka felt more at ease with the situation. Unlike his failed attempt to raise the issue with the military, the colonists accepted the danger and shared his outrage at what had happened, and were dedicated to helping them.

But he dreaded what they all knew was coming. The tension as Proxima neared the horizon was intense. They all expected an attack once it got dark.

They had infrared gear for almost everyone, and the rest were holed up in the administration building as the last line of defense. They'd turn on the floodlights in sequence once the attacks started, hoping to temporarily blind their attackers, but expected them to get taken out by shots from the attackers quickly, so they needed to be prepared to take advantage.

Everyone was wearing their environmental suits, as a breach of the dome was a near certainty.

Soka was walking along the improvised inner barrier. It was not great. It had been many years since Soka had served as an engineer, but he could see all kinds of weaknesses. Hopefully their attackers did not have a lot of heavy equipment.

"How are you holding up, Soka?"

Vincent came up beside him.

"I'm good. I think."

"I know you're not used to battle. Most here aren't. Just keep your head down, and take your time aiming."

Darkness was creeping closer and closer. Vincent headed to one of the laser mounts while Soka was hiding behind the wall.

Finally he heard the first shots, and as he looked out through a hole, he could see plasma fire from what must be a light plasma cannon starting to punch holes in the dome.

In response, the mining lasers rapidly tore through lines of the landscape outside, crisscrossing in the hope of burning anyone unfortunate enough to be advancing through.

The plasma cannons were limited to where they'd punched through, while the lasers could do substantial harm outside without opening further holes in the highly heat resistant dome as long as they didn't heat any given point for too long.

The beauty of a laser, Soka thought. Most of the energy passes straight through a translucent surface.

But the plasma cannon kept firing.

Soon there were several gaping holes in the dome, and people started working their way towards them.

The lasers took out several of them. Soka could not hear them scream as the air in the dome was rapidly thinning, and his EV suit muffled what little sound got through, but he could see the lasers burn their flesh and cut them to pieces, and he could imagine their screams anyway.

Now that there were already holes in the dome, there was no reason to hold back, and soon all the three mounted lasers pointed at the same group of attacking soldiers working their way through the holes.

He heard screams over the radio as the plasma cannon had fired on one of the laser mounts. He could hear Vincent yelling to take it out, and both the remaining lasers fired towards the source of the plasma. Soon the third one rejoined—the laser was intact, and someone new had taken over the firing.

Soka was shaking. He could see the plasma cannon blow up, but he could also see soldiers who had used the opportunity to get through the dome, and there was fire from plasma rifles everywhere. He tried to remember Vincent's advice, and took several deep breaths, and slowly aimed at one of the soldiers running towards the outer barrier, and pressed the trigger.

The soldier dropped to the ground, clutching his chest.

Behind him one of the floodlights turned on, and several of the soldiers pouring through the holes stumbled, others got shot at. A couple made it almost all the way to the outer barrier before they too got shot.

Soka tried aiming for another as the lasers tore through a whole line of soldiers.

He could see them trying to drive a small armored vehicle through the hole, only for all three lasers to get focused on it, turning it into a fused together barrier, slowing the flow of soldiers through the dome as they struggled to get past.

Then the flow stopped as abruptly as it started.

A few uncertain soldiers who had made it inside didn't know what to do and were picked off as the soldiers outside the dome started to retreat. The mining lasers picked off at least half a dozen more of the retreating soldiers outside.

Then it was over.

"This was too easy," Zo said over the radio.

"Much too easy," Vincent added. "They'll try again—these people were just cannon fodder used to probe our defenses. Hopefully they won't try again tonight… We need to assess damage. Quickly."

Soka sank down. He thought about the man he'd shot, and his eyes teared up. Then he thought about the attack the other night. The man whose head he'd blown off. And before he knew it, he was sobbing.

This wasn't what he'd signed up for.

Rob found him like that a few minutes later, and helped him up.

"Come. Let's go inside."

They walked together into the administration building where the crew and First Triaton and a few other colonists were gathered.

"I'm certain they'll attack no later than dawn."

Vincent was almost yelling, for no apparent reason. No one was disagreeing with him.

"But this was too easy," he continued, at a more normal volume. "We know there's a damn destroyer in orbit. Likely two. They're bound to have more material here. This must have been a test. I'm telling you, we have to expect the next attack will be much worse. We need to decide how we get out of here."

Zo stood up. "I agree with Vincent. It must have been a test. As far as I am concerned, our only hope is to either prepare for an escape with the ship that is here—I know you don't like that First—or we need to sneak someone back to get *Black Rain* ready, so we have a backup, and so we can make an unexpected escape before they get the idea to bomb it."

"We won't have time to sort *Black Rain* out before the next attack. But I agree we need to get it ready." Vincent nodded at Zo.

"Mons. Clarice. Think you can handle getting back there in one of the all-terrain vehicles? I'm worried you might get spotted, but with some luck they're too focused on preparing their attack, and in those you might get there in an hour. If we send you now, you'll get there before it gets light."

Mons and Clarice both nodded, and got ready to leave.

These Earthers amazed Soka more the more time he spent with them. How they could be so ready to run out there and into danger was something he did not understand. Even when he served on a Centauri ship himself, military operations were always so meticulously planned. Slow and cautious and backed with overwhelming force. And this crew. This crew would just decide and then act instantly.

Slow and cautious, he thought to himself. *Something doesn't add up.*

Chapter 26

"Got everything we'll need?" Mons looked over at Clarice, who was putting the last of the equipment into the back of the all-terrain vehicle.

"Yeah, think so. We should have most of it on the ship anyway. Just a precaution."

"Okay, I'm ready. Let's go."

They steered the vehicle to the opposite side of the dome to the one the previous attack had come from. First Triaton had managed to boost the power output of their antennas and gained a connection to the mapping satellites in orbit, and they had a decent resolution scan of the Centauri forces on the ground. At least until the destroyers figured out what they were up to and took out the satellites or upped the gain on their crude jamming attempts.

Mons had plotted out a course that should just keep them from being spotted directly by the enemy forces. But of course there was the very real danger they'd be spotted by scans from the destroyers overhead.

The data they had from the satellites also included passive scans of the surrounding space, and they thought they'd timed things to minimize the chance of being spotted, as the two destroyers appeared to do periodic overlapping sweeps. If they timed it right, they'd pause for two five-separate-minute intervals when the chance of being picked up was greatest. It would not obscure them entirely, but standing out as a small, slightly less dark spot on a dark rocky background was better than being lit up massively due to the heat from the engine.

They got help to open a gate, and drove off in relative silence. Clarice was usually quiet anyway, and Mons didn't particularly feel like talking. It was a tense twenty-minute drive until their first pause. They would not know immediately if they'd been spotted, of course. They'd need radio silence, or they'd be noticed for sure, and their first warning they'd been noticed by the destroyers would likely be a missile barrage they'd have little hope of evading.

***

"Missiles, incoming!"

Rob looked up when he heard the yells, and saw the plume from at least half a dozen missiles heading for the dome.

The sky was still dark but slightly glowing near the horizon where Proxima Centauri was about to rise. Alpha Centauri A and B were just barely visible, seemingly entwined.

In the near darkness the missiles stood out clearly. To Rob they looked a bit like burning arrows, the exhaust leaving a glowing trail that soon went dark. Moments later they punctured the dome, which was compromised anyway.

Two rockets exploded on impact with the dome and tore additional huge gaping wounds in it, and about a third of the dome started buckling. The integrity lost by the multiple holes and the twisted structure.

The rest hit buildings on the outer perimeter, taking out two of the laser mounts.

Rob heard screams on the radio that quickly died down. He started running towards the collapsed buildings, and met Centauri colonists busy suppressing the fires. His first instinct was to help with triage, but he realized he knew nothing about which injuries the Centauri would prioritize.

It doesn't matter, I'll do what I can, he thought to himself. He went from person to person, leaving behind those who appeared to have minor injuries for the colonists to handle. He felt bad when each face he didn't recognize made him grateful it wasn't one of his crew.

He ran into Zo and Vincent who were also helping, and finally one of the Centauri doctors. He asked how he could be of the best help, and the doctor pointed him to a couple of patients with injuries for him to assess.

***

"The ship is right over there," Mons whispered to Clarice.

The vehicle cabin was pressurized, and they'd opened their face plates to avoid the risk of using the radio even on low power.

"See any sign of people?" Clarice whispered back.

The situation just made it feel right to whisper even though nobody could hear them.

They'd been lucky so far, and hadn't run into anybody, nor had any missiles shot after them. The ship stood as they left it.

"Let me off here, Mons. I'll sneak up to it and run a security sweep. I'll wave when it's safe to drive up."

Clarice left the car, and moved from rock to rock up to the ship. Mons saw her slip inside, and almost held his breath while waiting, until she came out and waved. He drove the vehicle all the way up to the ship, and together they hauled the crates in, and closed the access.

Clarice brought life support up quickly, and they started assessing the damage. It was not too bad. The main engine damage was the worst. There was a leak in a compartment about halfway up the ship that they were able to quickly seal before their air pressure dropped again. They'd need to do more to it before they'd be ready to take off, but at least now they could work without their full suits.

***

Rob saw too many dead people.

For every injury he helped assess and start treatment of, he saw three to four colonists lying limply on the ground, or charred, or with limbs severed, sometimes enough so that he was unsure of exactly how many dead he had seen.

The Centauri worked fast and efficiently in going through the wreckage, and quickly declared there was no point going through the rest.

Rob was about to object. There were still dead bodies there, but someone pointed out to him they had no time. If they were to stand any chance at all, they needed to focus on improving what little defenses they had, and heal those who could be healed.

They were again left wondering why, if their attackers were able to do this, they didn't level all the buildings. Surely they had enough missiles?

He saw Vincent again. "Clearly they want something with us," Vincent said, and walked on shaking his head.

***

Mons thought he was close to fixing the engine. Clarice reported the bridge was okay, and the computer systems passed the diagnostics.

He heard her gasp over the internal comms.

"I switched on passive scans, Mons. I can't tell what's going on, but almost I'm certain an attack has started. Heatmap in direction of the colony lit up like crazy. Either there's a fire or they were hit by missiles…"

We won't have much time. If they don't come soon, they won't come at all.

Chapter 27

Zo was waiting for the next attack, expecting it to be more missiles, but instead they faced a range of vehicles coming in across a broad angle. Clearly the missiles had been intended to both destroy enough of the dome and enough of the outer defense perimeter to allow them to drive their vehicles in to protect their men this time.

After the first attack, their attackers knew exactly where the weaknesses and strengths of the improvised defense were.

They all started shooting, and the one remaining laser mount took out several vehicles before one of the attackers managed to take it out with an RPG shot from the back of one of the vehicles.

Soon the first vehicles hit the gap in the outer defense perimeter. They drove right over the remaining corpses.

"Fuck you," Zo yelled, as she lit a Molotov Cocktail and ignited the explosives they'd littered along the outer perimeter on her insistence.

The Centauri were very helpful, but they were not very inventive like this. The mine had plenty of suitable explosives, and she'd pointed out they didn't need fancy bombs to make the vehicles break down and help reinforce the destroyed outer perimeter. For a moment she thought about Grant. Grant would have loved this. *The dumb bastard,* she thought to herself, angry about his betrayal, but she still missed him at times, and right now she pictured how he'd have probably charged the attackers with improvised explosives at the ready.

They quickly took out the soldiers trying to get out of the broken vehicles as well as several of their comrades trying to climb over the vehicles from behind.

But Zo also saw colonist after colonist get slaughtered. They were outnumbered to start with, and their attackers were better trained and better prepared.

The rage was rising in her, and she threw explosives as if they were rocks, and followed them with plasma salvos to set them off. She took out a group of the attackers that way.

She yelled at the others to do the same.

Eventually this attack attempt also ended with a withdrawal.

"We better expect another missile attack next. I got the distinct impression they thought they knew how to beat us this way. These people are idiots. Why the hell did they not fire more missiles to soften us up more first?" *Or to just kill us all?*

Vincent is right, she added a moment later. *These are definitively not professionals.*

"See if any of them are still alive," she yelled over the radio.

She heard another plasma rifle shot.

"I thought they were fleeing?" said Zo. "Who shot?"

"They are. I caught one. Shot the fucker in the leg."

Vincent, of course.

"Where are you, Vincent?"

"I see you; I'm bringing the asshole."

They dragged their captive into the administrative building, and once inside the airlock, they pulled off his helmet.

Zo gasped. "Tell me, First. I'm not too familiar with your species. Do any of your people look like this?"

Inside was a white man, light brown hair, blue eyes.

"No. We all have roughly my skin color, some variation but none as pale as this. And none have eyes like that. He looks like an Earther."

"That's what I thought too. Just making sure it's not my preconceptions..."

She turned to the man.

"Care to tell me what you're doing in a Centauri uniform attacking a Centauri colony, coming from a Centauri ship, before I let the very human man over there show you how good he is at hurting people?"

Zo pointed at Vincent, and saw Vincent do his very best to look like he was *hoping* the man would refuse to cooperate.

"We were told that if captured, I should tell you 'Mr. Terrell sends his regards, and regrets that you have to die.'"

The man seemed to be trying to appear tough and forced a smile, but it rapidly disappeared when Vincent took a step towards him and grinned.

Zo held up a finger and Vincent stopped.

"The ships?" Zo asked.

"They're ours. We built them. Mr. Terrell built them, I suppose. They only look Centauri on the outside... Some weapons... we procured. Fooled you well, didn't it." He forced a smirk, but Zo was not fooled—he was terrified. "Doesn't matter if I tell you, they'll destroy this place soon enough, and kill all of us."

"Really. We've repelled you a couple of times now. Clearly Mr. Terrell wants something from us or he'd just have destroyed the entire colony from orbit."

"He wants you to know he's the one killing you. And he wants to be sure he knows who you've told, so he can kill everyone you've been in contact with. He doesn't care about you. Just as long as a couple of you survives long enough to tell him what he needs. *Traitors*."

The man tried to spit at Zo.

This guy has seen too many bad movies.

She stepped aside before he succeeded, and instead Vincent planted his fist in the man's face.

"Vincent, *what the fuck*. He might have more to say."

"Sorry. He had it coming." Vincent shrugged.

Zo did not for a second believe Vincent was sorry. The man had passed out, and she asked the Centauri for a medic while she conferred with First.

"Should have known it was these bastards, First. I'm so sorry we've brought this down on you."

"It doesn't matter, Captain Ortega. These people need to be stopped, and it would not be honorable to avoid helping you just because the enemy was different to whom we thought."

He looked sad, but showed no hesitation.

"We stand with you until the end."

One of the Centauri medics gave the man a stimulant, and Zo turned to him again as he woke up.

"Tell us what you know. Unless you want Vincent to hit you again."

Vincent took a step closer, so he could breathe down the man's neck. He grinned, clearly relishing the ability to intimidate their captive some more. Zo didn't feel comfortable about Vincent acting this way, but she suppressed her feelings—they couldn't afford taking their time to talk him around.

"I don't know much. We've trained in the Alpha Centauri system mostly, moved around. Done training exercises destroying various small ships Terrell got hold of."

"Is that what he told you? That they were training exercises when you murdered that freighter crew in cold blood?"

"What? No. We've attacked ships controlled by drones. We wouldn't kill humans. Except for traitors like you."

"Bullshit. We saw your handiwork, and picked up some pieces of the charred bodies you left behind, and followed one of your scouts, you scum."

The man seemed uncertain whether to believe them or not. It seemed clear he did not *want* to believe them.

Zo was both disgusted and intrigued. Terrell appeared not to even trust his own crews to believe in his cause enough to be happy about shooting at human crews.

Just like he treated us. Getting them on the hook with a lie, and hoping it sticks.

"What will they do next?"

"I don't know. Honest… There are more missiles, though. I'd imagine they'll fire more missiles, and next time they'd be dumb to send the vehicles in without looking for explosives. That shit won't work again."

"Yeah, you guys were pretty dumb weren't you," Vincent interjected and grinned. "Real green."

Zo took his point, and once again raised a finger to Vincent to get him to stop.

"You didn't have any experienced officers?" she asked.

"Uhm. I don't know. I think most of the guys were recruited from freighters and from Earth. There were a couple of ex-military, but not many. Terrell promised us military units would start coming around when we prove the Centauri threat is real."

"At least it's good news they don't have any better than this so far," Zo said and turned towards Vincent.

"Do we need this clown anymore?" Vincent replied.

"I'm done. But that does not mean you get to hit him again."

"*Aww.*" Vincent gave her an exaggerated look of disappointment.

Chapter 28

"Incoming!"

The loud yelling was coming from outside. Rob put his helmet back on and grabbed his plasma rifle and rushed out.

As he left the infirmary, the first thing he saw were more incoming missiles. The first slammed into the building right in front of him, and blew up all of it. Rob was thrown onto the ground, but forced himself to get up and look for cover.

There were people running all over, and more vehicles incoming. Rob tried to fire at them. The resistance was in total disarray. About a third of the buildings in the colony had been leveled.

They were being pushed back, with most seeking cover behind the administration building and a handful of other buildings near the center of the colony.

There was a lot of yelling over the radio, and Rob struggled to keep track of all the conflicting reports.

He shot one of the attackers in the chest, and kept running. *I don't even feel bad about shooting them anymore,* he thought to himself, and it made him shiver for a second. He thought he saw Zo and Vincent, but it turned out to be two Centauri. One of them had her head blown clear off before he got to them. He turned and shot repeatedly at the location the shot had come from without taking the time to aim properly.

All that fueled him at this point was fear and anger, and a sinking feeling that there was no way out. Nothing at all they could do.

He finally spotted Zo and Soka, and ran for cover behind the same building they were hiding by.

A vehicle rounded the corner, and four or five of them there all suddenly had only one goal: To stop it. To kill the driver. Take out the wheels. Shoot anyone inside it.

Rob had no idea what he was doing. He was reacting by pure instinct, and somehow his instincts were leading him the right way. The soldiers in the vehicle were killed in seconds. He did not know who got the kills, and it didn't matter.

Zo ran to help a group of Centauri from being overrun, and Rob watched her just run at them with her rifle in front, firing shot after shot as the inexperienced attackers panicked instead of taking the time to aim. Zo picked them off one after the other.

He saw Soka firing at another group, and moved to join him, lining up next to him and trying to pick off the first of a group of six of the soldiers charging them. He hit the man in the leg, and watched him fall and the one after him stumble over his body.

Soka fired and fired and eventually hit one of them. "Slow down and aim," he told Soka over the radio.

The remaining four were almost on them and Rob and Soka shot the same man almost simultaneously, one in the leg and one in the chest, and Rob swore when he realized they'd wasted an opportunity to take out someone else. The callousness of that thought made him shiver again.

Rob saw one of them lift his pulse rifle and aim at Soka's head, and without thinking about what he was doing, he jumped, and pushed Soka out of the way.

So this is what burning plasma feels like, he thought, as he was hit, and everything went black.

***

Soka didn't have a chance to react when Rob pushed him aside. He fell and rolled, and when he looked back, Rob was on the ground. Soka rushed over to him, and grabbed his shoulders, then he realized there was a gaping hole straight through where Rob's chest should have been.

Soka had never been a man to rage. He got angry like everyone, but he always remained composed, and let the anger slowly burn away at his insides until it subsided.

But this time he felt rage, and the rage grew until he felt like he became nothing but rage. He lifted his plasma rifle and started firing like a madman at the three remaining men.

He did not know who had killed Rob, but it did not matter, because he killed them all before he even knew what he was doing. He'd not even particularly liked Rob. Rob seemed to have a problem with him, or at least be wary of him. They'd spoken very little.

Yet Rob had not hesitated to save his life, and the only way Soka felt he could repay him was by letting the rage control him and take out the men who'd cost Rob his life, and then to find the next group and run at them with his rifle spewing plasma, without paying any attention to the risk he was taking.

He was screaming and shooting and running and shooting some more.

He heard Vincent yell at him over the radio to fall back at least three times before he realized it was meant for him, and he looked around and saw there were only a couple of them still confronting the attackers out there.

He started backing off while he kept firing, until he got behind the administration building and turned and ran towards the workshops at the other side of the colony where Vincent told him to get to.

"Rob is dead," Soka yelled. "He's dead." He repeated it again, and this time his yelling turned into something more like sobbing.

Soka turned to fire a few more rounds towards the attackers coming around the side of the buildings, before he kept running while others laid down cover fire.

He almost ran straight into Zo.

He couldn't look her in the eyes. Just turned, and found cover, and lined up to keep firing. It was the only way he could keep going.

Emotions like these were entirely new to him. He'd seen death before. He'd had close friends die. Relatives. But this brutal mass murder was too much. Rob throwing himself into the line of fire to save someone he hardly knew was too much.

He didn't realize at first that he was crying. It was only when he found it hard to see as he was aiming for another attacker that he realized his eyes were all wet, and the tears were dripping down his face.

Zo grabbed his arm. "Come. We're pulling back further."

He followed her and Vincent, and turned back once more just in time to see the administration building blow up in yet another missile attack.

"They seem intent to destroy the entire colony," Vincent yelled over the radio.

"We can't stay here," Zo replied.

It was trite and obvious. The place was being flattened. *Of course we can't stay here,* he thought in anger.

Dozens of people *would* stay there, on Proxima Centauri b, a planet so insignificant it hadn't even been given a proper name yet. This would be their burial ground.

We will avenge them, thought the Centauri who had never before in his life wanted to avenge anything.

Chapter 29

Zo and Monique held the line by the shuttle while Vincent helped the Centauri get into their ship. It was a last, desperate move.

They didn't even know if Mons and Clarice had succeeded in getting the *Black Rain* ready, but they figured they'd stand a better chance if they gave Sovereign Earth two separate targets.

And, thought Zo, *maybe we'll draw the fire away from the colonists.*

After all, it was them Terrell had a reason to hate.

Jonas had been put in the shuttle between the attacks, to be ready in case they needed a rapid retreat, so as soon as the Centauri were ready, Vincent would be the last person to get onto the shuttle, and then they'd fly in something like an erratic half circle towards *Black Rain* in the hope it'd take Terrell's people too long to realize where they were headed.

The Centauri would fly in the opposite direction, away from the destroyers on a path to try a slingshot around the planet and towards the gate. It provided the destroyers with a convenient target for quite some time before they'd have sufficient speed and distance, but it was the best shot they had. *Hopefully they're not callous enough to prioritize murdering the colonists*, Zo thought.

"They're ready, Cap."

Vincent got back to the shuttle and jumped inside, and Zo followed him.

They waited for the Centauri ship to lift off before they headed off as well.

Zo watched their scans anxiously, when a massive cloud of dust covered everything.

"The fuckers bombed the colony," yelled Vincent. "I guess they're getting tired of trying to keep any of us alive."

"But they still had their own people there!" Zo replied.

"Doesn't seem like they cared."

"Shit, missiles," Zo yelled.

Zo could see at least a dozen missiles incoming, and started evasive maneuvers, but they didn't appear to be the target, and she got a sinking feeling as she dropped the shuttle down as close to the ground as she could.

Behind them the Centauri ship turned into a giant fireball and broke apart.

The bastards murdered every last one of them. Every single colonist had sacrificed their lives to save them.

And Rob, Zo added to herself.

The ship almost slammed into the side of a ravine, but she pulled up at the last second. They had to survive. They had to retaliate and stop this evil bastard. She didn't much care about anything else at this point.

"Have they picked us up yet?" she asked Vincent, so she could concentrate on flying, hugging the surface as best she could, at the risk of having no margin for error.

"No sign of it, but it can't be many minutes before they either find us or realize where we're headed."

They were only a few minutes out when the dark sky was lit up by another round of missiles, this time clearly split between them and *Black Rain*.

Zo almost screamed. Not in fear, but anger and frustration. The shuttle had only light weaponry, but nevertheless Vincent succeeded in destroying one of the missiles, and Zo pulled up hard just in time for a second to hit the ground instead of them. The third was still closing in when she could see the plasma cannons on *Black Rain* firing, taking out one missile after the other.

Zo put the shuttle down almost on top of the ship. Vincent and Soka took Jonas' stretcher in, while the others secured the door.

"Faster! Faster!" Zo yelled. "We have seconds before they'll try again."

"Welcome to *Black Rain*, your ride today may be a bit bumpy as the weather report suggests missile rain, and we'll be taking off before you've reached the bridge, so please hang on wherever you are, you have *ten* seconds."

Zo had never found the sound of Clarice's voice as appealing as that moment, as she practically threw herself at the nearest straps and clipped herself to the wall. *But fuck you for making a joke of it,* she thought, and couldn't help cracking a small smile.

They could feel the ship start moving and the g-forces increasing as the main engine ramped up.

"If we survive this, I'm going that girl a spanking," muttered Vincent opposite her, after having just managed to lock Jonas' stretcher safely in place.

"Oi! That's the captain's job," Zo told him, and instantly wished she hadn't drawn attention to her attraction to Clarice. Vincent said nothing, but she could see him smirk, and she in turn tried to kill him with a stern look and hoped she wasn't going red enough for it to be noticeable.

"What are you guys complaining about? I'm here on a fucking stretcher with a back injury," Jonas yelled from his position strapped down on the floor.

Zo tapped her contact display into the bridge systems and brought up the tactical display and their front view.

"Clarice, what the hell is that?"

They were flying at an altitude that'd still be dangerous in the little shuttle, and Clarice was doing it with *her* ship.

"Welcome, Cap. Don't worry, while we waited, we analyzed the map data carefully, and plotted out a course, and I did some... light surgery on the navigation system. We'll survive."

"Well, we'll survive the flight pattern... Don't know about the destroyers," Clarice added.

Vincent laughed a deep rolling laughter she'd not heard before. Zo was briefly worried Vincent had lost completely lost it. But something about the insanity of what they'd been through, and Clarice's chirpy jokes and Vincent's crazy laughter was infectious. Zo just barely managed to stay serious. Mostly.

That girl is crazy, Zo thought. She wouldn't have it any other way. *But if she destroys my ship she'll pay.* Of course, if she destroyed the ship, they'd all be dead.

The destroyers had started moving, but she could not yet tell whether they realized they were planning to circumnavigate enough of the planet to then adjust their thrust and let themselves be slingshot out in the direction of the gate, or whether they were just following the *Black Rain's* current path without much thought for the orbital mechanics of it.

She hoped the latter. Changing direction of those huge ships was not easy, and every second of delay in reaction where their pursuers kept accelerating in the wrong direction would increase their chance of survival.

They picked up a feeble further attempt at firing missiles at them, but they'd racked up enough speed that they easily outdistanced the missiles.

"They're accelerating fast," Clarice announced, but Zo knew she'd understand that meant little right now. The destroyers had significantly more powerful engines, and could accelerate faster, but they'd worked up enough of an advance that they were now constantly almost over the horizon, and in a moment, they'd be out of view of the destroyers for a few minutes until the destroyers' speed caught up enough to start cutting the distance.

And it was almost time to lift the nose just a tiny bit towards the gate. By the time their altitude made them visible to the destroyers again, it'd be a real problem for the destroyers to change direction fast enough to avoid losing valuable time.

"See you later, bastards!" Clarice announced over the comms in an upbeat voice that got not just Vincent but all of them to burst out laughing as they were handling the g-forces as best they could.

Chapter 30

Soka had been quiet ever since they'd gotten on the ship. Now they were all gathered on the bridge, except for Jonas who was strapped into the medibay, still facing a few days of recovery.

He was struggling to figure out how to deal with what had happened. The death of all the colonists, of course, but mostly Rob and how he had reacted with blind rage afterwards. It puzzled him why he was so much more affected by the death of a single person, an Earther even, than the death of many dozens of the colonists. The total eradication of the whole colony.

He felt sad about that, but it didn't make him tear up the way thinking about Rob's sacrifice did.

"As soon as we're through, you have the course changes. Make sure we execute them immediately."

Zo's instructions to Clarice and Mons barely registered with him.

Zo—and the rest—had hardly acknowledged Rob's death yet. They seemed intent on ignoring it as long as they were in the middle of the escape. Soka could accept that. The destroyers were still accelerating, even though they clearly had no chance of overtaking them before the gate.

The minutes they had to themselves after entering Alpha Centauri space would be essential in accelerating in a direction the destroyers would hopefully not anticipate, and to get them into a position where they could hope for protection from the Centauri fleet. Though Soka was still anxious about whether or not they could convince them after the last attempt.

They passed through the gate. It always disoriented Soka for a moment. There was no physical sensation per se, but it felt like going "blank" for a moment. Like you'd lost a few seconds. He was not even sure if it was a real sensation at all, or if it was just a psychological reaction to knowing they had suddenly moved a vast distance.

He knew the Earthers were curious about how the gates worked, but as far as he knew, *his people* didn't really understand the principles very well either. They knew a lot about the engineering tolerances, and which parts were safe to experiment with, and they knew a quantum entangled pair of particles was necessary for them to work, but it was unclear even what physical principle was at work.

Once through, the ship immediately flipped and accelerated hard towards one of the other gates.

One of the ones leading out of the system, and which Earth ships had no authorization to use. It was bound to provoke a reaction from the Outpost in the system, and Soka believed that was what Zo was hoping for. Any Centauri ships heading towards them running into the fake Centauri destroyers would force the Centauri to deal with the threat—they could fail to recognize that they were fake if they scanned them.

But Soka could not focus on their escape. There was nothing he could do about that anyway. So instead he kept replaying over and over again in his head, those moments when he looked down and saw Rob with a hole instead of a chest, and the rage and the running, and the men he shot.

He felt like he was changing then and there. He could not go back and unsee Rob's sacrifice, or undo the rage. And it was still burning in him. He wanted each and every one of the people following them dead. He wanted to see it up close. He wanted to pull the trigger over and over.

How can I deal with that without turning into a monster? Maybe that's why they are so focused on their work.

To not have to think about what had happened or how they *wanted* to react.

"The first destroyer is through," Mons announced.

Clarice started a countdown for a course change.

They all waited patiently for the destroyer to adjust course to match theirs, and run through their relatively lengthy process to spin up their main engines to maximum acceleration, and the moment the destroyer was done, the *Black Rain* spun 180 degrees and launched a full missile salvo.

The missiles would be insufficient to deter the destroyer, but it made them start altering their course, and Clarice rotated *Black Rain* again, and started a maximum acceleration burn approximately on a right angle to their original burn, slowly adjusting their course by combining their original momentum with their new thrust.

There would be several more course corrections. If they were lucky, they'd manage to slingshot around Alpha Centauri Bc, a small rocky planet on the outer edge of the system's habitable range, getting them on a rapid final course for a station in the outer system.

Soka knew they were entirely dependent on the destroyers sufficiently missing their course corrections for long enough that they gained a bit of an edge each time. The course corrections they'd come up with were designed to be confusing enough so that it would not be obvious where they were headed, and to allow them to attempt to run dark on the final legs and hopefully not be spotted.

They all knew it was a long shot, but every second they gained opened up new options.

Meanwhile, they were all confined to the bridge—the corrections would be frequent enough and involve assorted nav thruster corrections that it'd be unsafe to move from their stations.

Leaving Soka stuck with his rage and mourning in private—he couldn't well interrupt any of the crew to talk about it in the middle of this. In his mind he started composing angry letters and strongly worded admonitions to the diplomatic corps and military for the reaction he had gotten before they ran away.

And, he added in his mind, *for their failure to react speedily this time.*

They were still being jammed by the destroyers, though Vincent had estimated they'd be out of the range of the jammers after another couple of course corrections, assuming they kept increasing the distance. For now, it had prevented Soka from being able to make another attempt to reach someone. Anybody.

Their scans did show a couple of Centauri ships moving towards the Proxima gate, but way too late. They did not seem in a hurry, and either did not notice or did not care about the chase, or perhaps they were confused about what was going on. Either way, Soka considered it gross incompetence, and when they did get radio contact again, he would certainly take great pleasure in elaborating to someone suitably high up on exactly the extent of this incompetence.

This brought a smile to his face for the first time since he'd gotten back on the ship. He was going to end careers the way he'd ended lives. Fast and brutal, and driven by rage. *Maybe that's how I'll control this,* he thought. *By channeling it into arguments so devastating his opponents could do nothing but concede.* It sounded stupid to him the moment he'd thought it, but it still made him feel better.

He straightened out in his seat, as if he was standing up tall, and shaped words into daggers in his mind. They were going to pay. They had let a bunch of Earther terrorists run rampant, and denied their ships even existed. They needed to pay.

Either they knew the ships were there and thought it was something above their pay grade, or they'd not bothered checking. Nonetheless, they'd let a bunch of backwards savages—as much as he had grown to appreciate the ingenuity of the *Black Rain* crew, there was still not a doubt in his mind that this was a suitable description for Terrell's crews—destroy ships, and a colony, in their space.

It made him fear for the future if the Earthers could manipulate them so easily.

Chapter 31

"We're out of the range of their jammers," Mons announced unceremoniously, as if it was not of tremendous importance.

There was still no doubt that Terrell's destroyers could see them on scanners; in fact, their tactical display showed regular "pings" as they detected active scans, so trying to establish radio contact would not give them away any more.

Zo turned to Clarice. "Try to see if they'll relay our connections to Earth, please, Clarice."

"Nothing, Captain, they're rejecting our connections."

"Soka, try to see if they'll let you talk to your outpost at least. If they're being difficult and won't let us talk, they should at least honor your diplomatic codes and hear what you have to say."

Soka nodded, and sat by the console next to Clarice.

He tried to direct a call to the Lady Xine first, his superior. It did not go through.

He then directed a call to the military liaison at the local outpost.

"Yes?" a brusque voice answered. No video feed was being sent.

Soka sent his credentials and asked to speak to someone in charge.

The video feed was enabled and Soka looked at a very serious woman in a military uniform.

"This is Squadron Commander Mera'li Scirrrn Three. You may speak to me."

Soka started explaining what had happened to them, but was interrupted shortly after he mentioned the colony on Proxima Centauri b.

"You claim you were attacked by Earthers pretending to be us? And you expect me to believe these Earthers are capable of fooling us?"

She gave a derisive snort, before continuing.

"Look at this video we received from the colony you claim were attacked by these Earthers."

Soka gasped. He was looking at a video that seemed to show the *Black Rain* coming in low over the colony and firing missiles at it. A lot of it looked exactly how he remembered the destruction caused by Terrell's people, but it had been faked to appear to be caused by them.

"We received that video along with a distress call from the colony. We also received confirmation from two destroyers in the Kzari Squadron that they were in pursuit, and have seen them follow you when you came through the Proxima gate. Care to explain?"

Soka furrowed his brow. The Kzari Squadron was a black ops squadron. They would not generally identify themselves, but if Terrell's crew had succeeded in faking their idents, it would explain why Soka had been shut down when making claims about ships earlier.

The officer he spoke to would have thought he'd be revealing state secrets. But it raised a big question to Soka over how they had obtained the codes needed to pretend to be from the Kzari Squadron.

"I fully believe the colony was destroyed by Earthers, Soka, but I think we both know it was by the ship you are on. I am sure you are making these ridiculous claims under duress. Let your captors know they have not fooled us, and your only option is surrender."

"Commander Meera, I assure you I am not under duress, and that video is fake. You know how easy it is to fake such videos."

"Video is easy to fake, yes, but we also have the testimony of the Kzari Squadron captains."

"They are not Kzari Squadron. They're lying to you. Scan the ships. Ask to send an attache aboard their ships. They'll refuse."

"Of course they'll refuse. They have every right to refuse. They do not answer to me. Our long range scans showed nothing out of the ordinary and we have no reason to send a ship to get more detailed scans."

"They'll refuse because those ships are full of Earthers."

"Ludicrous, Soka. If it is as you say that you're not under duress, then you are complicit unless you attempt to take control of the ship and force their surrender."

"I will do no such thing. These are brave and honorable people. The colonists of Proxima Centauri b died out of honor to defend them and ensure we were able to tell the truth. One of their crewmates died to save my life."

"This utter nonsense… I am shocked that you are protecting these murderers. You have made your choice. There is a warrant out for the ship and its crew. Your name will go on it as well."

The connection went dead.

Soka tried to reconnect, but the relay refused his codes. He tried to get a connection through to his home, to see if his wife could help, and it was also rejected. He didn't really expect otherwise, but it was worth a shot.

He started tearing up. It shocked him that they were so unwilling to listen to the truth. That they could not see that they were being fooled.

Clarice put a hand on his shoulder. He tried to pull himself together, he knew the Earthers found such displays of emotion to be weak. Rob had dismissively called it "girly" once, and Soka had been confused, because it sounded like Rob was trying to insult him, the way a Centauri might accuse him of crying like child, but it made no sense to him. He never got close to Rob, but thinking of him now just made Soka more upset, and once again he pictured him there on the ground in the colony, with the gaping hole in his chest.

"Guess they don't want to talk to us," he heard Zo say from behind. "You did what you could, Soka. It's not your fault they're so up their asses and think humans are too dumb and primitive to fool them like this."

Soka turned towards her, and didn't quite know what to say. He'd been rude and dismissive about Earthers' capabilities as well. He was certain they were all primitive savages, and while he'd learned that some of them certainly were primitive savages, he'd been impressed by the crew. Especially Zo, whose forceful manner was just what he liked in a woman. He'd also been amazed to see the men being so strong and feminine. On one hand he found it disconcerting and out of place, but he also found it intriguing to see them able to step up and do the same things the women did, and it had made him resolve to try to toughen up as well.

"We'll find a way," Zo added.

Chapter 32

The Lady Xine-Zor Li'mor Four sat in her office looking out the window at the artificial lake in the park in the colonial administration compound.

Her intelligence reports were troubling, and she was awaiting her staff so that they might properly account for what sounded like a total mess, if not outright nonsense, coming out of the Centauri system.

A destruction of a colony was nearly unheard of. Along the borders to one of the more unruly major powers nearer the center of galaxy, perhaps. But out in the outer reaches, these things just did not happen.

And to be told an Earther ship was responsible. "Total madness," she thought to herself. Those savages had hardly mastered basic intra-system space flight before they received the invitation to connect in the Alpha Centauri system. They had built a reasonable trade network in their star system after learning how to build gates, she understood, and for a primitive civilization they had potential.

But to destroy a colony?

They'd bribed a few traders, and gotten enough agents into Sol to know what the Earther military capability was like. A basic precaution, of course, with no hostile intent. It made Xine certain she knew how limited and primitive their armed forces were.

The video was shocking enough. The testimony from the Kzari Squadron officers even more so. She had not known the Kzari Squadron even had anyone in the system, but then again, she was not privy to their operations. She had made some discreet requests, and been told to mind her own business. *That was fair enough*, she thought.

"Apologies, everyone is here for your meeting."

Her assistant stood by the door when she turned around.

"Send them in."

Three people entered. First a heavy-set but tall and quite handsome general she had met once before but could not remember the name of, and did not care to learn, as the one thing Xine did remember about her was that she had been exceedingly boring. She was accompanied by two of her staffers from the intelligence section.

"Hello again, General, how are you?"

"I'm well, thank you, my Lady."

"How are the husbands?"

"The entire family is excellent, my Lady. Though the children are annoyed at being stationed out here. They'll learn to deal with it."

Lady Xine smiled to pretend to care, and turned to her staffers.

"What is the latest status?"

"Soka'li Em-Sckirrrnie Three attempted to contact you. The call was rejected as per your instructions."

Xine did not want to risk being seen to have any loyalties to Soka given the current situation. She'd decided it'd be best to restrict his access to the local military contacts only, to keep her hands entirely clean, given it had been her decision to bring him in. A decision she was now regretting.

"What did he want?"

"He tried to convince them the Kzari destroyers are secretly Earthers in fake ships, and that they destroyed the Proxima colony, my Lady."

"What? Outrageous!"

She slammed her hand on the table. *Such lies and deception from my own envoy.*

She did not know Soka personally, other than their one meeting, but he had an unblemished record, and she was astounded when her staffer showed her a recording of his ridiculous excuses.

To deny the video from the colony was one thing, but when it was corroborated by testimony from officers from the Kzari Squadron it was another matter entirely.

"General, as you can see, we are dealing with a crisis. We cannot let this stand unanswered. These Earthers clearly engineered this business with their freighter as an excuse to give those terrorists free hands, and now they've managed to turn one of our own."

"What would you have me do, my Lady?"

"Prepare a punitive expedition. It is the standard response. You know this."

"My Lady! The last time we executed a punitive expedition was a century ago."

"When was the last time one of the savage civilizations dared attack any of our colonies, General?"

The general was quiet for a moment.

"You are right, of course. I cannot even recall such a thing happening in my lifetime. Certainly not with the aid of one of our own. Who knows what knowledge he may hand over to them."

That worried Lady Xine too. Soka had been a diplomat for decades, but he'd been an engineer for decades before that. He undoubtedly had lots of knowledge the Earthers would love to get their hands on that, while decades out of date, would still be a huge step up from the scraps they had allowed the Earthers to see so far.

Who knows how it may mess up a civilization that backwards.

"We need to teach these savages a proper lesson, General. I want you to prepare to disable a few of their local gates, and give one of their colonies the same treatment they gave our Proxima colony. Obliterate it."

The general nodded.

"If that doesn't teach them, we'll have to destroy the Centauri-Earth gate and leave them to their barbary."

Destroying the gate would effectively give the Earthers a couple of decades to reassess their choices while waiting to see if they'd be allowed another gate. She was hopeful a couple of decades of introspection might teach them to behave.

It was centuries since the last time someone had been fully cut off that way, and many more since anyone had been handed a permanent ban after a second round of infractions once the next gate was opened. Xine had read about it during her training, a long time ago, but it was ancient history.

As she understood it, further decades of pleading via radio had continued, complete with news about how knowing there were others out there, but being cut off had cause their society to fracture and crumble, and how being allowed to reconnect was their only hope.

There were several stories like that in their history books. Societies that had been allowed back in their good graces but had suffered decades of decline, war, and chaos during their bans, as civilizations that had rapidly become used to the idea that there was adventure and wealth and knowledge out there had turned on each other; fighting over who were at fault for getting them disconnected; fighting over resources or attempts to build their own; fighting with xenophobes who saw the disconnection as a new dawn and those who wanted to fix the flaws in their society they thought had been the cause of the ban.

Some had seen entire religions founded dedicated to the Centauri after their civilizations had fallen in the aftermath of a ban.

She had never once imagined she might be at the focal point of what was already close to becoming a historic event, and she did not like it—she felt fear at not knowing how the history books would describe her, and she'd never desired notoriety in the first place. That was why she was a civil servant willing to serve in the provinces rather than a politician trying to climb the ranks in the Central Worlds.

Xine hoped it would not come to a ban for Earth. But from what she had seen, she did worry Earth would not quietly accept the eye for an eye of a punitive expedition.

But what is the alternative, she thought. *A colony for a colony. Children must learn somehow. The Earthers must learn.*

Chapter 33

The bridge was quiet. They were all there. Even Jonas, who was now able to sit up for short periods of time.

They were intently watching the main display, which had very little on it right now. They had gone dark, and there was only so much useful information they got from purely passive scans.

As Soka understood it, based on what Clarice had explain to him, they had not been gaining enough distance from Terrell's destroyers, and so they were worried that continuing their planned course corrections would reveal their final destination too soon.

Instead they'd slightly changed course, going into their planned slingshot around Alpha Centauri Bc, but at a speed and angle that'd just barely allow them to execute a brutal maneuver to change course while out of view of the destroyers following them. They'd use its atmosphere to bleed enough speed to change course and get into a tight orbit around one of its moons instead, maybe giving them the option of landing and hiding.

Zo had looked at Clarice as if she thought the course corrections involved were entirely insane, and had it not been for Mons backing her up and the impressive escape from the Proxima colony, Soka would have been certain Zo would have rejected the whole thing.

He had discreetly looked over Clarice's work as well, and though his orbital mechanics were rusty at best, and had never been very good, he was impressed.

The maneuver worked, but Soka almost vomited, and the entire crew complained loudly about the g-forces they'd suffered as a result.

They hid in a crater that was small enough that Zo again had looked unhappy when Clarice and Mons had shown her the scans, but again she'd yielded.

Zo confided to Soka after they'd made the landing that she was quite pleased to see Clarice actually cooperating with someone instead of doing all the calculations herself, and she also told him she thought Mons was flourishing under the attention Clarice was giving him. Well, "flourishing" was Soka's word. *I don't think she'd ever say that word,* he thought.

So there they were. Sitting at the bottom of a crater, watching the tactical screen for any signs of active scans that might pick them up. Everything that might cause external EM emissions to show up had been disabled. No active scans. No engines. No floodlights. Which meant there was nothing to see on their external cameras but bits of alien night sky, and darkened crater walls.

"You know, this is the first time we've had to sit down and talk since that meal when we first met Soka." Clarice looked around at everyone.

It was true. Since then there'd been someone or other running around to get something done, or they'd been in a middle of crisis after crisis.

"We've not had a chance to have a drink for Rob." Vincent's voice was gravelly and he spoke with a much lower volume than usual.

"You're right," Zo added. "Let's have a drink for Rob. And for the colonists. But only one, we can't afford to let our guards down. And don't forget to keep an eye on the screens."

Clarice rolled her eyes. "My augments will alert me if anything happens."

Vincent volunteered to bring a bottle. Zo reiterated that it'd be that one drink and one drink only. They'd need to be ready any moment.

Soka was slightly bewildered. He did not know what role this drink had to play in remembering Rob. He asked Jonas to explain to him.

"It's just a custom from Earth," Jonas told him. "We drink for social bonding. And so we drink to mark special occasions. And there are few occasions more special than to mark the loss of a friend."

Soka nodded. It seemed odd to him still. His people did not attach any meaning to having drinks. They were pleasurable of course, but you drank to drink, nothing more.

"I don't think any of us got to know Rob very well," Zo said, with her glass raised. "Many of us keep to ourselves a lot. I guess living so close to each other works best for people who know how to compartmentalize."

"But I knew him perhaps better than the rest of you. The first time I met him, in fact, was before any of you joined the crew. He wasn't crew back then. I ran into him while he was a medic on Io colony, and I'd gotten hurt real bad. It was back when my crew was killed, and I was hunting down the bastards who did it."

"Is this a long story, Cap, because I'm not sure I can look at this drink much longer?"

"Fuck you, Vincent. Drink up, for Rob, then I'll tell the story."

Zo lifted her glass again, and they all drank.

"To Rob!"

"Now, will your grace be patient?" Zo glared at Vincent.

"Sorry. I'll be quiet."

Zo started talking again.

"I'd killed one of the mercs who got my crew, but he'd lodged a knife in my abdomen, and I nearly bled out getting it out and sealing it up as best I could with a gel pack."

"I almost crawled to the infirmary, where Rob saw me. The bastard looked right at my gaping wound and then looked me straight in the eyes and asked me 'So, what seems to be the problem?' Complete deadpan. I was so dumbfounded I didn't even realize he started cleaning the wound and applying anesthetics while keeping eye contact with me the whole time."

Zo grinned. Soka had not seen her smile like this while he'd been aboard.

"It was only when he told me to start counting to ten I realized something was up, and I passed out just as I was about to ask him what he meant."

She paused for a moment for effect.

"Asshole had given me a sedative, and the pain in my abdomen was so bad I didn't even notice the injection. When I woke up, he'd fixed me up. So when I had finished my 'mission' and needed a crew, I knew where to look for a medic."

She was still smiling, but it looked to Soka as if she was tearing up. Everyone else was quiet.

The silence felt oppressive to him. He wanted to talk, but he couldn't bring himself to. He couldn't imagine what it'd be like to lose someone they'd worked with or lived with for that long, but he still did not understand this ceremony of sorts.

It made him sad. And once again the image of Rob filled his mind, but this time he remembered him alive. One of the few, superficial exchanges they'd had during the very brief time he'd known him.

And then Soka also teared up.

Chapter 34

"Captain, I have a proposal."

Zo had been discussing how to proceed with Vincent, but stopped and turned to Soka.

He looked very serious.

"Okay... Tell me."

"I may be able to help you upgrade the ship."

"What do you mean 'upgrade the ship'?"

"You may not be aware, but before I was a diplomat, I was an engineer. I worked in the fleet for forty years."

"Forty years?! How old *are* you?"

"I'm only 132."

Vincent looked on the exchange with bemusement. He would never have guessed Soka was older than his 40s, so he was surprised himself, but Zo's face made it incredibly hard for him not to burst out laughing.

"Okay, I'm going to want to get back to that subject"—Zo was shaking her head—"but back to the more important part. You can help us upgrade?"

"We're not allowed to share knowledge about propulsion, weapons, or navigation, but given the circumstances I believe the survival of this ship is essential to both our peoples' interests. My engineering knowledge is a few decades out of date, but from what I know of your technology level, I should still have knowledge significantly more advanced than you. I propose I work with Vincent to review what we might be able to upgrade here and now while we're waiting out the destroyers anyway."

Zo nodded.

"Of course. Anything we can do. Just don't leave us stranded here without a working engine. Vincent, you heard the man. Get to it."

Vincent walked Soka over to one of the terminals, and they started going over the engine first.

Soka told him he was a bit rusty, but would do his best. Vincent walked him through a rough outline of Earth engine design history to give him an idea of what they understood how to work with. Chemical engines had dominated for a very long time due to fear of nuclear accidents, but eventually the sheer potential of nuclear tech had prevailed and the designs were not entirely awful, but Soka instantly started to point out ways to him in which they could improve the ship's engines that wouldn't be particularly invasive.

"It's really a very simple engine," Soka told him, and Vincent had the urge to punch him in the face given how long it had taken Vincent himself to learn how the engine worked. But he resisted and smiled, and asked Soka to explain the details to him.

He was glad he did. Soka had an incredible grasp of the technology that went way past Vincent's. Of course, Vincent was not an expert, but he knew enough to realize that what Soka was describing was definitely well ahead of Earth knowledge on the topic.

They started sketching out step by step plans together that'd be possible to do in a way that wouldn't risk leaving the engine disabled for long periods at a time, in case they needed a quick getaway.

It only took them a couple of hours to come up with a rough plan.

Vincent took it to Zo.

"And you're sure?"

"It all adds up, Captain. He does the math several times faster than me, but I've verified it, and I showed it to Mons as well, and he's checked the math as well and agrees it's safe."

"Okay, then. Go ahead."

Vincent told Soka to come with him, and brought Mons along for additional assistance.

"We're going to need to be quick. We really don't want to be spotted while we're unable to fly out of here."

He walked through each step with both of them again to make sure there were no misunderstandings, and they started the modifications. It went surprisingly smoothly. Seeing Soka work on the engine was like seeing an entirely different man. Vincent had just assumed he'd not be the type to want to get his hands dirty, but Soka dug in without hesitation. Vincent found himself looking at him and being impressed.

They finished the engine modifications that evening. There was still no sign they'd been spotted, so they'd thankfully not been forced to rush to put things back together.

They had detected faint signs of active scans that suggested the destroyers were still looking, but Zo authorized a very brief engine power-up to verify it would still light. They'd be unable to confirm if the output was as good as Soka suggested it should be, but it all looked plausible.

Vincent was pleased. If Soka was right, they'd be able to accelerate about twice as fast in theory. The biggest limitation at that point was that they'd be physically unable to handle that acceleration very long.

Once they finished up, Vincent and Soka sat down again to discuss the weapons and nav.

"I never thought I'd see anyone work an engine that well in a dress," Vincent told him.

"I still don't understand why you Earther men all act and dress like women," Soka retorted.

Vincent grinned. He saw himself as open minded. It was not that he was unfamiliar or uncomfortable with men who dressed feminine, or with non-binary people or others that were different to his own norms. He'd more than once seen someone he found attractive, though he considered himself straight. He found Soka unusual, but it wasn't that he minded.

But he realized he had not really thought about it that way—that Soka was simply a typical Centauri man, and that he was what the Centauri considered masculine.

I guess maybe I'm not as unbiased as I assumed, he thought, and resolved to try to do better.

"You dress feminine to us, Soka."

"Ah, I hadn't thought about that. Embarrassing, given my diplomatic duties."

"I just had a realization that I've been making the same type of dumb assumptions myself," Vincent replied. "Guess we both need to stop assuming things. It's a nice dress, though."

They returned to their work, and came up with several improvements to the plasma cannons as well. The design was just a scaled up version of their plasma rifles, so they were able to rig up and test it in their cargo bay, though Vincent hoped Zo wouldn't get too annoyed at the damage they ended up doing to one of the walls.

"You keep delivering like this, and I might just develop a crush on you," Vincent joked, and had to explain to Soka what he meant, and that it was a joke, and came to wonder just how much of what they said that Soka completely misinterpreted.

They upgraded the front plasma cannons without incident. They were reassembling one of the newest plasma cannons when Vincent nearly crushed his foot with one of the generators. Even with the very low gravity on this moon, the generators were heavy enough to cause damage.

Soka threw himself and caught it, and Vincent looked on in amazement as Soka casually lifted the generator back in place.

"Are you okay, Vincent?" Soka looked at Vincent with concern.

"Yeah, no... I'm okay. Just surprised. How strong *are* you?"

Soka smiled gently at him. "I'm not particularly strong. I think we're in general quite a bit stronger than humans. I've never really thought about it."

The rest of the upgrades went without incident, and Vincent went to tell Zo what he'd learned.

Chapter 35

Zo told him they would be ready to move soon, and so if he wanted to make another attempt to reach someone, now would be the time. They'd be fine to break radio silence for a short while as they were setting off, as their engine would make them highly visible for any active scans anyway.

Soka wanted to badly, but he wasn't sure if he'd get through.

"We can try scrambling our idents," Clarice suggested. "The relays seem to let Earth ships communicate without much authentication. I wonder if the blacklisting is just against our ship ident, not anything fancy."

Soka agreed it was worth a try, and Clarice dug out her fake ident program. They'd make their attempt as soon as they'd boosted off the moon and started their full acceleration burn.

***

Zo gave the go ahead soon afterwards, and they launched. The launch was uneventful, but Soka ached under the acceleration after the welcome low gravity break on the moon. Shortly afterwards it was time to test the engine improvements, and the g-forces increased substantially.

"Good job," Zo told him.

At that moment he wished he hadn't done such a good job; they'd all suffer for hours on end for a bit of extra speed.

Once Clarice had prepared the comms system, Soka was up.

It didn't seem worthwhile to try to talk to anyone in his chain of command again. The only person he'd trust to resolve this would be his wife.

He tried connecting to her, and to his surprise the call went through.

"Soka! What are you mixed up in?"

It was odd to Soka to suddenly hear his native language instead of English.

His wife looked upset and angry, and Soka was suddenly not sure if he wanted to continue the call.

"What have they told you?"

His wife recounted the same story he had been presented with, and Soka repeated what had really happened.

"But that *can't be,* Soka'li."

"I swear to you, my love, it is what happened. You cannot believe what they told you."

He knew she didn't truly believe the accusations, or she'd never have taken his call.

"I do not, but I also cannot believe what you have told me, and either way this has shamed our family. How are you going to fix this, Soka'li?"

Soka hung his head.

"We'll find evidence…"

"We?"

"The Earther crew and I."

He knew the moment he'd said it that his wife would not be happy.

"How can a bunch of savages hope to solve this?"

She had raised her voice and turned her head to the side, in an attempt to hide her anger. Soka was glad the others could not understand what she said.

"They've shown themselves to be surprisingly resourceful, my love. You should see how they've outmaneuvered the ships that are following us. For that matter, if the ships following had truly been ours, we'd not have stood a chance… They'd have overtaken us in no time, and I'd have been dead already."

His wife nodded. Soka knew she'd come to realize he was right about that, and that if he was right about that there was no way the ships were what they claimed to be. If she'd be able to convince others of that… Maybe it'd be enough.

"There is something you must do for me, please," he said.

"What do you want?"

"Plead my case to the Lady Xine. Make her understand there's a real threat, and they must deal with it."

It was all he could ask.

His wife nodded, and Soka started feeling all emotional, and wanted to end the call before he'd start crying.

"Tell everyone I miss them."

"Good luck, Soka'li."

She ended the call abruptly, and Soka sat quietly for a moment before turning to talk to Zo.

"I don't know if it'll help at all, Captain."

Soka shrugged. He tried to seem positive about it, but he was not even sure if his wife believed him fully, but more importantly he worried she'd just get in trouble when she tried to bring the issue to the Lady Xine.

Maybe he'd doom his family too.

That was what he feared most of all. He was fine with risking his own life. He'd seen a lot, and had a good life so far. He wished he'd get another century or two, but if he died, he'd die having seen things most people never would.

But his family meant more to him than his own life. He'd seen too little of them lately as it was, but he was used to being apart. He was not used to fearing for their security. His postings had always been safe and secure.

He knew his wife would take precautions. She was much tougher than him, and was used to thinking strategically. She must have already thought about what to do the moment they told her about the accusations.

"All we can do is our best, Soka. Nobody asks for more than your best. What did you tell her?"

Soka recounted their conversation. Explained that his wife would go to their local administrator.

"Lady Xine is responsible for about two dozen systems, I think, with gates in the region the Centauri system belongs to. She was the one who ordered me to join you. And she's responsible for our forces in all of those systems. It's not a high ranking position—this is a far outward-lying territory after all—but she's ambitious. I'm a bit worried her ambition will make her overreact to show her strength."

He looked at Zo for signs of what she was thinking, but he was still awfully bad at reading Earthers.

"What do you think she might do?"

Soka thought about it for a moment.

"There's a system of punitive actions if someone attacks us. They might attack an Earth colony."

"If they do, it will be war. Earth will never let that stand unanswered."

Soka was surprised.

"How can you be sure, Captain? It's a proportional response. Won't your people understand that?"

"Because that is how Earth responds, Soka. We get attacked, we hit back, hard. It doesn't matter if someone on our side hit first. We hit back. And if the other side attacks again, we keep hitting. Even when it's not the smart thing to do."

"Then it is even more important that we prevent this from escalating, because any retaliation to a punitive expedition will be treated as a new provocation and reason for a harsher response. You're expected to understand it's a just punishment, and back down like civilized people."

Soka noticed his hands shaking.

He'd thought about this as about their own survival, and maybe the security of his family, not as potentially causing war. But he could tell that Zo was serious.

Chapter 36

Soka's wife did not waste a moment of time. She ran a large transport firm, and so had considerable resources at her disposal.

She had their fastest ship brought to her within the hour, during which she arranged for her husbands to take on the necessary duties, suited up in her most impressive suit, and set off at a bruising speed through several gate transfers to visit the Lady Xine in person.

It was clear the local administrator wanted to make an example of someone, she thought, and she would not have her family pulled down into the mud by some upstart administrator out in the outer reaches.

She arrived at the first moon of Thestias where the Lady Xine was based in half a day. She was pleased. She knew it had taken her husband more than two days to get there, but he'd traveled on a normal passenger transport that cared about comfort and not pushing their passengers back in their seats so hard during the acceleration between gate transfers that it'd hurt for days, and he'd had to transfer between ships a couple of times.

The Lady Tyra'ki Em-Sckirrrnie One was determined to make an impression, and she marched into the palace without an invitation, and when challenged by the security guard threatened him with the loss of his job, and walked on while ignoring his insistence that he would shoot if she didn't stop.

The last she heard of him was when he reported to the Lady Xine's assistant that someone was on their way in.

Moments later she was facing an angry assistant telling her why she needed an appointment. She waved the assistant away, before flinging the doors to Lady Xine's office open.

Lady Xine was at her desk, with a gun on it.

"I see you've been told I'm here," Lady Tyra told her, and nodded to the gun.

"I was informed some crazy person was on her way in. It seems my guards are useless."

She fingered the gun on her desk, and smiled coolly.

"Don't worry, I'm only here to talk. You won't need that, but feel free to hold on to it if it makes you feel safer."

Lady Tyra took a few steps closer, and stopped, straightened up and set her feet near shoulder-width apart in the kind of power pose that terrified most of her employees. It did not seem to have much of an effect on Lady Xine, but she didn't really expect it to—she just wanted to demonstrate her own confidence.

"Then talk!" Lady Xine's face was stern, but calm.

Tyra introduced herself.

"You're Soka's wife, then?"

"That is correct. He called me. Did you know that?"

Lady Xine looked like she was trying to stifle a little gasp of surprise.

"Is that so. No, I didn't. But then I'm sure you caught my little gasp. I'm impressed—I thought we'd blocked his access. I'm rather less impressed by the local security. This conversation is already very enlightening. You'll be pleased to know I'll already be firing at least two people thanks to you."

"I'm sure you can guess what he's told me."

"I've heard about his delusional conspiracy theories, yes."

Lady Xine rolled her eyes in an exaggerated and totally unnatural fashion.

"I believe him."

"Of course you do. You're his wife. Unfortunately I don't have the luxury of trusting him."

"Does it make sense to you that the destroyers following him have failed to catch up to and apprehend an Earther ship if they are truly ours? Are our forces really incapable of catching a slow, primitive Earther ship?"

"It is not my role to question the Kzari Squadron. You know that very well. If you thought this was such a convincing argument, you'd have just sent me a message, not made a show out of flying here in person and marching into my office."

"I'm not asking you to question the Kzari Squadron. I'm asking you to apply logic. They could overtake an Earther ship with ease. You know that. They have far more powerful weapons. How is it my husband is on a small little Earther ship that can challenge supposed Kzari Squadron ships?"

"Maybe they had confederates. Maybe the Kzari Squadron had other concerns. I cannot know. It is not my business."

"But now you *are* curious. You wonder why it's not been flagged."

Lady Xine's security finally arrived, and flanked Tyra.

"I have said what I came here for. I'll leave willingly. Think about it."

She turned and walked out, with the security following her closely.

***

"What she said makes sense. Something seems off here, General."

The Lady Xine had called the general as soon as Lady Tyra left her office.

"It does not matter; we do not have the authority to question the Kzari Squadron."

"But if these are not Kzari Squadron?"

"How do we determine that safely? You see the problem, right? If we send someone and demand access to those ships, and this crazy person is wrong, we both lose our positions. If we're lucky."

Xine knew the general was right. They could not afford to challenge this. But if Lady Tyra and Soka were right, they'd bomb an Earther colony on bad intel.

On the other hand, Xine thought, *even if we decide to believe them, the attack was carried out by Earthers.*

Did it matter if the Earthers in question were sanctioned by the Earth government rather than allowed to attack due to the incompetence of the Earth government?

Their own government certainly would not allow any of *their* people to fly around attacking other species colonies. Even the idea was preposterous.

So is it not acceptable to carry out the punitive expedition to Sol regardless?

She did feel a bit bad about it, but she told the general to keep preparing anyway. It'd take them days to get all their ships in position. *There is no rush after all. There is still time to call it off if new information came to light.*

In the meantime she would have to have the guard that let Lady Tyra walk straight past fired, and her security shored up. She hated being confronted like that. She liked to have a dossier on her visitors lined up and ready before a confrontation, so she could control the situation from start to end. That required notice and preparation, not people marching straight in and surprising her.

She ordered her assistants to assemble a dossier on Lady Tyra immediately, along with her entire family, just in case they decided to meddle further.

Chapter 37

Zo hated hard burns at the best of times, but she'd never felt like this before. The engine improvements Soka had carried out with Vincent meant they were accelerating far faster than they normally would. But that just meant the pressure they were under was accordingly more brutal.

Vincent told them this was what being in a fighter felt like.

"Fighter pilots sit on an engine and a bunch of weapons, with life support tacked on," he had said. "Really just a missile with a compartment for the pilot."

The limiting factor on a fighter was the g-forces the pilots would survive. And so increasingly the fighters were drones, or supported by swarms of drones, as much as a lot of officers had emotional attachments to putting humans in their fighters.

They couldn't handle this very long. They had drugs that could ease the effects of high-g somewhat, but it was not sustainable, and there's only so much you can do to keep a body caught in a virtual vice from collapsing. Zo knew some extreme augmentation proponents replaced body parts to handle high-g better. Reinforcing parts most affected.

I wonder if Clarice would ever go that far, she thought.

They wouldn't need to deal with this for long, though. This speed meant they could outmaneuver the destroyers now that they knew they were not Centauri.

They'd picked a new destination, and were headed for one of the intra-system gates, to bring them in towards a small station orbiting Alpha Centauri B—Toliman—close enough to orbit only that star.

The station was not on the official maps. Soka had brought it to Zo's attention quietly, and with a sense of embarrassment. It was an unofficial trading station that they generally did not like informing non-Centauri about, and that Earthers certainly would not have been allowed access to yet anyway. Zo was unaware there was such a thing as an unofficial trading station, but she found Soka's apparent embarrassment entertaining.

"Don't worry, Soka, we won't judge you. Or your species. We have plenty of seedy stations in Sol system."

She could tell Soka was intrigued, but unwilling to pursue the subject. Maybe one day she'd show him one of the smaller belt stations. She shuddered briefly as she recalled her last trip to one. *Just not Styx,* she thought. *Even if it's under new management.* She recalled they'd not even known they had faced the station owner while escaping—she'd first found out during their trial.

Their scan had showed the destroyers were still lurking, clearly they knew they must have lost *Black Rain* near the planet, and that it was only a question of time before they'd show up.

But even though the destroyers were now accelerating hard—harder than the *Black Rain* used to be capable of—the distance between them continued to increase, and there was no indication the destroyers would catch up.

We still need to figure out how to provide evidence, though.

They could not just run back to the main Centauri outpost until they did. They'd get arrested, and according to Soka it was unlikely they would get a fair trial given what he'd been told so far.

"We're about to pass the gate, Captain."

Zo looked at the tactical display. They had enough of a speed advantage that after they passed the gate, they could afford to reduce the acceleration for a while. As soon as they were through, she told Clarice to slow down, and enjoyed the reduced pressure.

"Whoever was standing on my chest got off it," Vincent said and laughed.

"Shit, who'd thought we'd be able to accelerate that fast," Mons added.

"Enjoy it for an hour, people, then we resume, and longer this time." Zo was happy too, but didn't want anyone to get complacent.

Happy was an understatement. It was amazing. If they'd be able to bring the improvements back home, they'd be heroes. And they hadn't even tested the weapons improvements yet. Zo itched for a chance to see what they'd do to Terrell's men.

Even more so she hoped for a chance to use them on Terrell himself. Of course they didn't even know if he was in the system.

What a coward. Always letting others take the risks.

Of course they had to survive first. But she was still feeling the rush of having seen what the improvements made them capable of.

She brought up the external cameras. She remained transfixed by the very idea of being in an alien system, and now they were about as close to an alien star as their heat shields could handle.

Toliman was a quite orange main-sequence star, somewhat smaller and a lot dimmer than the sun, but they were closer to it than she'd ever been to the sun, and it took up what felt like an absurdly large portion of the viewscreen without any magnification.

She could see Alpha Centauri A, Toliman's companion, as well, if she panned. It looked like a dim, distant sun noticeably bigger and brighter than the rest of the sky, but the same diminished size she'd gotten used to seeing the sun take up when in the outer solar system. It messed with her perception of space to be able to pan from one sun to another this way.

They were three days out from the station Soka had sent them towards. They'd alternate between maxing out the acceleration, and easing up for periods to allow them to recover and safely attend to biological needs, but she didn't want to let up too much—the more speed they gained over the destroyers, the more time they'd have before there was a risk they'd catch up.

It'd be a brutal three days. But three days of pain was worth it if let them find a way to resolve this problem.

She hoped they'd manage to ditch the destroyers entirely. They'd set their course out towards nowhere. They'd adjust it hard as late as possible to intersect with the very rapid orbit of the station. It'd bring them about as close to Toliman as Mercury is to the sun. Their ship was not shielded for long term exposure to those kinds of temperatures, and beyond the stress on the hull they had no way to bleed that much heat, so every part of the ship would gradually heat up. But the station was shielded for it. They could cool down when they got there.

Once they'd see the station, it should be too late for the destroyers to catch up until it came back around. Their calculations suggested even if the destroyers were to burn as hard as they could, they'd have at least a week to catch up.

Zo smiled. They had a chance now. She stretched and enjoyed the relative freedom for the hour until they resumed the brutal acceleration burn.

There would still be a few hours until they expected the destroyers to pass the gate. She tensed up as the countdown started to their next hard burn, knowing the pain would come, focusing on her breathing and clearing her mind.

The engines roared, and the pain in her chest was there again. The feeling of being crushed against the seat. Struggling to fill her lungs because she had to work several times as hard to expand her chest.

This is how you win. By getting up and taking a beating again and again.

Chapter 38

As they ended the final burn, Toliman was all they saw from their external cameras even when zoomed fully out, not because they were that close—it filled about three times as much of the sky as the sun would on Earth—but because it was right there in front of them and the glare was unbearable even on a screen.

Why the hell can our screens handle this much brightness? Clarice thought. She had to adjust the brightness down before they could even see the station.

The core of the station was a fairly typical spinning wheel layout to generate decent perceived gravity without the sheer volume and cost of a station the size of even Vanguard, with a non-rotating docking area, and a synchro-mesh type transfer unit that'd spin up to match the rotating side while moving across between them. *Just like Styx*—the station they'd finished their previous year's adventure in.

But what they looked out on was nothing like Styx, or any other station in Sol space.

Closest to Toliman, the station was "covered" by a massive heat shield leaving the other side perpetually in shadow. To radiate away the huge amount of heat from the surface of the shield a number of massive cables stretched out like the tentacles of a giant jellyfish flung outwards by the rotation of the station ring.

Why is getting rid of heat in space so damn hard? She knew the answer of course—there's no convection because there's no convection medium. You only lose the heat you radiate away.

Once inside, it was clear the station's insides were also unlike anything Clarice had seen before. Even the main Centauri outpost was boring in comparison. It had been big and fancy and been the closest Clarice had seen to feeling like it actually was a self-contained world, but it had been too close to an Earth station in appearance and experience.

They'd also not gotten a chance to run around in it.

It'd been like a guided tour of a scaled up Vanguard II full of people who, granted, were alien, but who still all looked surprisingly close to human. Even the restaurant Soka had taken them to had felt like it wouldn't have been out of place on Earth, somewhere "exotic" with weird food.

But this station, which apparently didn't even have a name, but was just "the station nearest Toliman," was something entirely different.

It was small, cramped, and dirty, but so far Clarice had counted six species other than Centauri. Six species no humans had ever seen before. She was taking full advantage of the recording capabilities of her augmented eyes, and looked forward to showing the recordings back home.

Good thing I don't have to stare, she thought. She captured well past a standard eye's field of view while looking around normally.

Clarice couldn't stop grinning. And running around and poking at things like a little kid, or a lost puppy. *With Soka chasing after me like a frustrated, stressed-out parent.* The thought made her fail to suppress an uncharacteristic giggle.

"Careful, Clarice. Not all of these people will be happy to see a stranger."

"I can look after myself, Soka." She continued her earlier imagined scenario by replying to Soka in an exaggerated little girl voice.

Soka didn't react to the voice, to her disappointment. But he sighed, and Clarice patted his back.

They were all exhausted after the crazy burns to get here. Because of the orbit, they'd been accelerating all the way there, rather than decelerating at the halfway point. They'd moved in an arc that let them intersect the station close to its nearest point to the nearest gate, and there was practically a celebration on the bridge when they did their latest course adjustments and it was clear the destroyers following them had realized where they were headed and had given up.

"We need to be prepared for them to adjust and meet us on the other end, though," Zo admonished.

The station was in a very tight, very fast orbit around Toliman that the destroyers had no hope of catching up to, and so they'd have seven to eight until the destroyers would be able to meet them when they were coming back around the other side of the star. How soon depended on whether they'd burn hard for the nearest intersection point. They needed to be prepared to leave no later than that point. They could outrun the destroyers now, but that wouldn't help if they were sitting in the station.

Clarice was not thinking about any of that as she was running around the station looking at all the different goods for sale, and asking Soka about which things were safe for her to try eating—to which the answer was often "I don't know," and grilling him about various devices for sale.

She also made him act as a translator, as most people there had no reason to have integrated English.

It took her a few hours to work her way around the full commercial deck, at which point she finally allowed Soka to rest.

"I keep forgetting you're an old man," she said and laughed, and Soka pouted.

"I'm sorry, it's just we had no idea you people live so long. I'm still not used to it."

"I know. I do look good for my age, don't I?" Soka's smile returned.

Clarice was pleased to see her good mood appeared to have carried over to him too. She enjoyed spending time with him. She was wildly curious about everything she saw and heard, and Soka to her was the gateway to all of it. She loved his dramatic mannerisms and the way he dressed more feminine than her, often walking around in what would definitively be considered a dress on Earth. She'd of course probed him about his dress sense, and how the Centauri dressed in general, and found it hilarious when Soka told her about his exchange with Vincent and pointed out to her how feminine Vincent would be considered by his people. To Clarice, every little difference like that made the experience more exciting.

They found a little café, and Clarice watched as Soka carefully conferred with the proprietor to find out what Clarice could safely eat. She listened to the strange sounds of the Centauri language, and marveled at how Soka could switch so effortlessly and could speak English without accent after just a few days.

They picked out some baked goods as the safest option, and Soka presented her with a creamy cake that she insisted on trying before he told her what it was made of.

She was both disgusted and excited when she learned a primary ingredient was a churned worm found on a distant system Soka was unable to pinpoint an Earth name for.

"See, Soka, that's why I didn't want to know. I'm not sure I could have eaten it if I knew that. But it was delicious. And now I can say I've eaten alien worm-cake."

Clarice loved showing off her willingness to try things others found disgusting. It was a matter of pride for her that she knew most of the crew found certain things disgusting. The alien worm-cake was definitely a new highlight.

She took Soka's hand, just as a friendly gesture, as she'd learned Centauri expected to hold hands when walking with someone, and she relished in truly trying out the local culture.

"What's that," she said, and pointed at a shopfront she'd not noticed earlier.

"They do augmentation," Soka said.

Clarice immediately started dragging Soka there.

"Tell me more. What exactly do they offer?"

Chapter 39

Mons wandered the promenade looking for supplies. Zo and Vincent were a bit further down from him. They tried to check in regularly.

He'd need to find Soka to be able to actually negotiate the purchases, as none of the Centauri merchants he'd found so far spoke English, and certainly none of the others.

It was a pretty pointless exercise as long as Soka was running around with Clarice, but he'd promised he'd be back to help out soon, so Mons kept looking around with a distinct lack of curiosity.

He wished he had Clarice's ability to see excitement in everything new, but Mons was first and foremost practical. He wanted to ensure they had enough fuel, and enough food, and he was more excited by the potential to restock their rapidly depleting stores than looking at ugly aliens.

And they were all ugly. He didn't pay much attention to them. The Centauri at least looked human.

Then again that was part of the reason for their damn problems. If they'd been less human-looking, Terrell's people would stand out far more.

Though, he realized, *we've only seen a couple of them in person. So it doesn't really matter anyway. They could've just used masks, or filtered the video if the Centauri had looked more alien.*

Just as he was thinking that, he noticed something odd. The next shop down had someone in it that looked human. And not like the Centauri looked human—the Centauri all had skin close to bronze and slightly shimmering. This man had skin that was much too dark, with hair in cornrows. Admittedly he had not seen all that many Centauri, but he'd never seen any Centauri that looked close to this at all.

We should've asked First Triaton to expand on how varied Centauri appearance is, he thought to himself. Maybe he was just being overly worried.

He looked for Zo and Vincent to see if he could get them to have a look as well, but they'd disappeared into some shop or other, and the man started moving.

Mons decided he had to follow him. If there were humans here, they needed to know if they were aligned to Terrell. The man disappeared into another shop, and Mons waited outside, pretending to intently study some product he didn't have the slightest idea of the purpose of.

He turned his back as the man came back out, but instantly worried that the man might have noticed him. After all, Mons had noticed him, and Mons with his pale skin would certainly stand out if he caught a glimpse of it.

He pushed it aside and kept following the man while looking around for any of his crew.

The man walked up a pair of stairs to the level above, which held mostly cabins and offices. Mons followed him and spotted the man entering what appeared to be a closed office. There was no good place there for Mons to wait without very obviously loitering in a way that would be suspicious.

Mons looked around for somewhere he could hide and still be able to see the man when he exited. Nothing stood out.

It was too late anyway. The man came back out, with four other humans. This time he was sure—two of them were white, one looked Asian. None of them were close to being able to pass as Centauri.

"There he is," one of them yelled almost as soon as Mons had noticed them.

Mons started running, and they chased him. He ran as fast as he could while looking desperately for somewhere to hide, but unlike the market level there was nowhere for him to duck in here. He looked back and saw them close in on him. Just as he tried rushing down the stairs two of them overtook him, and he was knocked unconscious.

***

When Mons woke up, he was tied to a column in a storage room. There was no furniture there, and not much storage either. The men who had chased him down were there, as was the man he had followed.

"What are you doing here?"

Mons kept his mouth closed. One of the men punched him in the stomach.

"Why did you follow me?"

The man he had followed stared straight at him. When Mons still didn't talk, he was punched in the face.

"We can continue, you know. And you're just slowing us down. Not many ships come and go. We'll ask around and find out who you are anyway."

It was the man he had followed who spoke.

"I'm just a tourist," Mons answered. He didn't feel very brave, but he was also adamant he would not risk giving up anything.

One of the men laughed.

"Uh-huh. Always with the attempts at comedy. Why do people always do this? It just makes the people interrogating them angrier." He sounded partly amused, partly genuinely annoyed at the response.

The man who had laughed punched Mons in the face.

"You see? Makes us angrier."

Another man entered and walked over to the person Mons had been following and whispered something in his ear.

"Ah," the man said. "Lucky for you, we have friends who *do* talk. You came with the *Black Rain*, didn't you." It wasn't a question.

Mons instantly wondered if this meant they were Terrell's men for sure, or if they'd just obtained information about their recent arrival.

Who else would be out here?

But this was the type of station he could see would attract adventurers hoping to bypass Centauri rules and get hold of products they had not yet been authorized to trade in.

Then again that also makes it exactly the type of place someone like Terrell might want to have people in. Looking for weapons or information or technology he could use to get the power he craved.

"We'll be back. Don't get too comfortable."

Mons was left in the room to himself, the light turned off. The room was entirely dark to the point that even when his eyes adjusted as best they could, he could see nothing.

He envied Clarice's augmented eyes and her infrared vision right now.

And he wondered how long it would take any of them to realize he was gone. It was a small station. Once they figured out he was missing, it couldn't take them long to track down the most likely places he might be. *They will find me soon.*

But his captors undoubtedly knew that too, which would mean his friends were in danger, whether or not it was Terrell's people. They'd definitely want to ensure his friends were not going to be a threat as quickly as possible.

He tried to get loose, but these were not amateurs. They'd zip-tied his arms and legs together, and chained him to a solid column tightly enough that he saw no way to get loose.

Was that a weird sound? Something moving? Or maybe that was just his imagination. *I hate everything about this,* he thought, desperately hoping it was just his imagination.

Chapter 40

"I don't know if this is a good idea, Clarice."

Soka looked like he was attempting to be a stern parent. Clarice smirked at the thought of him trying to stand up to his children like that.

"Do you have children, Soka?"

"Yes, I do, actually."

"Does that *work* on them? Ever?"

She laughed.

"I'm a big girl. I've done augmentation before, Soka. You've seen my eyes, haven't you?"

She made her eyeballs change to a pulsing rainbow. She knew full well her eyes freaked Soka out.

"Yes. Yes, I've seen your eyes. Stop that, please. It's very disconcerting."

"He said the scan shows the integration net is fully compatible with human physiology, right? And that if something goes wrong it'll just get rejected and break down and get flushed out?"

She'd had Soka help her translate the available augmentation, and one thing had immediately stood out at her. The clinic offered integration nets of the type Soka had explained to her the Centauri used to pick up new languages.

She could learn Centauri. Maybe other alien languages. And lots of Earth languages. She instantly started wondering if she could hack the interface and find out how to feed in other knowledge as well. She'd lost track of how many times she'd fantasized about hacking her own brain. Any brain, really.

It was pretty clear Soka thought it was a mistake that he'd told her the moment she started talking about getting the treatment.

"But they haven't *tried* it on humans, have they?" Soka's objections kept getting meeker, as he'd recognized it was almost certainly futile.

"He did say they'd tried it on other aliens, and it'd never caused a problem."

"This is a cheap, low end clinic on a third rate station where they're not subject to any kind of monitoring, Clarice. Please don't do this. The captain will kill me if anything goes wrong."

Clarice smiled. "I'm sure she will." She knew that would not calm Soka at all.

"Ask the nice man what we can trade for this."

Soka sighed, and obliged, and discussed the matter with the man in charge.

"He says that since he hasn't done this to humans yet, he's willing to strike a deal. If he can have your DNA, a blood sample, and some brain scans, he'll do it at no cost."

"I like this guy. Is he a guy?"

Soka shrugged. "I don't know, and I'd rather not ask."

The alien running the clinic was not Centauri. Soka said he thought he might be from near Procyon, a couple of gate hops away, but he wasn't sure. He was bipedal and looked like a hominid, but with a hairy face and six thick claw-like fingers.

Clarice had asked Soka about why all the species she'd seen had been relatively humanoid, even the ones that had clearly evolved along very different paths, such as the reptile-like aliens she had seen.

He'd explained to her that the current hypothesis was simply that it was a significant local maxima of developmental options fairly close to the global maxima. Energy efficient, and allowing for a proportionally big brain, and limbs that allowed for efficient manipulation.

"There are exceptions," he told her. "A few other significant clusters of species." She had made him promise he'd show her images sometime.

Soka kept trying to discourage her to have the operation, but she wore him down.

"What is the recovery time like," she asked him to relay.

"He says it'll be a couple of hours. You'll likely get nausea, and your balance and language understanding will be affected. Then you should be fine. But full integration of the first language datasets will take a few days."

The man said something else, and Clarice looked to Soka.

"He'll throw in my language and his own, he says."

Clarice almost jumped up and down and insisted to Soka that he'd tell the alien to go ahead.

Soka sighed, but did as she asked, and soon he was standing beside her holding her hand while the man applied an anesthetic and inserted a probe into her brain through the nose.

"You'll be awake the whole time," Soka explained, relaying the man's instructions.

The alien man pointed to a display, and Clarice was delighted to see the inside of her brain. She could not move her head at all, but with the field of view of her augmented eyes she could still look at Soka, and he looked like he was about to pass out.

"Relax, Soka, I'm fine. See, it's nothing to worry about. Look at the screen. Isn't that *awesome?*"

She considered faking distress, but thought the better of it—she didn't want to give Soka a heart attack.

The operation was surprisingly quick and painless. The alien had her say a few things while he watched a monitor, until his computer emitted some signal that he explained via Soka meant it had located the appropriate sites to inject.

She could see him injecting something at a few different places around what she hoped was the language center of the brain, and Soka explained it was nanotech that'd construct the overlay network around her brain tissue that included additional processing, and that enabled integration of languages via a low bandwidth electromagnetic link through her skull.

Clarice looked forward to demonstrating it to everyone. She was sure Zo would absolutely hate it, but she'd live. She imagined just suddenly switching to speaking Centauri to Soka while they were all together.

Soka and the alien doctor had to help her to a seat afterwards—she struggled to stand, much less walk. The alien doctor's hand was furry and cold as ice, and even that she loved. Not the sensation—the sensation was gross—but she loved to have had it.

"Thank you. I know it freaked you out to help me do this, Soka. You're a good friend." She flashed him a broad smile, and he gave her a faint smile back.

He held her hand a bit too hard, but she let him. It was more for him than for her.

It's funny, she thought, that *foot cycle torn.*

She tried to talk to Soka, but only gibberish came out.

Soka looked alarmed, and she could hear him talk to the doctor, and then try to explain to her, but she didn't understand.

Clarice tried not to panic. This was what the doctor had said could happen. It was only temporary. She tried breathing in and out as calmly as she could, and held onto Soka.

Maybe ten minutes later she tried to talk again.

"Soka, can you understand me?"

"You scared me so much, Clarice. The doctor said it was okay, but you scared me so much."

Soka looked like he was trying not to cry.

"I feel great. Don't worry."

It was true she felt great, but she had been terrified too, and didn't want him to know just how close she had been to screaming and crying. But *he* had managed to stay calm, and there was no way she was going to panic when *he* managed to stay calm.

Chapter 41

"Where can we find weapons dealers in this place? I'm sure there are plenty."

Vincent had cornered Soka after he came back with Clarice.

Soka looked hesitant, and slightly intimidated by Vincent, who was right up in his face.

"Any advantage we can get matters, Soka. The upgrades we did are great, but anything else we can do to keep these bastards from taking us out matters."

Vincent was always looking for an edge. He didn't like a "fair" fight.

A fair fight is a bloody fight, he often said. In his view, the bigger the advantage one side has, the quicker and more decisive the victory, and hence less need to actually cause harm.

At least as long as the side with the advantage doesn't consist of an evil, sadistic bunch of assholes.

So when Vincent saw an opportunity to get hold of more weapons, he grabbed it. An alien space station outside of government control seemed like as good an opportunity as any.

"Let's at least look. I don't even know if we have anything to trade that these people will be interested in."

"I have it on good authority you might be able to trade your DNA and a blood sample or two. You're curiosities."

Vincent looked at Soka, trying to determine if it was an attempt at a joke, or if he was serious.

"What do you mean?"

"Sorry, I shouldn't have said that. I promised Clarice I wouldn't tell."

"Clarice? What is she up to now?"

"I really can't tell… I'm sure she'll tell you when she's ready."

Vincent shook his head. He really did not care. He was sure she'd picked up some piece of tech or other she'd be overly excited about in a way that Vincent just couldn't be about technology.

"Come on. Show me, Soka."

He dragged Soka with him, and Soka took him to where most of the technology and equipment sellers were based.

Vincent didn't immediately see much of interest. A lot of advanced tech, but he didn't spot much in terms of weapons.

Soka asked around cautiously, and got some hints and a couple of tips, but overall the sellers were under the impression that while the Centauri governments kept hands off the station, they were not so flexible when it came to tolerating weapons sales, and so if anyone was prepared to deal with them it was likely it was only to arrange to meet off-station elsewhere in the system, which wouldn't do them much good.

Vincent grumbled, but kept looking. Finally Soka got a tip about someone who might be able to arrange a "private viewing." The location looked like a regular coffee shop. Regular for the station, anyway. A grubby little room with a couple of tables and chairs, and a small counter to order at. The decor looked like it'd been stolen from an office. Soka asked the man behind the counter, and gave the name of the person they'd spoken to, and they were asked to wait.

Soka sat down at one of the tables, while Vincent insisted on standing up, but leaned at the table. He did not trust these people, and wanted to be ready for anything.

The man who came out looked Centauri, but something looked off about him, and Vincent wasn't quite sure what. He looked taken back when he saw Vincent, but then most people here were surprised to see humans.

"Talk to him in your language," Vincent whispered to Soka.

The man answered in English when Soka introduced them.

It heightened Vincent's suspicion, but it was not conclusive—if he was Centauri, he might have been trading with humans.

"You've integrated English, huh," Vincent said, and grabbed the man's hand, and stood close. "Or maybe you're human."

"I don't know what you're talking about."

The man couldn't quite stand still, and it made him look nervous.

"I think you do."

Vincent withdrew his hand, and held it up. It had patches of bronze makeup and glitter on it.

The man hit out at Vincent and bolted out the door, and as Vincent was about to follow him, he ran straight into a furry, squat alien that was on the way in.

Soka apologized for them both, but by the time they were out the door, the man had disappeared.

"I'm worried. A human here is weird enough. I'm not surprised one tries to pass as Centauri, but running…"

Vincent got Zo on his radio, and explained what had happened.

"Let's check in on everyone."

Zo called him back a couple of minutes later.

"We can't get hold of Mons. He went out looking for supplies a couple of hours ago, and nobody has seen him since."

"Shit. Maybe the guy that ran knows something. I'm coming back."

They'd gotten a set of cabins next to each other to stay in while there; the docking section was not really meant for regular access, and apparently the station management frowned on people sleeping on the ships. The cabins were small, but well kept—functional and decorated in a boring neutral style—if they hadn't known better, they might have mistaken it for a low end Earth airport hotel.

When Vincent and Soka got back everyone was there, crammed into Zo's cabin, which could barely fit all of them in.

"So what do we do?" Monique asked.

"We'll need to search, but since only Soka can talk to everyone here, we have a bit of a handicap," Zo said. "We'll need to use him effectively to ask if anyone has seen anything."

"That's not strictly true," said Clarice. She grinned, and spoke a few words haltingly in Soka's language.

"When did you learn that?" Monique asked.

"Learn, and learn…" Clarice looked over at Soka. "I'm integrating it."

"You're what?"

Zo leaned towards her, as if she didn't hear clearly.

"Soka and I found a place."

"You've had *brain surgery* on a seedy space station in the middle of nowhere on a whim?" Zo sounded angry, and Vincent grabbed her shoulder.

"Let her talk. It seems like she's fine."

"I am. I'm fine," Clarice said. "My Centauri isn't very good yet, but it's boat rapidly." She shrugged. "Doc said I might mix up words for a bit. *Coming* rapidly. I can help asking around if Soka can just help tease out a few phrases with me first."

Zo shook her head and sighed in an exaggerated manner which told Vincent that Clarice was in for a serious conversation later.

"Okay, then. We split up in groups. Let's check in with each other regularly."

Chapter 42

"I want to be there when Zo talks to you about this language integration later."

Monique looked at Clarice with a very serious expression which she didn't manage to hold for more than a few seconds before she burst out laughing.

"What is it with you, girl?" Monique shook her head. "You're brave, I'll give you that. But who is crazy enough to do this kinda stuff on a whim?"

Clarice's eyes briefly pulsed red, and Monique went silent. Monique knew Clarice had some sort of enhancement done with her sight, but she didn't realize Clarice had both her eyeballs replaced.

"Shit. I didn't know *that*."

"Yeah, Clarice is quite the cyborg." Vincent sniggered. "You should've seen your face, Monique."

Monique didn't quite see the humor. She really didn't understand how Clarice could have taken this kind of risk on a strange space station, having tech added that might not even have been tried on humans before, but she also didn't understand how someone could have risked losing an eye either. She wasn't against augmentation in principle, but she saw it as the kind of thing you might do if you'd already lost a body part.

Why not add some extras back in if the damage was already done, she thought to herself, *but what kind of person replaces perfectly good body parts?*

And messing with her *brain*? That was well over the line for her.

They were going one way looking for Mons or anyone who had seen him or any other humans, while Zo and Soka went the other direction around the circular station concourse. Jonas' back was still too weak for him to walk for prolonged periods of time.

There were a couple other floors too, of course, and they'd deal with that if they got no leads on the concourse.

Clarice's first attempt at talking to the shopkeepers and passersby were halting and met with requests to repeat herself or laughter, but it improved rapidly, and Monique was astounded to listen to the difference. Even though she didn't know the language, it was noticeable how much smoother it flowed after only a few repetitions, and how the sounds changed from quite different to those she spoke with, to nearly indistinguishable.

It was still weird to her, but she had to admit it seemed to *work*.

I just hope it doesn't leave her with brain damage, she thought, as they were walking to the next shop.

Clarice stopped another passerby, and finally they got a lead. The woman—at least Monique thought it was a female—said she'd seen a couple of men who looked not that different to Vincent around the station. She wasn't sure where, but suggested a couple of places they could try.

In the second shop the woman had suggested, the shopkeeper recognized Mons when they showed a picture, but did not recall any other humans, and he had no idea where Mons might have gone.

It was getting late, and they were having no luck. The places on the concourse were closing down and they were not getting anywhere.

"We'll have to continue first thing in the morning," Vincent said. "We can't go busting in doors."

They contacted Zo on the radio, and she agreed.

The walked in silence back towards the cabins.

***

Mons did not know how many hours he'd been tied to the column. He'd managed to get down into nearly a sitting position, propped up a bit by his back against the column, so at least his legs did not take all the weight.

He'd been in darkness the whole time.

Every now and again he could hear talking in an adjacent room. He desperately needed the toilet, and he needed something to drink. At one point the door opened briefly and someone looked in at him.

He told them he needed the toilet, and pleaded for water, but whoever looked at him either didn't understand or didn't care.

The door closed again, and he was in darkness again for what seemed like several hours, but Mons was not at all confident about how long it was. He tried counting to make time pass, but lost count again and again as he got tired. At some point he pissed himself, but was too tired to care.

Finally someone came in. They quietly showed him pictures of his crew. One after the other. Clearly taken surreptitiously.

"Do you know these people, scum?"

He refused to answer once again.

"You can answer, and get water, or refuse and get punished."

He refused again, and the man kneed his groin.

Mons tried doubling over in pain, but he couldn't. He pissed all over himself again. His eyes teared up.

"Do you know them?"

Mons looked at the pictures again. It was all of them except Clarice and Soka.

He grinned, and was punched in the stomach.

"Okay, okay," he said. It didn't matter if they knew that he knew them. He'd give them that. Since they'd let him know they were unaware of Clarice and Soka.

"I know them."

"Names?"

"Water."

The man motioned to someone else that Mons had not noticed had entered the room, and the man brought a glass of water and let Mons drink.

"Names?"

Mons gave their names, knowing not much would show up on a search. Except for Monique—he made up a fake name for her, not wanting there to be any chance they accidentally found out she was military.

"Why are you here?"

"We're tourists."

"The comedy routine again, huh. Guess you need to soften a bit more."

The man had a plate of food brought in, and placed outside his reach.

"Think about it. We'll be back soon."

Mons tried to spit on him, but ended up just spitting on his food.

Doesn't matter, he thought, *it's not as if I can reach it.*

The men left, and the light went off again.

Mons started humming to himself to pass the time, while he tried to forget about the food in front of him, which seemed to be some sort of fowl.

Smells just like chicken, he thought, and started laughing hysterically at the lame joke, while at the same time wondering if even alien fowl would taste like chicken.

Chapter 43

They started the search again early the following morning. Zo and Soka started by going to the clinic where Clarice got her language integration implant done, on the odd chance that he might have dealt with other humans.

"How could you let her go ahead with it, Soka?"

"'Let her?' Do you know Clarice at all, Captain?" Soka asked. "I am sorry, but I don't have the fortitude to deny her anything. She would make an excellent diplomat."

Soka looked at Zo and tried to think of additional ways to convey that he really could not imagine how anyone could possibly talk Clarice out of something like this.

"I really don't like her obsession with augmentation. Pointless risks," Zo answered.

"So you never did anything reckless at her age?"

Zo opened her mouth to answer, but closed it again.

"Aha, I thought so, Captain."

"I said nothing."

"Exactly. You said nothing."

Soka gave her a smile that he thought perfectly conveyed that he knew that the reason the captain said nothing was that she'd have to either lie or admit that she'd engaged in plenty of reckless behavior. He wondered what she might have been up to, and made a mental note to try to tease the truth out of her about this when they were under less pressure.

They got to the clinic, and Zo took up position near the door, legs apart, head up, with a hand on her plasma pistol, that Soka thought looked excessively aggressive. He apologized to the proprietor for the intrusion, and asked him about any other humans or "human-like" people.

"If I'd seen any, I wouldn't have offered your friend to pay with her DNA and blood sample, now, would I?"

"No, that suggests you either haven't operated on any, or just that they refused the same deal," Soka told him. "I suggest you think hard. We're short a crewmate and our captain, over there, is not as gentle as I am."

Soka hoped he sounded tough, but he knew deep down his voice was too soft and tempered to intimidate anyone.

But hopefully Zo's "I'm ready to shoot up the place" stance by the door would make the man take him seriously.

"I don't think so… Maybe… There might have been someone in here a few orbits ago. Asking about integration tech in really bad Centauri. I'm not sure. You hairless soft-skins all look the same to me."

"That's not very helpful. Do you know where he might be, or what ship he came in with?"

Zo came over, and started lifting her plasma pistol.

"Patience, Captain." Soka put a hand on Zo's shoulder.

"See, she is losing patience. I suggest you give us an answer."

"Okay, okay. He chickened out. Didn't even have scans done to check compatibility. But I've seen him a few times with others. Hanging out over there."

He pointed out the window at a bar across and a bit further down the road.

"Thank you very much. *She* will be back if we don't find them."

Soka smiled and bowed slightly to him, and led Zo out. He translated what the man had told him, and they walked over to the bar.

"You have a look, Soka. If they're there, they'll spot me too quickly."

Just as she was saying it, a light-skinned humanoid that was very clearly not Centauri exited the bar and walked straight past them.

"That makes things so much easier. Come."

She took Soka by the arm, and rushed after the man. They followed him down the road, and up to the floor above, and hid in the stairwell as he met up with two others.

Zo called Vincent and told them where to find her and Soka.

"Will we wait here for them?" Soka asked, and was hopeful he would not have to run after the men and engage in any kind of fight. Thankfully Zo was sensible.

"There's no point in rushing in now," she said. "They've had him for a day. Another few minutes is unlikely to make a difference, but if we screw this up, that will."

Vincent, Monique and Clarice joined them about five minutes later.

"Okay, everyone. There are at least three people in there. We don't know if Mons is there, *so don't kill anyone* until we're sure, please."

"Why are you looking at me, Cap?" Vincent said.

"You *know* why I'm looking at you."

Vincent looked proud that the captain had singled him out. Soka was still unsure about reading human expressions, but Vincent was not exactly subtle.

They snuck up to the door, and Zo tried to peek in. She saw nobody in the front room, and motioned for Vincent to kick the door in.

As soon as he did, Soka could hear yelling from the back room. The door flung open, and Vincent and Monique started firing, trying not to hit anything vital. Two men went down and screamed in pain.

Zo jumped the counter, and was about to look into the backroom when another man showed up in the door opening.

"Sorry," was the last he heard as Zo shot him point blank in the chest.

"What was that you said earlier, Cap?"

"Needs must. Besides I'm the captain. My privilege."

"Sure thing, *boss*."

Vincent and Monique followed Zo into the back room, with Soka climbing over the counter and eventually looking in to find they'd subdued two more men by the time he did.

And there was Mons, chained to a column, beaten, bloody, grimy.

Soka gasped, and went over to him.

Mons looked down at him and just smiled.

"Someone, help me get him loose."

Monique came over and together they carefully blasted through the part of the chains behind the column and got them off him, while Vincent held Mons up so he didn't collapse on the floor.

"They were Terrell's men," Mons said, and fainted.

They found a bench to put him down on, and got him some water. Vincent splashed it in his face, and he came back to it.

"You said they're Terrell's. Did they say that?" asked Zo.

"I overhead them."

Mons' voice could barely be heard. Vincent gave him some water and told him to sip it slowly.

"They're just low-level goons. They didn't seem to know anything about us. They were just here to prepare some mission and try to obtain more weapons, and thought we were after them. Their bad luck. I think this is where they must have made deals for whatever weapon they used to attack the freighter we investigated."

Mons seemed to be trying to smile again.

Soka looked around the room, and back at Mons, who was grimy and smelled of urine, and had clearly been beaten and mistreated. He could not understand how Mons could even think of smiling.

"You don't get it, do you, Soka?"

It seemed Mons had noticed his confusion.

"These people keep losing because they're so paranoid they keep beating themselves by resorting to aggression when they don't have to, and in doing so reveal themselves. It's hilarious really."

He coughed some blood, dried it off with his hand, and smiled at Soka, who felt sick.

"I used to think the same way."

Chapter 44

After freeing Mons they had no further problems. They managed to find a few reliable suppliers to barter with to replenish their supplies. No weapons. It seemed that while the Centauri government was fine with allowing the station as a minor outlet for behavior that they did not strictly *condone*, and that might well violate assorted agreements, they really did draw the line at weapons.

Zo had Soka discreetly enquire in several places, but they'd all consistently informed him that military ships did occasionally come and check, and the few people who had tried running weapons out of the station had been quickly and brutally put out of business.

Just like when Vincent had taken Soka around, they found some that hinted they could set something up, but not *on the station*, and since that would do them no good, given they needed to be prepared to engage the moment they left the station, they didn't push their luck.

Hopefully it won't be a big problem, Zo thought, *thanks to the upgrades Soka helped us do.*

Zo was more concerned that they were getting close to the point in the station's orbit around Toliman where the destroyers would have a shot at intercepting the station, which incidentally was the last point they'd dare try to leave.

Soka had managed to convince the station owner to give them access to high level scan data of arriving ships. He'd given a stupid story about wanting to ensure they could meet "friends," which Zo was sure the station owner had seen straight through, but they'd offered some computer parts that he seemed pleased with as a trade, and it was not like they had asked for anything sensitive they could not get by leaving the station and running scans themselves.

They'd considered leaving sooner, and discussed the issue at length over the last few days, but they'd be leaving at a trajectory and speed which would require far too lengthy burns to get them back inwards towards the main cluster of gates. They needed to get back before the Centauri fleet might do anything stupid.

And before Terrell kills more people.

Timing their departure right would let the station orbit do a lot of heavy lifting.

They'd spent the last day or so getting everything ready for a rapid launch, and had double and triple-checked everything they could think of to ensure they were ready for a hard burn possibly facing off against the destroyers nearly head on.

The advantage they had was that to intercept the station at this point in the orbit, the destroyers would need to be at a fairly substantial speed, and so if they got past, there was a good chance they'd have a clean run at the nearest gate.

But that's a big if.

The counter was that if the destroyers were ready, and fired missiles at them, they'd be accelerating straight towards a missile barrage, and their time to react to avoid them would be accordingly shorter.

Zo could feel she was nervous. She didn't often feel nervous. She'd tense up. Tighten her neck muscles in particular, often leaving with her a headache after a battle. But she rarely felt nervous.

This felt particularly high stakes. If they didn't get past, they'd be unable to find a way to prove what had happened.

Even if we get past, we might not be able to find a way to convince the Centauri we aren't responsible.

She dreaded the consequences of a Centauri punitive mission triggering an outright war with Earth. A war with a power clearly technologically superior would seem like an idiotic thing to do, but Zo was not convinced that would deter anyone from doing it.

And maybe we're already too late.

"Everything is ready, Captain."

Mons had practically snuck up on her as she had been deep in thought. She'd wanted him to rest, but he'd insisted on getting back to work after just a day of recuperation. He had bruises and a few cuts from his ordeal, but had refused to say much about it.

Zo had been surprised. He didn't strike her as the type to resist treatment like this.

Then again, she thought, *he's always been loyal to a fault. Maybe that's where he's found the strength.*

"Thank you, Mons."

Now it was a waiting game, and if their calculations were right, they would not have to wait long. A few hours maybe.

***

It took four hours before their feed of scanning data showed anything. When it did, it showed a single destroyer incoming at high speed.

"Where is the other one?" Zo asked.

"No trace of it," Clarice replied. "Maybe it's trailing behind."

"Or maybe they were smart enough to leave it loitering closer to the gate," Vincent muttered in an ominous tone.

"Doesn't matter right now, we don't have a choice. Request launch clearance. Let's get out of here."

Their launch clearance arrived promptly, and they started maneuvering out of the docking area. Everyone was strapped in and prepared for the hard acceleration they knew would come.

Soon they were looking at the screens and saw open space, while the tactical display showed the destroyer heading straight for them. It looked like it was moving quite slowly, but that was only because of the relative speed of the station's rapid orbit around Toliman.

They set a course at an angle that'd let them fire with their plasma cannons as soon as they were clear of the station, and would keep them sufficiently clear of the destroyer as it approached.

Vincent, Jonas, and Monique manned the weapons, as they all expected the destroyer to fire at them first chance it'd get.

Zo held her breath, waiting to give the order to fire, as they wanted to wait to see if the destroyer identified them first.

There was the burst of missiles from the destroyer.

"Weapons free!" Zo yelled.

"They're not aiming for us," Clarice yelled back.

They watched on the tactical display as the missiles the destroyer had ejected out of its torpedo tubes were heading straight for the station.

"Fuck. What are those lunatics doing?" Zo gasped. "Keep firing!"

The station had no time to prepare, and there were no signs their defensive weapons were hot. *Black Rain's* main plasma cannons were angled so they could have taken out missiles heading for them, but only one was positioned with enough of an operating angle to shoot at the missiles heading towards the station.

Jonas managed to take out one of them before the rest of the missiles hit, and the station shook.

"The... It is breaking up," Mons nearly whispered.

Zo confirmed what he had seen. The missile barrage had severed the docking ring from the habitat levels, and threw them apart. The people on the station would have no way to get to their ships.

Not that it mattered, because as they watched in stunned silence, not even Vincent firing their own missiles at the destroyer stopped the destroyer from firing their cannons at the habitat ring and breaking that apart too. If anyone survived in the segments of the habitat ring, none would have survived as the segments slammed into the cooling cables or the docking ring parts or other habitation ring segments, and broken into even smaller pieces.

They were accelerating at their top speed, and the destroyer and the wreckage of the station was rapidly disappearing in the distance.

"Did we record that?" Zo asked Clarice.

"Of course."

"Won't matter," Vincent muttered.

Zo turned to Vincent. "Won't matter?"

"They didn't believe us last time. Why would they believe us this time?"

He's right, she thought, *but we have to try.*

Behind them, their scans showed the destroyer was making no signs to turn. Instead energy flares suggested they were continuing to fire, eradicating every last part of the station.

Chapter 45

"What is the latest news, General?"

Lady Xine-Zor Li'mor Four was wandering along the lakefront promenade in the park of the administration compound. She was trailed by two of her aides, and the general had just joined her, whisked there by an assistant as soon as she arrived.

"You know the station innermost around Toliman, my Lady?"

The general's face was stiff, and the question was spoken quietly, and Lady Xine immediately got a sense of dread from the general.

She responded in an icy voice. "I know of *it*. Dreadful place according to all reports, but a useless *outlet* for less civilized people. *What of it?*"

"It has been destroyed, my Lady."

She had not expected *that*.

"What do you mean, destroyed?"

"Completely eradicated, my Lady. We've received several reports. The first showed it having been reduced to tiny pieces, no sign of life."

"Who?"

Lady Xine stopped walking and turned to the general who had pulled several steps away from her. She leaned forwards and clenched her fists in anger.

She did not particularly *care* for that station, though she cared in the abstract for the loss of life. She did however immensely care about what this meant as a sign of breakdown of her authority and that of the Empire, and for law and order.

"We received a recording purporting to show the Earther ship… 'Black Rain' I think, firing missiles at the station."

"The ones who destroyed the Proxima Centauri b colony? The ones with our envoy aboard? Why have they still not been apprehended? Or destroyed?"

"I don't know, my Lady. We're sending a bigger carrier group, but it's taking time to get them in place around the system."

"What about the punitive expedition?"

"Plans are proceeding at pace, my Lady. We need a few more days."

"These barbarians need to *burn*. You understand?"

The Lady Xine did not usually yell, but she yelled now. A flock of birds nearby took off in fear. Her attendants had wisely pulled further away.

"We also…"

"We also, *what*, General?"

"We received a very noisy message purporting to be from your envoy to *Black Rain* professing their innocence, my Lady."

"They would claim that, wouldn't they?"

"They repeated their claim of fake Centauri destroyers."

"So what? More lies."

The general shrugged, unwilling to risk angering Xine further.

Lady Xine turned and looked out over the water. She saw no reason to believe the ludicrous claims of whole fake destroyers full of people pretending to be theirs, when the much easier claim to believe was that Soka had betrayed them or been coerced into being a face for a small ship of murderers.

She would have to have them destroyed, and she would have to set a greater example for Earth. She'd consulted their data banks to pick suitable targets. She was considering Mars. The largest human colony, surrounded by several stations that could be blown up.

"It'd be an easy target," she mused.

"What's that, my Lady?"

"The punitive expedition. I want to have it wipe out every colony and station in Mars space. See to it that plans are drawn up."

It'd be proportional, she thought to herself. *A few million dead barbarians for a few hundred of hers. A reasonable ratio, that the Earthers would come to accept as a reasonable price or face being cut off.*

She had consulted their military intelligence. There were no military assets of consequence that would prevent them from taking out the Mars colony. There were those laughable tiny stations near the main gate to their system, but that was not a hindrance.

She waved to her attendants to take the general out of her sight, and continued her walk alone.

Chapter 46

"I think we got the message relayed, but who knows what the quality was like. Or if they'll listen." Clarice turned towards Soka and Zo.

Soka wondered if it would help at all.

They had quickly found out why there was only one destroyer approaching the station, as they picked up another on long range scan ahead, toward the gate.

Knowing this meant they'd face being jammed again, Zo had asked Clarice and Soka to get a message through about the attack.

Soka would record a statement and attach their video, and Clarice would work with Vincent and Jonas to try to boost power to their transmitters to at least get a highly compressed message passed to the gate relay.

It was hard for Soka to remain calm while recording the message. He knew it'd likely be disregarded as yet another lie from a crew that was already suspected of the destruction of the colony, and he had to watch their recordings again to ensure his account was accurate and precise and aligned with what they sent.

They bundled up everything they had, and ordered and prioritized data and testimony about the attack on Mons and the destruction of the colony. This was in order to repeat the most critical elements in the hope that at least the essentials would get through before the destroyer ahead would realize they were trying to overpower the jamming.

It took them a few hours to get everything ready, and the transmission itself felt very anticlimactic to Soka. Clarice had pushed a button. A progress indicator had moved, stuttered, paused, moved some more, and finally reached 100%. And that was it.

They would, of course, listen for replies, but expected none. It was likely they would have to fight their way past the destroyer ahead, and had to expect other ships might also be on their way.

Now that the message been sent, Soka really wished he could go lie down and curl up and try to pretend everything was fine. But he couldn't, as they were still accelerating hard to ensure they had sufficient margin to have to deal with only one of the destroyers at a time. Instead, he was pushed back in the uncomfortable bridge seat, and listened to the chatter of the Earther crew.

It was almost comforting to listen to them by now. The integration of his English was complete, and he felt at ease using it as well as understanding it. The exhaustion that comes with constantly hearing a language you don't fully understand was gone. But more importantly, he felt he was coming to understand the crew. Mostly.

He listened as Clarice described how the destroyer ahead of them had flipped, and was breaking hard, clearly intending to be ready to chase them once they passed, and knowing their comrades would be doing the same.

Space is vast, he pondered, *but ironically we have nowhere to go, exactly because space is so vast. We can fly anywhere, but would get nowhere before running out of supplies unless we stick to the gate network.*

That meant the only viable paths followed a long and spindly web of orbital routes from each gate to various planetary bodies and stations and other gates, and now, with a destroyer in each viable direction, there was seemingly nowhere to go but straight into the maw of one of those enemy ships.

Yet this crew had challenged them and survived.

That kept amazing Soka.

He was torn from his thoughts as Mons reported a new signal on their scans.

"It looks Centauri," he said. "It's coming from behind, at an angle. It's definitively not the destroyer."

"Clarice, try hailing them." Zo sounded eager and hopeful.

"Nothing."

"Keep trying."

They all waited and looked at the data from Clarice's attempt to hail the other ship.

The message was Centauri, and Soka translated for the rest as it came in.

"This is the freighter K'tara. We were getting ready to leave when the station was attacked. We just got out, and burned as hard as we could at an angle. When we saw the destroyer hang back and totally break apart the station instead of making signs to turn, we angled back towards the gate. We've been at maximum acceleration since in case they'd come after us. We can't handle much longer."

The message was breaking up, but they caught it all thanks to plenty of redundancy, and Soka, as it came in.

"Clarice, what is going on with the signal quality?"

"The jamming from the destroyer ahead, Captain. Even with the extra power it's getting hard to get data through."

Zo turned to Soka. "You talk to them with me. It may add weight. We need to convince them to help us quickly. Introduce us, then translate for me."

Soka nodded, and started speaking to them in his language.

"K'tara, this is Soka'li Em-Sckirrrnie Three. I'm a diplomat and was sent to this Earther ship to investigate the destruction of an Earth ship. I am here with Captain Zara Ortega, and I will translate for her unless you have picked up the Earther language yet."

They confirmed they had not, and Soka proceeded to translate as Zo started speaking. She repeated their mission, first, then went on to talk about the colony.

"The people we found went on to destroy one of your colonies, and now this station. Maybe we can help each other."

Soka translated their response carefully. "They're saying they recorded our attempt to destroy the missiles headed for the station. They are attempting to relay the recordings through the gate, but they're facing interference."

"The destroyer ahead is trying to jam our communication. We think we got a message through, but last time we tried, they refused to listen," Soka relayed from the captain.

"We'll try to relay your message if you send it to us," Zo added and nodded for Soka to translate that too.

Clarice confirmed to them the ship was sending the data, and she tried to pass it to the gate relay, but there was no sign enough got through to the gate.

Soka felt both elated that at least one ship had made it out, and despair at the news Clarice gave him.

"Please, I implore you to come up with a strategy together with the Earther captain," Soka told the captain of the K'tara. "I will vouch for her integrity, and you have seen her try to save our station. It is imperative that we stop these terrorists, and that someone other than us bring news home of what is going on."

The captain of the other ship listened as Soka explained the whole affair from beginning to end in more detail, including how Rob lost his life saving him. Then Clarice transmitted all the data they had. Every little detail they thought might help their case and demonstrate their sincerity.

They knew the captain would likely also face the lies and fake footage when he tried to report what had went down, and so they needed him to believe and fight for what he'd seen.

"Okay. We're in," came the reply. "Tell us what you propose."

Zo grinned when Soka translated their response, and they immediately started formulating a plan.

Chapter 47

In the few days since he had been freed, Mons had struggled to sleep. He woke up during the night and felt the pressure from the acceleration and the bands he was secured to the bed with in a panic, thinking he was still tied up, until he realized they were just the normal bed straps used in case the ship needed a sudden change in direction.

It was no better when he was awake.

He was jumpy and struggled to focus. He had not told the captain. He did not want her to know, and he wanted to prove she could rely on him as before. He felt weak and useless.

Few things had made him happier—and a tiny bit hurt—than when he realized she was amazed he'd lasted. He'd beaten her expectations. A tiny bit hurt because he did not realize she thought he might break that quickly.

But he had taken the good side of it and embraced it. He cherished the feeling of serving well, and he was going to carry out this task well too, no matter how much he had to struggle to keep focus. No matter how weak he felt for finding it hard to overcome.

They had come to a rough agreement of an approach with the captain of the Centauri freighter, and Mons had been given the job of working out the details and overseeing the *Black Rain* side while Clarice worked out a suitable program for the Centauri ship to load into their navigation system to handle their side.

His part was the easy one. His job was pretty much to execute exactly what they would normally do in a situation like the one that was about to kick off.

He looked over at Clarice.

He was a bit jealous of her. And attracted to her. She was beautiful, with her black hair and pale skin and those eyes… Her eyes both freaked him out and made her more attractive. He could not fathom how anyone could have their eyes replaced, but the way she used the glow and color changes to emphasize her intentions and emotions made her seem even stronger.

He was jealous because he could see the captain thought the same way, and Mons' feeling of loyalty to the captain meant he felt unable to even contemplate acting on his attraction.

As if she'd want me anyway.

He sighed. But deep down he wondered whether he was more jealous of the captain or of Clarice.

"We're almost ready." Clarice seemed to have heard his sigh and interpreted it as impatience.

"Great. Everything is ready here," he replied.

"Give me a countdown as soon as the Centauri are ready."

Zo's voice brought Mons' focus fully back to the bridge and made him turn to check everything one more time.

A few minutes later Clarice started the countdown.

"3... 2... 1..."

The Centauri ship lit up on their tactical display as their nav thrusters started spluttering and their main engine cut off for a while, and restarted seemingly randomly.

Their direction changed abruptly several times, and they started accelerating in a direction that'd gradually change their course far out into the middle of nowhere.

"Give it a moment," Clarice announced.

A distress broadcast reached them from the K'tara.

The erratic firing of the thrusters continued. Their course had already changed enough that they'd pass far away from the gate if they kept going.

It continued for several more minutes before first the nav thrusters went off, and the main engine kept spluttering for several more, and then the main engine went dark too.

They waited quietly for several minutes, and then the life raft radio buoys came through loud and clear, announcing the location and a general distress message.

They waited a short while, in order not to appear too prepared and too eager, and Mons executed the burns to start turning them enough to intersect the buoys. Thankfully it'd not be too much. The Centauri ship had almost overtaken them.

It took a couple of hours for them to intersect. They started adjusting course to get a plausible match, and just as they got close enough, the transmitters went offline.

Mons held for the agreed time, and then fired the thrusters again, turning the ship back towards the gate, and they started accelerating hard again, letting the Centauri trader drift on its new course.

"Think they bought it?" asked Clarice.

"Hope so, but we won't know for hours," answered Zo.

If they bought it, the two destroyers would largely keep the same directions, believing they had a single target and no need to worry about the seemingly derelict Centauri ship.

If not, one of them would be compelled to adjust course to chase the K'tara.

The one in front of them would want to accelerate harder to be closer to the gate if the Centauri ship attempted to come at the gate from another angle. Or the one behind them could adjust course to try chasing them.

Mons counted up the minutes. Minute after minute passed without any sign of a reaction.

He warned the rest of the crew and slowed the acceleration burn. They waited again.

A few minutes later the destroyer in front slowed their deceleration.

He was so focused on the screen he hardly noticed Vincent and Clarice both cheering briefly.

They repeated that dance several times, carefully avoiding reducing their acceleration enough for the destroyer behind to start catching up too rapidly.

Both they and Terrell's crew could clearly see they'd meet the first destroyer long before the one behind them could hope to catch up.

"I can't believe that worked," Jonas said. "These people really are amateurs."

The mood on the bridge lightened considerably. By not braking further, the destroyer in front of them was creating a bigger and bigger window between it and the gate. The further out they were able to pull that destroyer, the more room it gave the K'tara to break for the gate.

Mons wished they could tell them, but they could not break radio silence—they'd only do so if things went wrong. Besides, even with only passive scans, the drive plumes from the destroyers would be noticeable enough for them to have a good idea how it was going.

Mons was pleased. Everything had gone right. His part had been easy, but he still relished in the feeling that he had again shown the captain could still rely on him.

A nagging feeling told him it was really himself he needed to convince, and he felt his mood getting gloomy again. *I just need some proper sleep,* he thought to himself.

Chapter 48

Jonas could still not quite believe that he could handle the g-forces created by their rapid acceleration without pain in his back so soon after his back injury. Being incapacitated even for just a week while his crew mates had fought for their lives, and his, had been torture on him.

Lying there in the infirmary in the Centauri colony, and then the shuttle, when they got ready for evacuation, unable to do anything while the battle had raged outside, had made him resolve to do everything he could to pay Terrell back when he recovered.

They were coming up on the destroyer fast, and everything needed to be right. They needed to engage it. Do as much damage as they could, and, assuming they failed to incapacitate that much bigger and more powerful ship, they needed to keep it occupied long enough for the Centauri freighter to get a decisive advantage.

Jonas worked with Monique to pre-program firing patterns to allow them to maximize damage on their projected fly-past. They were braking hard to pull the destroyer away from the gate, but they'd fly past each other at high speed, and the timing needed to be more precise than manual control could give, so the basis for their attack would be automated, with manual overrides as needed to deal with any unanticipated situations.

Jonas liked working with Monique. She was precise and to the point, like Vincent. It felt to Jonas as if it gave him an idea of how much of Vincent's way of working was down to the military training he and Monique had in common.

But she's a lot more attractive than Vincent, he thought, smiling to himself. Jonas found Monique intriguing, and wished he'd had more of a chance to get to know her, but while the crew had taken turns to check in on him while he was out of commission, they'd also been busy dealing with crises most of the time, and so he'd had little time with all of them.

He'd enjoyed the brief visits from Monique the most. After she left, he'd close his eyes and let the residual smell of the cocoa-butter moisturizer she used linger in his nose while he wracked his brain for what to say the next time she'd come see him. She'd been nice, but whatever he tried, she didn't open up with him, and it drove him crazy.

"You think we have any chance of taking out their engines, Jonas?"

"I'm not sure. We have to assume they'll flip before we're in weapons range, and will execute another flip while we fly past, so it'll be really tight. Maybe we can damage enough of their nav thrusters to affect them."

Monique looked him in the eyes quietly for a moment while seeming to ponder the implications, and Jonas found it hard to hold her gaze. She intimidated him a bit.

"What if we start changing course and get them to try to follow, and then hit their nav thrusters when their course is out of alignment with the gate?"

They went back and forth over the strategy for a while, and settled on a few different alternatives, contingent of how the destroyer would respond.

Jonas was happy.

He liked the excitement of flying at an attacking ship like this. They had a decent shot, but it was still a challenge. There were unknown and known threats ahead, but they were alive, and he was healed, and the situation did not seem desperate. Just exciting.

This was what he'd left Earth for. He looked over at Vincent, who did not look nearly as excited, but closer to bored. Jonas did not let it get him down.

"Ready, everyone, we're within their weapons' range in minutes." Zo brought him back to Earth, so to speak. *What a silly thing to think in space, in another star system even,* he thought. Zo continued. "Time to give them a surprise. Clarice, Mons."

Jonas was particularly looking forward to this. He'd not seen the details and there'd been no time to chat about the plan, but he knew part of the prep Clarice and Mons had done with the Centauri captain before they pretended to take on the life pods was to have the Centauri rig them.

"There they are, Captain," Mons announced.

The tac display lit up as the buoys which, thanks to the hard braking the *Black Rain* had carried out, were now well in front of them, started flying off in random directions. The capsules had small thrusters intended for very basic navigation and what little thrust the limited capacity for fuel provided, but it was enough to separate them from each other significantly.

What was more important was that they were loaded with munitions from the Centauri ship.

Effectively, they were becoming smart mines, separating and realigning with the destroyer, and then using what they had left of reaction mass to randomly change direction while remaining in the destroyer's flight path.

They'd be visible on the destroyer's active scans, and they'd almost certainly realize what was up and destroy most of them before they did any damage, but hopefully the two dozen of them would keep some portion of the destroyer's weapons capacity focused on the capsules while the *Black Rain* closed enough of the gap and started their firing run. With some luck, maybe a couple might make contact.

"Full speed ahead," Zo yelled.

The main engine cut out briefly, and they were jerked around as the nav thrusters quickly rotated the ship so they were facing in the direction of travel again. Not that it made a difference to their tactical screens. And looking at the exterior camera views was pointless at this distance.

Then the main engine turned back on, and their heading adjusted so they'd cut straight in front of a destroyer and then passed at fast, and rising, speed.

Jonas looked over at Zo and she was grinning. *She is as excited about this as me,* Jonas thought, and triggered the first phase of the targeting programs he'd been working on with Monique.

In front of them, the destroyer did a flip of their own, as he'd predicted to Monique, so they were meeting front to front. On one hand, this made them vulnerable to more weapons systems. On the other hand, this meant the destroyer would lose precious time for acceleration towards the gate if or when they discovered the K'tara. Every minute would improve the odds for the Centauri freighter.

He looked over at Monique and met her gaze again. She smiled at him.

Jonas knew she probably didn't mean anything by it, but between Monique's smile and feeling like they were finally on the offensive, Jonas *was* happy.

Their forward plasma cannons started pulsing. It was mostly for show. At this distance they wouldn't do much, but hopefully they too provided an additional distraction.

They launched a missile barrage, programmed to a very wide spread and erratic course corrections.

"Our friend is away," Mons announced as the Centauri freighter re-engaged their engines and emptied their own torpedo bays towards the destroyer before doing a hard burn on a course that'd require a slight course correction to hit the gate, but that kept them further away from the destroyer while *Black Rain* engaged it.

"I wish I could see the faces on that bridge now," yelled Vincent.

The plasma cannons on the destroyer lit up, and five of the capsules were destroyed in the first round of fire.

All of their first missile barrage were taken out in the second.

The destroyer was tearing through the capsules as they launched their second set of missiles.

They did not have enough missiles aboard for more than a couple more rounds.

"Brace!" Clarice yelled as one of the destroyer's plasma cannons was now targeting them instead of the capsules, and the ship shook as the nav thrusters kicked in while she tried to adjust their course.

They were hit.

Chapter 49

"What is this I hear about a Centauri fleet buildup?"

The speaker was a heavy-set, older, black, three-star general that General Weaver didn't know the name of.

Another general stood up. "We *warned about the possibility of this* before the gate had even opened. It was obvious they had ulterior motives."

General Aziz was known to most there to have Sovereign Earth sympathies, and despite her diminutive stature and a face that made her seem like a friendly grandmother, her voice was as sharp as knives and anyone who heard her speak knew instantly not to cross her.

"Oh, shut it," Weaver heard someone mutter, but he couldn't tell who.

Weaver took the word. "They've sent a communique talking about a destruction of a base on Proxima Centauri b. As far as I'm concerned, we have no ships in that system—they've told us in no uncertain terms we're not allowed to use those gates yet."

"Frankly, we had no idea there even was a colony in that system." General Weaver looked around the table with a puzzled look on his face.

"So what does the destruction of it have to do with us?" the older three-star general asked.

With each exchange, the volume of voices in United Sol Military Command war room increased.

They were not physically there. It was a VR meeting room, bringing together top staff normally stationed across the Earth, mostly based near the major space ports, and in low Earth orbit.

There were people from the colonies on standby, but the latency even with the gate relays did not really allow live participation from further in a group setting without being immensely frustrating, so the colonies were mostly reduced to listening in. None of the highest ranking generals were normally out there unless there were any conflicts that needed special attention anyway.

"They claim an Earth ship destroyed it," someone yelled out of order.

"Preposterous. You know it's an excuse for war. We need to prepare our own war fleet now. And blow the damn gate." Aziz was banging on the table as she spoke.

"Yeah, yeah. I know your Sovereign Earth sympathies and your desire to blow the gate up," someone yelled. Again Weaver could not tell who. The chairperson seemed to be giving up keeping control at this point, and Weaver all but abandoned trying to keep track of who was speaking at what point.

"I'm politically neutral as the rules require, you know that," Aziz replied. *Her* voice he could always recognize. "Besides Terrell acted alone. No link to Sovereign Earth was proven."

"Have they said *which ship*?" someone else said.

"Some small courier or freighter named 'Black Rain.' What the hell kind of name is that anyway?"

"Do we have anything on that ship?"

"There's a classified note regarding it."

"Open it. Do we have someone to concur?"

The classification assigned required three ranking generals to open it. Two others immediately agreed.

"Confirmed," the chairperson said, and opened and started reading the note. "Apparently they were sent on a covert mission to investigate that attack on an Earth ship."

"And now they're blowing up Centauri colonies? Ridiculous. But if they are, I'm sure the bloody Centauri had it coming. We need to close that gate." Aziz banged the table again.

He did not quite get why the people making this simulation had even made that possible. *Does it just register if I bang my desk?* He wanted to try it but didn't want to add to the chaos that already made it hard to keep track of who the hell was speaking.

"Fuck you. But we do need to pull ships in towards Earth as a precaution."

Weaver didn't catch who it was, and was getting increasingly frustrated.

"Fuck you too, but we agree we need to pull ships in." Aziz seemed to be settling down.

Weaver finally spoke up. "I concur. To pulling the ships back in, not to the expletives. Can you two please act like adults. And put the fleet on a war footing. As a *precaution only.* I assume we agree *anything else* will require council approval."

There were murmurs of agreement all around and the chair called for confirmation. The resolution to pull the fleet back towards Earth and to put it on a war footing as a precaution was approved unanimously.

Chapter 50

"Welcome, my Lady."

Lady Xine had just disembarked at Outpost 164A-79, the primary outpost of the system the Earthers called Alpha Centauri, and she detested it before even having seen more than the docking area.

It was not the outpost per se, but the combination of the tedious travel to get out to the outer reaches. She had been quite pleased with the relaxed pace of her desolate provincial administration, but this conflict had made her start reconsidering, and made her wonder if maybe she should aim for a promotion to one of the inner parts of the Empire, if not one of the busy Central Worlds. And this... This was a reminder of just how backwards some of what she administrated was, and made a promotion seem all the more appealing.

But there was this problem with the Earthers.

Not once in her half a century long career had she needed to personally get involved in a matter like this. Not once had they faced a destruction of a colony. And not just a colony, but a space station too. If she messed this up, she'd be stuck out here forever. She might not even keep her administrator position.

Granted, the station that had been destroyed was a seedy unofficial station that was merely tolerated as a means to provide an outlet to prevent resentment to grow into pressure for an unacceptable rate of change. In one way she was quite pleased it was *gone*. But the *way it went* was completely unacceptable. And of course she did not *like* loss of life. Even the loss of people who frequented a station like that.

The destruction at Proxima Centauri b was much more politically sensitive, but blame for that was also much less likely to fall on her. There'd be no warning of the scale of the Earther problem before that.

The destroyed ship, she thought, *that was nothing. A mere nuisance.*

She was led to her assigned chambers, one of a handful of "luxury suites" on the station, but the handful of rooms that made up the suite were hardly what she considered luxury. She looked out over the "outside" space.

She had a view of the beach on a little circular river of sorts, or lake perhaps, as it met itself in what looked like the ceiling from her vantage point. *It is amusing how normal terms for geographical features become inadequate when the geography loops back on itself,* she thought and allowed herself a brief smile.

There were clouds obscuring a reasonable section of the ground up top, but it still felt *so* small. Her mood soured again.

She had some time to freshen up before meeting her generals, and got out of her uniform. Her husband had suggested she travel in something more comfortable, but Lady Xine preferred to stick to something that intimidated and showed her strength when traveling on official business.

A woman should not show that kind of masculine weakness, she thought to herself as she stepped into the shower.

She'd read up on the Earthers during the travel here, and she'd found their conception of gender and sexuality both irritating and amusing. Their insistence on pursuing equality fascinated her, but the thought of Centauri men demanding to be treated the same as women sounded appalling to her.

I mean, consider the whole affair with Soka. I should have given the job to a woman.

She'd been convinced he was a good choice, and he turned out to be a simpering turncoat.

She had nothing *against* men. She respected her own husband.

But for some types of posts…

She'd barely gotten dressed before one of her aides knocked on the door to ask if she was ready for the meeting.

When she strode in, they rushed to their feet. As she looked around, she didn't recognize any of them. They introduced themselves in turn and she smiled and nodded, and ignored their names.

A bunch of provincial nobodies, but this was a simple mission.

"You have an easy job. Prepare to burn Mars to the ground. Destroy every station in Mars space. Send a clear message. It should be trivial. We've overcommitted forces to this to account for every contingency, but our intelligence on Earth space is solid."

She paused briefly, before continuing.

"At the same time I want a task force to *get me the Black Rain.* I read on the trip here that the Earthers in some cultures used to put heads on stakes by city gates as a warning. I want their heads on stakes."

Her generals looked suitably intimidated, and she grinned. "Metaphorically, of course. Is the *Black Rain* task force ready?"

One of them nodded and gave her a "yes" that sounded like a whisper after her booming voice.

"Then catch the bastards," she yelled while clenching her fists and baring her teeth, and the general who had answered her nodded and got up and almost ran out of the room.

"The rest of you, get the punitive mission ready. And get me a report by the hour to explain who is responsible for making it take so long that I had to drag myself all the way out here to deal with this."

They nodded their agreement.

"What are you waiting for?"

Chapter 51

They were reeling from the plasma cannon hit, but Zo kept her focus.

"Status!" she yelled.

After everyone had given their reports, it seemed they had escaped pretty well. Minor damage to their thrusters but they should still manage to outpace the ship.

They fired another barrage of missiles while the destroyer was tearing through the remaining capsules.

Their furious acceleration had brought them up close enough that several of the destroyer's plasma cannon batteries was unable to aim at them, and Jonas and Monique's targeting program focused their fire on the plasma cannons still directed at them first. They took out two more batteries.

"Hold on, they're starting to flip, taking evasive action."

The massive ship had stopped its main engine and fired their nav thrusters. They started flipping back to face the gate. Clearly, they had realized they had little time to prepare to accelerate to keep up with *Black Rain* as it'd pass them. *And they don't realize,* Zo thought.

"Now."

Zo grinned. Everything so far, apart from that plasma cannon hit, was going as planned. The destroyer had turned, so now they turned until they their front plasma batteries pointed just right so that Jonas' targeting program could focus most of their firepower towards the enemy engines.

Just as they hoped, their upgraded weapons were powerful enough from this distance to start overheating the engines of the enemy ship. They could detect a big buildup of heat.

"I think we did it. Looks like it's going to blow."

Zo held her breath. If it blew now, it'd be close. They risked damage, and if the ship didn't disintegrate, they were about to pass the front at a relative speed uncomfortably low for facing the destroyer's main batteries.

Suddenly the ship shook.

"Did their engine blow? Clarice?" Zo yelled.

"We were hit by a plasma cannon. Shit, it damaged our main engine. It should be able to light, but diagnostics suggest only two of our four main thrusters are operational."

Two thrusters.

They'd be slower than the destroyer behind that was rapidly catching up. If they ran towards the gate, they'd outpace it, but if they didn't finish this destroyer off there was still a chance it could get within weapons range of the gate before the Centauri freighter got through…

"Their engine appears damaged, but it survived."

"Fire up ours. Get us closer. Let's finished the damn job."

Zo looked around at everyone. They knew what it meant. It was dangerous enough to try to make another pass. It also meant allowing the one behind get closer, possibly close enough to be within firing range.

It also meant giving them more chances to get shot at.

Their remaining main thrusters burned at full, and the destroyer seemed intent at not turning again—maybe they'd realized it was more important to run for the gate and stop the real Centauri.

All the more reason for them to disable or destroy the destroyer before they got their chance.

They let loose with the plasma cannons, trying to damage the destroyer's weapons' systems further before they got a shot at the engine.

"Missiles incoming," Mons announced in an eerily flat and calm tone.

"On it." Monique took control of the rear weapons platform and with the augmented targeting system she took out the two first ones almost instantly.

"Need help here." The rest of the missiles were at awkward angles, and while Vincent took over one of the plasma cannons, Clarice tried rotating the ship slightly, but was limited by not wanting to get them far enough out from the destroyer to present a target to more of their weapons.

Vicent blew up a third missile, and Monique a fourth, but the two last ones were getting too close.

"Brace!" Mons yelled. This time he sounded worried.

Zo checked the status herself. They were down to one of their main thrusters, and had to use nav thrusters to compensate for the uneven thrust.

"Coming up on the engine." Jonas launched their firing programs again, and this time they seemed to be doing more damage to the already weakened engine assembly of their enemy.

The first engine blew within seconds, and the shockwave pushed them significantly off course.

"Pull away!"

Clarice reacted to Zo's order almost immediately and had the ship reorient and accelerate away as fast as they could with their remaining thruster.

The second engine blew soon afterwards, and they could see from the heat buildup on their scans that the explosion started cascading through critical systems of the destroyer.

It started what might have become a spin thanks to the uneven thrust of the remaining main engines if the forces and explosions didn't start tearing the ship apart.

They watched on the screens as the destroyer broke up, and went dark surprisingly rapidly apart from a few fires where escaping atmosphere was still fueling the reactions.

Then those fires too went out. For a moment the bridge was quiet as they looked at the scans and the images of the wreckage.

"I hate to say it…" Zo's mood had changed significantly in a very short amount of time, "... but we now have a new problem."

With their own engine capacity down, they would not stand a chance of making it to the gate before the other destroyer was on top of them.

"Ideas?" Zo asked.

"Only one, and it's a shit one."

Zo turned to Monique.

"Spit it out."

"Hide in the wreckage," Monique suggested. "There's nothing else here."

"You're right, that is a shit idea," Vincent replied.

"Hold up, Vincent, we don't exactly have many alternatives," Zo replied.

"But they'll spot us," Mons added.

"Maybe. Anyone else got a better idea?" Zo looked around. Nobody spoke up.

Mons was right that they'd probably get spotted, but they could not outrun anyone in this state. If they played dead at least there was a chance they'd not get blown to pieces before they had a chance to fire at the destroyer. Or they'd come up with something.

They turned, and limped back towards the wreckage, and when they got close enough, they shut their main engine and maneuvered between the pieces with their nav thrusters only, until they found a suitable location, at least somewhat shielded.

The destroyer was so close it was likely they'd get good enough scans even with the wreckage to be able to see right through this.

But what else can we do? Zo thought

She gritted her teeth.

Today is not the day. We've survived worse. We can take out another one of these bastards. Maybe Terrell is on that ship.

The thought of blowing up a ship with Terrell on it raised her mood a little bit, but only until she then realized it meant if they were destroyed or captured, it'd be by Terrell personally. Her eyes narrowed and her forehead scrunched up.

The hell he will.

She turned towards Clarice.

"Before we go dark, any sign if the Centauri ship made it?"

"They're close, Captain. They'll be through in good time."

"Send them a final message. Tell them 'Good luck.'"

Clarice looked back at her and nodded.

It struck Zo that there was one final reason for them to make sure they survived this. The wreckage of that destroyer out there was the only hard evidence they had. The only thing the Centauri could not doubt the authenticity of. They'd take one look at the thing out there and realize that it wasn't Centauri. It was far too primitive. Never mind that the *Black Rain* had killed it, which should be evidence enough. They'd also find engine and weapons fragments. Maybe corpses.

They couldn't die without ensuring there was evidence left over.

If nothing else, we need to make the Centauri understand what they are facing before Terrell manages to trigger the war he claimed he wanted to prevent.

Most of the ship's systems went dark, and the ship went quiet.

Chapter 52

With only their passive scans to rely on, they were, while not blind, severely limited. They could not tell if the Centauri freighter made it through the gate or not—but they assumed it did. They could not say much about the incoming destroyer other than the movement they saw by passively monitoring the radiation from its engine plume and the periodic "ping" as their passive monitoring picked up the destroyer's active scans.

They waited in the hope of some miraculous opening to disable it, or an opening to flee, but none was apparent.

Clarice could hardly sit still. They might have data, but she felt blind, and she of all people on the ship had sight far in excess of anyone else thanks to her augments. But she was also used to so much more.

Then they had their answer, and she wished they didn't.

A large complement of missiles was converging on them.

Zo yelled for full engine power, and Clarice took evasive action as best they could.

Vincent and Jonas did their best to target the missiles, while Monique fired at the weapons platforms to at least hopefully reduce their capability for doing more harm.

It was working. They were limping but got out of the way of the missiles long enough to take out all of them.

Clarice grinned. She'd pulled off a couple of crazy turns in between parts of the wreckage of the other destroyer, and felt very pleased with herself for a moment.

She stopped grinning when they were hit by plasma cannons hard enough that the ship spun, and she focused on getting it under control.

"The last main engine is out, Captain."

That's the end of it, then, isn't it, she thought, and bit her lip. It was trite, and she felt annoyed at herself for even thinking it, but nevertheless the thought that came to mind was *I don't want to die like this.*

She desperately adjusted the nav thrusters to try to hide them, when they received a message from the attacking destroyer.

"Stand down or be destroyed."

Everyone turned to look at Zo.

"This is not the end. You hear me?" Zo told them while she looked around the bridge.

"Clarice. Soka. Hide. *Now!*" Zo's voice was cold and hard.

Soka objected. Clarice was not sure why. But Zo pointed out he was their best hope of convincing his people. Clarice was not about to object. Unlike Soka, she understood. Her eyes were an asset the enemy did not know about. As were her computer skills. And she was smaller than most of the crew. She'd be easier to hide, and better suited to try to get them free. And Soka. Soka was the one on their ship most likely to be able to convince the Centauri of the truth.

Clarice led Soka rapidly off the bridge while she heard Zo take the comms and announce their surrender. They grabbed environmental suits, in case they'd need them, and got in, and packed a bag with mag grips and weapons.

"What is the plan?" Soka asked in a trembling voice.

Clarice wished she could reassure him. But she couldn't.

"There is no plan," she said. "We need to make it up as we go along. For now our priority is to stay alive and get onto that ship."

"Get onto the ship?"

"Someone needs to free the rest, right? Besides, they might well destroy the ship when they leave for all we know. Even if they don't, we wouldn't have functioning engines."

Soka looked as if she'd told him something entirely insane.

"Soka, I get you're not a soldier. Neither am I. But they'll be taken aboard, because clearly Terrell, whether he's here or not, want to see his prize. So they'll be alive for a bit, but we don't know how long. That means we have a chance. We get on that ship, and each crew member we free improves our odds. Then we figure out what to do."

Soka nodded, but Clarice could tell he was not convinced.

"Hush. They'll be coming soon." Clarice put a finger to her lips.

They could hear sounds through the hull. Someone had attached something. The airlock doors were probably about to be forced open and have a flexible tunnel attached to make the evacuation easier.

"We need to be ready at the other airlock. We need to find a way across and in, or we're screwed. Quiet, okay?" Clarice had switched to Centauri. *I bet most of them can't speak much Centauri*, she thought. After all, the alien she got the language net integrated from appeared to not have done it for anyone else. Not that it'd matter—if they were overheard, they'd be in trouble either way, but she liked having a secret language of sorts.

Clarice led Soka along the hallway towards one of the storage bays where the secondary airlock was. As they got there, Zo announced at low volume over internal comms that the boarding party was about to enter, and wished them good luck.

They put on their helmets and entered the airlock, and flipped the switch. Air was pumped out and the exterior door opened. They looked out into the darkness. They were in a shadow of wreckage obscuring the orange light from Toliman, and so it was hard to see much at all, but they could not risk turning on their helmet lights.

Clarice stretched her head out and looked towards the primary airlock. As she expected, there was a tent-like tunnel stretched across and attached to their hull with magnetic strips to provide enough of a seal to allow the boarding party not to have to worry about fitting their captives with full suits.

There seemed to be no one outside of that structure, which meant their only worry was whether or not the security team on the destroyer was competent enough to monitor their cameras to see if anyone tried to do what Clarice was about to.

She felt like holding her breath.

Then she told Soka to follow her lead, and took two mag grips from her bag and handed one to Soka before she kicked off towards the destroyer. They both attached without a problem.

They were there, and could move closer to the airlock, but they still had the issue of getting *in*.

Clarice opted to wait. She had an idea, and hopefully the worst case was that they'd get captured after all.

The tunnel shook gently. She assumed as they were bringing the crew over.

She waited.

Finally it stopped, Then the mag strips attaching it to the *Black Rain* detached. She moved as close as she could to the closer end of the tunnel that was still hanging where it was, but starting to fold in as whomever was inside it in a suit was pulling their way towards the ship to bring it inside. Soka followed.

Clarice brought out her plasma pistol and Soka followed her lead.

I hope they don't have friends inside waiting for them, she thought.

The tunnel was almost in when Clarice grabbed the underside of it and yanked hard. The person inside stumbled and got caught up in it and Clarice didn't wait but fired several times straight into the dark figure in the collapsed tunnel.

She motioned for Soka to help her get them inside, and hoped no alarms had been tripped yet.

Inside the airlock she flipped the switch and waited for the repressurization. Clarice looked at the person they'd taken out. It was a young man, not much older than her. Her shots had burned clear through his suit and torso in three places, and he'd have died fast enough she was hopeful he had not been able to say anything over the radio.

As soon as they were out of the airlock, she grabbed his helmet and flicked the radio.

"Say 'Airlock all clear,'" she whispered to Soka, in English this time, and Soka complied.

"Understood," came the answer.

Fucking amateurs, Clarice thought to herself.

The destroyer crew had failed in so many ways already. It was cheering Clarice up. They should have checked the ship computer for life signs. They should have had cameras on the evac tunnel. They should have had someone waiting by the airlock to confirm. They should have had access codes.

They got away with just having someone of the same gender—not even same *species,* though Clarice would be the first to admit Soka's English was flawless by now—give the all clear. She had a feeling they wouldn't even have noticed it if *she* had given the message either. She halfway regretted not having tried.

They still had a corpse to hide, though. And a crew to save.

And it was a big ship.

Chapter 53

Captain Nola'ti Ek-Tibarrlie Five was immensely relieved when they crossed the threshold into the gate volume. They had run intense active scans from the moment they had brought the ship back online, to keep track on how the Earthers were doing, and they had caught the destruction of the destroyer, but they could also tell from the diminished power output from *Black Rain* that they must be struggling.

She wanted to turn and fight, but she knew bringing news of the terrorist deception was more important than taking the risk. Nola had been a soldier in her youth, and while there was no formal rank involved now, she respected the position of Soka as a representative of their government as well as the leadership the captain of the *Black Rain* had provided while they planned their escape. She felt implicitly that her duty and honor was tied up into carrying out their wishes first, and show concern for their lives *second*.

That they had explicitly told her that her first and only priority must be to deliver the news made her more intent to do so, because she knew that implied in that was a willingness to die for this cause, and that had removed the last shred of doubt from Nola's mind.

When they got the final "Good luck" from *Black Rain* before the ship went dark, it was a moving moment, and Captain Nola vowed to ensure these people would pay, whether the *Black Rain* survived or not.

She only hoped she and her crew would be believed. Of course they had their own recordings and testimony, which would be delivered by transmission as soon as they were no longer being jammed, and in person.

More than that, unless that trailing destroyer heading for *Black Rain* made an exceedingly thorough attempt to destroy every piece of wreckage, there'd be evidence left over of a destroyer that could not possibly be theirs. All the scans suggested the wrong types of alloys, and surely there would be bodies left behind. Somewhere. Something this barbaric scum would fail to clean up.

But that would have to wait. They reached the gate with no further incident, and passed through.

As soon as they got past, all their alarms went off. A destroyer was waiting right on the other side, far closer than regulations allowed. She was immediately suspicious. Another enemy that the *Black Rain* had been unaware of?

"Hail them."

"They're ignoring us," her comms officer replied.

"Scan them. See if they match ours."

"They're firing!" her weapons officer yelled.

"Evasive action."

"They're not ours, Captain. Same profile as the other ones."

Captain Nola's mouth pulled together in a wry smile.

"Well, then, we don't need to hold back. Maximum acceleration. Full missile spread. Cannons free."

They were not quite as well armed as it had seemed the *Black Rain* was, but they only needed to be able to make a run to the nearest outpost, and the captain was confident the ship shooting at them would not want anyone to take too close a look.

They also had engines capable of more thrust than she'd seen *Black Rain* deliver, and a crew better suited to high-g than any Earther, and she'd seen *Black Rain* outpace these destroyers with seeming ease.

Don't get too complacent, she reminded herself. *They can still get in lucky shots.*

They counted down the missiles left from the destroyer's first barrage, and took out two of their plasma cannons.

They can, but they won't get in enough, she thought, as she plotted the route towards Outpost 164A-79.

One of the destroyer's plasma cannons did get in a lucky hit and took out one of theirs before it was destroyed in turn. Most of their weapons were facing forwards, which was not very helpful. Their missiles could of course turn, but it'd buy their followers a lot of time to target them.

"Let's do a spin-shot."

It was a trick they'd tried only a couple of times before. Her navigation officer had also served in the military while younger, and they'd shared an enthusiasm for crazy maneuvers. Within a span of seconds they cut their main engine, spun 180 degrees, fired a full complement of missiles and their forward plasma cannons, continued the rotation, and fired the main engine again.

It took very precise timing to prevent the spin from messing up the aim of their weapons, or their weapons fire from messing up their navigation, but they pulled it up perfectly. It was disorienting, more so now than when she was younger.

The destroyer was following them too closely, or trying to, to have time to react before the missiles slammed into it.

They waited for everything to clear. Their tac display showed the destroyer was still somewhat intact, but had stopped accelerating and was turning. It might not be over, but they clearly made an impression.

Nola felt it was appropriate to gloat a little bit.

***

Clarice and Soka were sneaking through the fake Centauri destroyer trying to find where their crew was being held. But so far, no luck. The ship fascinated her, despite the urgency of their mission. It seemed to be a relatively basic but large Earth freighter retrofitted with fake hull plating to match the profile of a Centauri destroyer, but without really expanding the usable interior space much, and with weapons and extra propulsion pretty much bolted on.

Despite her disgust at what they'd done, Clarice was impressed with the way they'd basically hacked together a sufficiently convincing facsimile of a Centauri destroyer from parts which would be hard to trace—normal freight ships, basic plating, commercially available engine and weapons components. She recorded everything with her augments, of course.

The upside was—if they made it home alive—this knowledge would be incredibly valuable. They'd be able to find ways of distinguishing them from the real thing.

But for now they were stalking through hallways with minimal lighting. And thankfully no people. She wondered how many were on this ship. They knew there had been quite a few given the number of people who had swarmed the colony on Proxima Centauri b, but who knows how many were left. *Assuming it's one of the same destroyers,* she thought, realizing they did not know how *many* Terrell might have.

She found a staircase, and they ascended it quietly. There was nobody in the hallway it led to either and Clarice was getting frustrated. This ship was big, but they needed to find *something* soon. Maybe a computer console she could hack into, or a map. *What part of the ship do they keep the brig in on a ship like this anyway?*

The answer was not at all obvious—this was not a custom-built ship. Trying to apply logic to it didn't work, because Terrell's people had been forced to retrofit a freighter space, and who knows how much thought had gone into making it *practical*.

They reached a corner, and when they peeked around it, they saw a guard.

At least something, she thought. She whispered to Soka to hold back, while she pulled her plasma pistol behind her and confidently turned the corner and strolled towards the guard.

"Who are you?" he asked.

"I'm here to relieve you."

"Really? My shift doesn't end for a couple of hours."

"Oh, I think it's over."

Clarice nodded down at the plasma pistol pointing at his groin.

"Care to tell me where you keep your prisoners, and I'll just disable you instead of castrating you."

She smiled, and let her eyes flash a menacing red. She then groaned when the man wet himself.

"The eyes. It was the eyes, right. What is it with you wimps and glowing red eyes? Can't one of you find it hot or cool instead of scary?" *Not that I'd like to attract this one.*

The man had suddenly developed a stutter, but managed to tell her where to look. There were three banks of cells, the first one on this same floor.

She smiled, and said thank you, then she hit him over the head with the butt of the plasma pistol. She got Soka's help to gag and tie him up with strips from her bag, before they hid him behind a cargo crate in a corner.

They found the first banks of cells alright, but they were empty. Clarice swore quietly to herself. If that guy had lied to her and pointed them to the wrong locations, she was going to go down there and make him *watch* her shoot his groin off, not just threaten it.

Then I'll feed him the charred remains.

They found the nearest staircase and made their way up two more floors. They almost fell as the ship started accelerating.

"Shit," she whispered, "they must be going after the Centauri ship... I hope they're too far away."

There was, of course, the possibility they'd run into trouble, and that Terrell's men still had a chance to get them.

There was also the possibility they'd take them wherever they were hiding these ships. Clarice was not sure whether she felt that was a good thing or a bad thing. As much as she wanted to see Terrell again and hurt him, she also wanted to live, and the best way to escape seemed to be to get as close as possible to the Centauri Outpost and draw attention to themselves.

"Look, Clarice."

Soka pointed around the next corner. Another detention block.

And two guards.

They waited patiently as the guards made their checks, and left, and slowly snuck up to their cells, where they found everyone but Zo.

Chapter 54

Jonas was the last one to be let out from the cell block. They melted the locks with a plasma pistol.

Clarice distributed the limited amount of gear they'd been able to pack between the crew.

"What do we do now?" Jonas asked, unsure who was in command.

Technically it would be Mons, if they followed ship seniority, but Mons seemed equally uncertain. Monique was military, and Jonas was certainly willing to follow her, but Jonas had noticed how Monique had held back more since the colony.

Clarice spoke up first.

"We need to find Zo."

"I agree, but we also need to start getting control of this ship, in case things go really wrong," Monique replied.

"Monique is right. If we don't figure out what they're up to, it might not matter by the time we find Zo." Jonas desperately understood Clarice's wish to look for Zo, but they needed to focus on the mission as well.

"How about this." Vincent stood with his hands clasped behind his back, as if inspecting his troops. Despite not even having any military background Jonas felt an instinctive urge to straighten up and stand at attention.

"We split in two groups. I suggest Monique, Jonas, and Clarice head for the bridge. According to the intel from the guard Clarice took out, the last detention area is near the bridge anyway—it's probably where they have Zo. Mons, Soka, and I start seeking out key systems, starting with disabling and sabotaging the engine. Anyone disagree?" Vincent looked straight at Monique, and so did Jonas.

They went back and forth on the details a bit, but Monique offered no serious objections, and they all agreed that Monique and Vincent would be best placed to lead their respective groups given their military experience. It might have been good to have Clarice on the team doing sabotage, but Mons had a good understanding of the engineering as well.

And as Clarice said to Mons, admittedly clearly because she was desperate to save Zo, "If you can't hack into the systems, just shoot them."

They didn't need subtlety. They needed to strike fast and hard and ensure this ship could do no more damage.

"But please don't take out life support," Clarice added.

Monique went first, with Jonas next, and Clarice following behind him. He had been more frustrated than scared when they were brought over to the fake Centauri ship. The people who boarded them were stern but not brutal, and joked with each other while they'd handcuffed the crew and pulled them across, and the atmosphere was surprisingly relaxed, other than one comment:

"You'll see Terrell soon."

They didn't elaborate, including when Jonas had asked. They didn't know if he was aboard, or if they'd travel to see him, and if so, where. Zo had tried to goad them into explaining their plans, unsuccessfully. She had been separated from the rest soon after they'd been locked up.

But Jonas had not for a second doubted that Clarice would find and free them.

He just hoped they'd find Zo alive and well.

In the meantime, he was finding it hard to focus on what he was doing, and not on the cat-like movements of Monique as she almost glided along the corridors. *Not cat-like*, he though. *Like a lioness.* It wasn't sexual, though he certainly found her sexy as well. It was admiration of her strength and mobility.

Through his years of training, one of the things he'd quickly learned was that strength and flexibility changes how you move. Everything from how you walk to how you carry yourself. You stand up straighter, you get more of a swagger, you tend to naturally engage your glutes and thighs more when you walk because they are proportionally so much stronger and exercising that strength just *feels good*. When you need to be quiet, you find it easier to stay on your toes… You tend to pull your upper arms more back and to the side because it feels good to engage your upper back and gives you a greater range to build up power behind a hit.

He could see all of that in Monique, and he was almost hoping they'd get into close combat with some of the guards so he'd get to see her in action.

He hoped he had what it took himself. He felt as strong as before, but had little opportunity to verify if his back was back to full strength or "just" to average human strength, or somewhere in between. Something in him made him worry he might hold back out of fear of another injury.

They worked their way up through several mostly unconverted floors that were primarily empty freight bays.

Finally they ran into someone. Almost anyway. Monique signaled for them to be quiet, and Jonas got his wish. She tiptoed up to the guard from behind and calmly broke his neck with a nearly elegant twist.

Jonas hated the sound as the man's neck snapped, and felt queasy at the implication, but the way she moved almost transfixed him.

She looked into the next doorway, and motioned for Jonas and Clarice to follow. It looked like there were maintenance panels for power distribution there.

"Take a look, Clarice, see what we can yank out or blow up."

Clarice went systematically through the panels while Jonas kept an eye out the door.

"One of them goes to life support, two are for lighting. One *might* be sensory data to the bridge."

"If you take out the lighting ones, is that all lighting, or will there be emergency backups?"

"I'm not sure, Monique, most ships would fall back on emergency lights fed from batteries or generators several places on the ship. It's likely there'll be some light left, but who knows on this weird *Frankenship*. If not, I have these."

Clarice's eyes briefly glowed like light bulbs, brighter than Jonas had ever seen them before.

"Okay, let's do it. Shoot them all. Apart from the life support of course."

An alarm went off as Clarice shot the first one. As she went through the others the main lighting went off, but as she'd suggested, some limited emergency lighting kicked in within seconds and lit the room and the hallway. Jonas peered into an eerie glow.

"Let's move. Quickly. Someone will get here to investigate before we know it."

Monique was right, Jonas thought. Someone was there already.

He lifted his pistol to shoot the guard that was suddenly right in front of him. He must have been coming towards them when the light cut out already, but he was too close and kicked the gun out of Jonas' hand.

Jonas' instincts kicked in automatically, and he kicked the man in the stomach with his left leg, and on the return, he rotated and slammed the leg to the floor to give him footing to bring his right leg up to kick the head of the guard who was now doubling over.

The guard fell backwards with a thump as Monique and Clarice came out.

"Nicely done."

Monique gave him a thumbs up, and Jonas grinned a bit too broadly at the validation, before he spotted the guard running at them from the other side.

Chapter 55

Mons would have preferred to go looking for Zo. But Vincent had been right—they needed one of the more technical members of the crew on each team, and while he felt a pang of jealousy at letting Clarice be the one to go for her, he did not want to get between Clarice and Zo. His desire to serve Zo well was more important than any selfish desire to be the one to save her personally. At least that was what he told himself.

Vincent was leading the way, and Mons was pleased about that. He was happy to be able to hide behind the much bigger man, and let Vincent deal with any physical confrontation ahead.

Soka was behind him. Mons occasionally looked back to make sure he was still there, as Soka tiptoed so quietly behind him he sometimes thought he'd stopped. Mons found him peculiar. Quite likable in his soft and somewhat subservient demeanor. On occasion, Soka had reminded Mons of himself.

Apart from the way he dressed. Mons thought he looked more like a woman at times, often draped in robes or kaftans. Mons had no objection to that; somehow a feminine appearance seemed to work for Soka, and at one point Mons had wondered if he was attracted to him, but he'd brushed the thought aside.

They were systematically climbing down towards the engine room and power plants.

"It's weird we haven't run into anyone," Vincent muttered.

"The crew must be quite small," Mons answered him.

"We still need to be ready."

They could feel vibrations and hear noise that suggested they were not far away, but that made it harder to tell if the hallways ahead would be clear of people or not.

Suddenly the light went out for a moment, before dim red emergency lighting kicked in.

"Hah! Bet that's Clarice," Vincent let out a little too loudly.

Mons struggled to adjust to the reduced lighting.

"No lights," Vincent said, as if reading his mind. "Let's not risk it. We'll turn on lights only when we need it."

They made it down another floor. Almost as soon as they got down, they heard voices loudly discussing the power outage.

"Bridge doesn't know what's up either. They're sending someone to investigate," the first voice said.

"Fucking bullshit. We should have had a much larger crew on this ship."

"Yeah, well, it was fine until that crazy attack on that Centauri colony. I'm beginning to doubt…"

The voice trailed off just as Vincent burst into the room they were in.

Mons kept well out of view.

"Gentlemen. You can put your hands up, or I can shoot you. Your choice. *Please* let me shoot you."

There was a brief pause.

"I'm disappointed," Vincent's voice came again shortly afterwards. "Come on in, no fighting spirit in these people."

Mons peered through the door opening, and saw two men with their hands up, looking terrified.

"Tie them up, will you, while I keep my gun pointed at them." He turned to the men and added, "You can still change your mind. For me?" Vincent pointed at his gun.

Mons and Soka tied up one each.

Unlike Vincent, Mons was pleased they had surrendered. He could handle violence when he had to, like when he killed Grant the year before. But that had been necessary—he'd betrayed them. Betrayed the captain.

Mons still had nightmares about how the room had filled with a mist of blood—he'd rather not experience a repeat. *Though we're still accelerating,* he thought, *so it at least wouldn't hang in the air like with Grant.*

"Where is the engine room?" Mons asked of the two men. His voice did not have anywhere near the level of power and menace that had come from Vincent, but the implied threat of Vincent still being there, with his plasma pistol pointed at the now restrained men made it enough.

They were practically there. Just two doors down.

The men insisted nobody else was there, but Vincent still took point again, and they snuck down the hallway, expecting a potential attack any moment.

Nobody came.

The engine room was loud, and almost dark. Vincent turned on a flashlight, and Mons and Soka followed his example.

"Your turn, Mons."

Mons looked around to see which circuitry to disable to shut down the engine in a somewhat safe way, while making it hard to fix. He started toggling a couple of switches, shutting down some higher level control systems.

"Bridge control should be disabled now. If they're not total idiots, they'll notice, so please be ready in case they find someone close enough to send here."

Vincent nodded, and pointed for Soka to provide lighting while he went to watch the door.

"Also, brace, because when I cut the engine, we lose gravity."

"I *have* been on a spaceship before, Mons." Vincent sounded insulted, but Mons just ignored him.

He opened a wall panel, and pulled out a couple more wires, before yanking out a circuit board.

"Soka, take this. Put it in a bag. I have a couple more to pull to shut things down, and then they shouldn't get it back up again without figuring out what I pulled and finding spares…"

"Hurry up, will you," Vincent said.

Mons was getting annoyed at his attitude. "Do you want us to be able to restart the ship again? Because I don't know about you, but I'd rather not be floating in space until we run out of supplies."

Mons closed the cabinet carefully, wanting to leave anyone coming to fix things guessing what he'd done. The boards he'd pulled were not essential to the running of the engine, but they were essential to the automatic diagnostics at startup. Without them, the engine would not pass self-tests, but even better, the self-tests would fail so totally they'd get no diagnostics to tell them the diagnostics equipment itself was what was at fault.

Mons smiled, and was quite proud of what he'd done. He wasn't as great at software and hacking as Clarice, but he had a mind for strategy and he understood how to get people to look in the wrong places.

He opened another cabinet, and shot a board straight through.

"Hey! What are you doing?"

"Don't worry. It's a non-essential backup function. It's a distraction. Someone will waste time fixing it and it'll do nothing."

Mons grinned now.

He left that cabinet open, and yanked a few cables going through the damaged board as well, as if it'd make a difference. But it'd make the cabinet look like the obvious thing to investigate and fix.

He opened a third cabinet.

"Get ready."

He tripped a switch, and the engine started spinning down. He pulled out a small fuse, and moved the switch back in position.

"All done. With some luck they'll be wasting a ton of time on the damaged board, and then a ton of time tracking down the fuse, and *then* it'll still not come up and they'll get no diagnostics… If they're as green as they seem, it'll take them *ages* to consider the reason they get no diagnostics isn't because of the engine but because the diagnostics boards are *missing*."

Mons looked at Vincent with his broad grin still on his face.

"Yeah, yeah. Well done, Mons. I can tell you're *very* pleased with yourself."

Vincent sounded sarcastic, but he actually smiled at Mons for once.

I'll count that as a win.

Chapter 56

"Behind you."

Clarice heard Jonas yell to Monique and spun around to see a guard about to shoot her.

Monique spun too, but before either of them had time to react, Jonas had jumped and kicked off against the wall and fired at the man right above their heads.

The guard slumped to the ground, and Clarice couldn't help but freeze and stare at him.

"You move fast. I'm impressed," she heard Monique tell Jonas, and turned to them. Jonas looked a bit too pleased with himself at the praise he got from Monique.

"Let's move," Monique added.

They rushed down the hallway they assumed would lead toward the bridge, and hoped they'd not meet too many others.

"Hey, let me take point," Clarice told Monique. "I can see better in this lighting." She made her eyes glow gently red to emphasize her point.

"Okay, but pay close attention. I don't want to have to explain it to Zo if you get hurt."

"I will." Clarice moved up front. For a moment the light fluttered. *Someone must be trying to bypass the ruined circuits,* she thought. But it didn't work.

They got to the next stairs, and judging by the markings they should be only about three floors below the bridge.

Clarice climbed up and looked around, and they entered a hallway with several rooms attached. The first seemed to have been repurposed as a state room of sorts, though distinctly lacking in luxury. Monique popped her head into the second room.

"Just storage."

They moved down the corridor as quietly as they could, and got to a guardroom. The men inside managed to lift their guns before Clarice fired in the wall right over one of their heads and told them to drop their weapons.

Jonas tied the men up, and Monique grabbed one of them by the throat.

"Our captain. Where is she?"

"There are cells down the hall. She's in one of them."

"Good boy."

Monique gagged him and his colleague, and they moved out.

"Why are there so few people here?" Clarice asked quietly.

"They must have lost more than we thought at Proxima," Jonas replied.

"Perhaps, or perhaps they're not crewing them with that many—after all these ships aren't here to win wars, but to attack defenseless traders and trigger conflict," Monique added.

Both replies made sense to Clarice. They worked their way down the corridor and found nobody else, before they got to the door that must be to the detention cells.

The door was locked, and Jonas shot it open with his plasma pistol.

"Is she there?"

Clarice was impatient and pushed past.

"Zara!"

Clarice felt a wave of relief as she saw Zo sitting in the cell, seemingly unharmed.

"Clarice…"

Zo's face lit up, and then she spotted Jonas and Monique as well.

"Happy to see you… all. Clarice…"

"Step back, Captain." The cell door did not look very solid, and Jonas cut through it with his plasma pistol with ease.

As soon as he did, Clarice slammed the door open and threw her arms around the captain.

After they'd been separated on the ship, it had finally hit Clarice just how much she'd missed her while they'd been locked up on Earth. She'd pushed it aside, and tried not to think about that evening…

Then this mission. This mission brought the memories she'd pushed aside back. She'd kept looking at Zo. Zara. Wondered.

And now she couldn't help it. She kissed her, and held her tight, and Zara kissed her back.

It felt just like how Clarice had hoped it would. A bit too much, in fact. She couldn't quite place it. She felt like she was floating.

Then she realized they were.

"Clarice!"

Zo smiled at her, and slid her hand through her hair.

She whispered "I wasn't gone *that* long. We'll talk later."

"You two done, or should we wait in the corridor?"

"Monique!"

Clarice went red. Zo drew attention away from her quickly.

"Business first, ribbing later, Monique. We got anything to do with the acceleration cutting off?"

"Hopefully. Vincent, Mons, and Soka went for the engine room."

"Great. Let's move."

***

When they had been taken aboard the ship, Zo had been pulled onto the bridge, and the first thing she did when presented with some young Sovereign Earth goon that insisted he was the "captain" was to spit in his face.

One of the guards kneed her in the stomach, but was held back by the captain.

"You're lucky Terrell wants you."

"Terrell is a cowardly piece of shit terrorist."

The Sovereign Earth captain just grinned at her.

"Put her in a cell. I have nothing to talk to her about."

Zo hadn't resisted when they led her down. When she realized they'd put her alone, she'd asked where the rest of the crew was. The man who locked up her up had been considerate enough to assure her they were fine, just locked up further down the ship.

They don't look like hardened soldiers at all, she thought to herself. More like children seduced into what they thought would be an adventure and getting in too deep.

She'd waited patiently. She had no doubt Clarice and Soka would find a way, and that they'd free her.

And they did, but Zo did not see it coming when Clarice kissed her. She'd thought a lot about their brief shared drink several times in prison, but she'd put it aside when this mission started. At first, not wanting to be distracted, and hoping for more relaxing time after they were done. Then they were thrown in deeper and deeper and there was no time.

Clarice's energy felt intoxicating but also was distracting her, and again she was forced to try to push the feelings aside.

"Let's go take this damn ship. There were only seven to eight people on the bridge when they hauled me there."

Zo kicked off and floated out now that the lack of engine power meant there was no gravity, and waved for them to follow her.

They climbed the stairs to the floor right below the bridge, which was a lot easier in zero-g.

Zo braced against the wall and unceremoniously punched a guard in the guts and then back of the neck before he'd even managed to turn to see who were coming.

She was in no mood for more bullshit. *It's time to end this.*

The upside of zero-g, was that inexperienced crew like this were even more likely to make stupid mistakes when trying to fight weightless, so Zo felt good about their chances.

They climbed the last flights of stairs, and Monique and Clarice took up positions either side of the door.

"Jonas, right behind me. Monique, Clarice, follow as soon as we're clear."

Zo triggered the door, kicked off against the back wall hard so she flew right in, and grabbed the left side of the doorway and swung by it and started shooting as soon as she passed the threshold.

She kicked off against the inside of the doorway as someone aimed for her, and Jonas came floating in and fired at one of the guards.

Zo watched as Monique and Clarice also came flying in at different angles, and then she turned to look for the captain.

"Hi there. I didn't quite like the accommodations, so I figured I'd come back for a chat."

The captain moved his hand towards the holster of his gun, but froze when Zo aimed at his head.

"Tell them to drop their weapons. Don't lose your head."

Did I really just say that, she thought to herself.

Chapter 57

Lady Xine was in a horrible mood.

She'd been inspecting the troops massing for the punitive expedition to Sol, and while she'd been there, she'd been interrupted to be handed several urgent messages.

One had been a request for a detailed report from the provincial administrator, someone whom Lady Xine disliked intensely. Apparently Soka's wife had succeeded in getting the provincial administrator's attention, and while he was a meek and unremarkable man whom Xine was certain she could pacify very easily, she could not ignore his request for a report.

He had insisted no punitive expedition should commence until he had reviewed the report, and as a result, Xine had ordered her assistants to compile the details urgently, but it would delay them by at least a day.

More peculiar were the reports of a battle between a destroyer that should not be there and a freighter near one of the gates. The destroyer had been beaten easily by a ship it should have had no problems with.

The report of the encounter made Xine raise an eyebrow. She did not like it one bit, and she ordered the freighter be stopped immediately; preferably alive so they could investigate.

But just as she was giving the order, she was given the latest message.

The freighter had beaten her to it and reported in at Outpost 164A-79 and the captain had insisted they had urgent evidence to provide.

Apparently refusing to provide anything until given an audience with the highest ranking officer in the system. Personally.

Xine had sighed, and ordered a shuttle back from the flagship of the attack fleet to the outpost. She'd have time anyway, while the report to the provincial administrator was being compiled.

"Where is this person?"

"Captain Nola'ti Ek-Tibarrlie Five is waiting for you in the conference room, my Lady."

Her aides led her to the conference room. The captain stood up straight and looked out the windows into the "outside" space on the station when Lady Xine entered.

"*Well?*"

Lady Xine's voice was sharp and made clear her impatience and annoyance that someone had insisted on seeing her instead of just giving a report to one of her officers.

"My Lady... We escaped the destruction of the station near Toliman."

"I heard this was about *Black Rain*. You saw the terrorists destroy the station?"

Lady Xine's attitude softened slightly. This was certainly worthwhile information.

"No, my Lady, we saw them try to *save* the station."

"Outrageous!"

Lady Xine slammed her fist on the table.

"We have sensor logs and camera output. You can go over our systems to determine they've not been tampered with. Our log systems have a cryptographic chain of custody all the way from the external sensors."

The captain did not seem fazed by Xine's angry outburst, and Xine was impressed she maintained eye contact throughout. If she was lying, she was good at it.

"Go on..."

"The station was destroyed by what appeared to be our own destroyers."

"Our destroyers would never..."

Lady Xine felt the anger rise in her.

"Listen!" the captain yelled, but before Lady Xine could storm out and yell for her attendants to deal with this insolent captain, the captain continued.

"I said they *appeared* to be our own destroyers. I did not say they *were* ours."

She lowered her volume. She had Lady Xine's attention now.

"They followed us, but could clearly not reach the speed one of our ships can. Another waited near the gate. We communicated with the *Black Rain*, and we concurred with their assessment that these were Earther ships made to look like ours."

Lady Xine could not believe what she was hearing. She'd been told this crazy story already, about the colony by Proxima. *Could it be true?*

"We tricked them into focusing on *Black Rain*, and *Black Rain* pulled the destroyer near the gate away so we'd have a clear run at the gate... They took the first one down, but they were damaged. I fear they may have gotten taken out."

She paused briefly.

"They told me you're probably planning a punitive expedition. You can't."

Xine looked at the captain, and could tell she meant every word.

"They're still Earther terrorists. Why should we not retaliate?" Her voice was calm and cold but she was curious.

"*They* want to stop these criminals as well. They're honorable people. They willingly risked their lives to ensure we could escape—and may well have lost them by now. Please at least go through the gate to Toliman. See the wreckage of the destroyer. Talk to the *Black Rain* if they're still alive. Please."

The last word was just a whisper.

Lady Xine did not enjoy watching the woman grovel like a little boy, but she had sounded sincere, and she could not very well ignore this testimony with the provincial administrator paying attention. The expedition was not quite ready anyway. She'd lose nothing by taking it seriously.

"Very well. I will personally take a few ships through to investigate."

"Thank you, my Lady."

The captain stood up straight again, and Lady Xine was pleased to see she pulled herself together.

***

It took only an hour to get two of the larger ships of the punitive expedition ready, and for Lady Xine to get aboard and onto the bridge of lead ship. They set course for the Toliman gate as soon as she was strapped in.

She'd briefed the captain that they might meet ships that looked like their own, and to be cautious, but from the testimony of the freighter captain they'd hardly need it. By all accounts these *facsimiles*, if the captain spoke the truth, would be no match for a real Atrycc class destroyer.

The Lady Xine braced herself when the main engines started. She hated traveling in a hurry like this. She didn't particularly like travel at all, but high-g acceleration was particularly annoying.

She understood the Earthers found high-g far more troublesome, and it quite pleased her to imagine these barbarians suffer worse than her, as they accelerated towards the gate.

"It shouldn't take us long to find them, my Lady," the junior officer who had been assigned as her aide aboard told her.

Xine didn't answer. She just wanted this affair to be over so she could make it back to her comfortable compound.

They passed through the gate without incident, and started long range scans. They found signs of a debris field, but no obvious drive signatures.

Xine ordered the ships towards the debris field with a sinking feeling. "At least the part about a ship being destroyed was true," she told herself.

Suddenly the alarms blared.

"Scans have picked up what looks like a destroyer. It's accelerating towards the gate. Weapons are hot."

Chapter 58

Zo made herself comfortable in the captain's seat of the destroyer.

"Clarice, get comms up and running if you can. Let's let the rest know we're in control."

"Monique, Jonas, once you've locked these people up, secure the bridge doors, and see if we can get internal scanners up and account for whatever is left of these clowns."

She felt in charge, and happy, and excited. And regularly distracted by thoughts of the kiss Clarice had given her.

This she enjoyed. Finally everything was breaking their way.

"Comms are up, Captain."

"All hands. This your *new* captain. If you're thinking of making some desperate attempt to retake the bridge, consider that we were locked up, and yet we took control in just a few hours. So listen up. You've been tricked. We were tricked by Terrell too; spent a year in prison because of the shit he talked us into. *Stand down.* Come to the bridge *unarmed.* You'll be treated fairly if you do. Try anything and I'll put you down the way your colleagues murdered the Centauri by Proxima before you bombed the remains."

"Oh, and *call first* before you come, so we don't shoot you," she added.

Zo was happy, but she was in no mood to deal with any more shit from these children.

She motioned for Monique and Jonas to monitor any activity.

"Only a couple dozen people on the ship total in addition to the ones we've locked up, Captain," Monique reported.

"Makes sense, these people were never meant to wage war, just incite one," Zo replied.

"Mons has made contact," Clarice reported. "He's asking if they should reconnect the drive."

"Tell him to go for it. And to stay alert in case any of the crew still wants to try something stupid."

Monique turned to her. "About half the crew has contacted us to tell us they're surrendering so far."

"Great. The comms is recorded and logged right?"

"Yes, Cap."

"Play it back over the loudspeakers. Let the rest know their comrades are surrendering one after the other."

This almost felt like it was going too smoothly.

Jonas reported the first group was by the door, and they all drew weapons as a precaution as Jonas let them in two at a time to get tied up and secured in the captain's chamber by the bridge.

"Welcome," Zo said to each group as they entered. "I don't expect you to believe you were lied to right away, but you've done the right thing by surrendering."

"Why do you bother, Captain?" Monique asked.

"Because we believed his lies last time too. I'm sure some of these people are genuine believers who knew exactly what they were doing, and they'll pay a high price, but if any of these were tricked into it like we were, I want them to have a fair hearing."

Monique didn't answer, but she nodded, and Zo felt sure she'd come to understand.

"Captain, a destroyer came through the gate."

Clarice sounded scared, and Zo didn't blame her.

"Real deal, or one of Terrell's?"

"Can't tell yet from this distance."

"Get an update on the engine from Mons."

Zo turned to Jonas. "How are we on the crew?"

"Almost everyone has surrendered… Got four more to lock up. What do you want to do about the rest?" Jonas asked. "About six of them, I think."

"Screw the rest."

Clarice informed her the engine should be operational again, and they checked diagnostics.

"Tell them to brace for acceleration. Over the private channel. Let's see how the crew that didn't surrender deals with that."

Zo smirked. She didn't *want* to hurt them, but if they were taken by surprise, it'd certainly slow down any attempts at sabotage.

"Lay in a course straight for the gate. Best speed. Scan them and report as soon as you know. Oh, and weapons ready."

"Now."

The engines came online nearly immediately, and they were kicked back in their chairs. Zo kept a close eye on the tac display, waiting to see how the destroyer they were facing would react.

If it was Terrell's maybe they wouldn't realize this one had been taken over. *If it is Centauri, will they shoot first?*

"Unknown destroyer, stand down or be *obliterated*."

The message came in English first, and then Centauri.

"They don't know either, or they'd have sent the message in just one language," she heard Monique say.

"Update on scans?"

"Still not certain. About 70% sure it's Centauri, but…" Clarice's voice trailed off. "They're targeting us!"

"Target them."

Zo answered their hail. "Unknown destroyer, this is Captain Zara Ortega of *Black Rain*. We've commandeered this ship. We will defend ourselves if necessary. Identify yourselves."

"Captain Ortega. This is Lady Xine-Zor Li'mor Four, local administrator for… this place. Cut your engines and weapons and we will drop our weapons lock."

"Agreed."

"You heard the *Lady*."

Zo was sure her voice conveyed just how up herself she thought Lady Xine had sounded, and did not regret that one bit.

"Is the ship secure?" Lady Xine asked.

"Mostly. Can I assume this means you now *believe us*?"

"While you started speeding towards the gate, our scanners confirmed the wreckage was not ours. That is… consistent with your story. You will not be arrested, but we will require interviews, you understand."

Zo sighed. *Just like last year,* she thought to herself. "Better not make a habit of this."

"We understand. If you send a shuttle, we're happy to come peacefully. Do be aware we have a couple dozen people locked up here and a few hostiles still potentially loose on the ship."

"Oh, no worries. We'll take good *care of them*."

"Now she sounded almost like you, Captain," Jonas commented.

"Oh, shut up." Zo grinned.

The shuttle arrived twenty minutes later, and they were asked to remain on the bridge while the soldiers aboard made a sweep of the ship. It didn't take more than half an hour before they'd located and taken care of the remainder of Terrell's crew, and brought Mons, Vincent, and Soka to them on the bridge.

"They treat you well?" Zo asked them.

"They took our weapons," grumbled Vincent, "but otherwise they've been nice."

Soka threw himself in Zo's arms. She didn't quite know how to react but patted him on the back before she gently pushed him away.

"I can't believe you succeeded," he whimpered.

They were brought back to the real Centauri destroyer, and soon Zo stood face to face with Lady Xine.

Chapter 59

Soka'li Em-Sckirrrnie Three—Soka to friends and family—was nervous when Lady Xine ordered him into the destroyer's state room to confer with him in private.

"I still have doubts, Soka. But so far everything has checked out. *We accept that it was this 'Terrell' that was responsible for the attack on the colony at Proxima, and the station nearest Toliman.*"

Soka started breathing again.

"Thank you... Thank you."

"I'm not *finished*."

Lady Xine's expression made Soka stop instantly.

"We also accept that your reports were truthful. As such, the warrants for you and for the crew of the *Black Rain* have been lifted."

Soka tried to stifle a smile, as Lady Xine still looked annoyed and he didn't want to anger her.

"After... consultations. We have decided that the punitive campaign will not go ahead. Even though the Earther lack of... control would still justify one, it has been pointed out to me it would draw attention to the fact these terrorists managed to convince several officials their ships were real, and managed to procure weapons we had not authorized the sale of, and that this *trade* occurred here, in this system, which is meant to be under our control, and so it would be... unfair to give them all the blame."

*She means under **her** control,* he thought to himself. *She is worried she'd get caught up in the fallout.*

Soka thought Lady Xine looked disappointed. As if she'd looked forward to an excuse to bomb Sol back into irrelevance.

"I'm so happy to hear that, my Lady."

"I thought you hated it out here, Soka."

"They've surprised me, my Lady... They're more... interesting than I thought."

"*Hmm.* Then I have a surprise for you."

Soka was puzzled. He had no idea what she might have in mind.

"I've convinced the provincial administrator that we need to learn more about the Earthers..."

Soka got a sinking feeling.

"I've recommended that you're assigned to accompany the *Black Rain* for the foreseeable future."

Lady Xine finally looked happy. A smile was spreading across her face, and the edges of her mouth curled into a smirk.

"But. I have a family."

"Oh, I'm sure your family can manage. Your wife has two other husbands to help out, does she not?"

Soka looked to the floor. He had *enjoyed* learning more about the Earthers, and he'd come to like and respect the *Black Rain* crew, but *serving there* with no end in sight?

This felt like Lady Xine was taking revenge for the nuisance he'd made himself.

"You'll be given leave to visit your family for a couple of weeks, and then report back here. Give my regards to your wife. I so *enjoyed* it when she came to visit."

She did not at all sound sincere. Soka wished he could say something. That he could stand up to her. But he had gotten the distinct impression Lady Xine would relish impressing on him that he *had no choice,* and he didn't want to give her the pleasure.

***

Black Rain had been towed back home by a Centauri ship, and was in a dock being repaired, and the crew had been brought back to Earth, and yet Zo was not happy.

They'd spent two days in debriefing with a bunch of military brass she'd not bothered to learn the names of. *Interchangeable bureaucratic morons,* she thought. Regularly.

On the upside, they'd been informed early on that everyone was "pleased" with the outcome.

On the downside, they wanted to go over every little detail.

It'd taken a lawyer and some not-so-subtle threats to prevent them from trying to open Clarice's head up to get at the integration augment. They'd negotiated an agreement to allow assorted scans and tests that'd keep Clarice busy for further days.

Zo had not yet gotten a chance to talk to her for more than a few sentences. But she did get a chance to give her a hug and assure her it'd all get taken care of.

She was pacing in her room, waiting for a phone call to go through to Colonel Williams, the man who had originally arranged their release and their mission, when there was a knock on her door.

"Come in."

It was Monique, and Zo motioned for her to come in.

"I can come back…"

"No, I'm just holding for Colonel Williams."

"Ah. I'm actually here because I've just spoken to him."

Zo lowered her phone.

"He's promised he's working on getting the bureaucrats out of the way."

"That's great. Can he get it done *now*, before I'm bored to death?"

Monique smiled.

"It'll be fine, Captain. There's one more thing… Colonel Williams and I."

"Yes?"

Zo was not sure she'd like what'd come next.

"We agreed this mission was a success… And that we learned a lot from Soka."

"I'm sure you did."

Zo was not sure what she meant by that comment, but she felt she needed to say *something*.

"The Centauri have asked if Soka can stay."

That was definitively not what Zo had expected. She was not sure how she felt about it. Soka had been a perfect guest, but he'd not been particularly *useful*.

Actually, that's unfair. He did help upgrade the ship. She was sure those "upgrades" were one of the reasons Colonel Williams had graciously offered to ensure repairs were taken care of by the military.

"You'll be compensated, of course, as you'd be carrying out a service for the government."

Maybe it wouldn't be so bad to keep him aboard, Zo thought.

"Also, we'd like for me to stay on board as well. You need a new medic anyway, and I have field medical training. And tactical training. Please."

Zo didn't know what to say. She respected Monique a hell of a lot more than Soka, but she was a serving military officer.

"What exactly would that *mean*, Monique? You want us to keep acting like some sort of black ops?"

"Most of the time we'd just do whatever it is you guys do, while discreetly looking for hints of Terrell—I assume we both still want him." Zo nodded, and Monique continued.

"As long as what you usually do is nothing *too* illegal. It isn't usually *too* illegal is it, Zo?"

Zo just smirked and turned and looked through the window.

"Hello? Hello?"

It was from her phone.

"Sorry, Colonel Williams…"

"I've just spoken to Monique."

"Yes. I understand, sir."

"Thank you, sir."

"She can come. But this will *cost* you."

She hung up and turned to Monique.

"This is the first time I'm getting *paid* to take on new crew members. But don't expect that means I'll go easy on you."

Zo looked up at the sky, and the perfectly ordinary single yellow sun hanging up there, and wondered where they'd go next.

If you enjoyed this book . . .

First of all, I would appreciate it very much if you would rate this book and leave it a review. Whatever you liked (or didn't like), as it will be very helpful to other readers as well as to me.

Of course, I hope you liked this book enough that you want to see where Zo and the crew go next. If you do, then there are several ways you can stay up to date with what is happening with Galaxy∞Bound:

There's my website, at galaxybound.com where I post information on upcoming books. The site is also a blog where you can find posts about my writing as well as the occasional free short story.

My website also lets you sign up for my mailing list. I promise I'll send you *at most* one message per week, and that often includes early looks at new short stories and other material before it gets posted anywhere else.

You'd also be most welcome to follow me on Twitter: https://twitter.com/BoundGalaxy—I post about my writing as well as retweet lots of interesting stuff about sci-fi and space. And I'd love being able to talk directly to you there.

www.ingramcontent.com/pod-product-compliance
Ingram Content Group UK Ltd.
Pitfield, Milton Keynes, MK11 3LW, UK
UKHW010827200825
7484UKWH00028B/446